A HOUSE OF DEATH

"What can you do now?" asked Miss Columba. "He's dead. It was an accident."

Miss Silver shook her head. "You do not think so, nor do I. Two people at Pilgrim's Rest have died violently, perhaps three. Are there to be more deaths? If you can believe your brother's death was an accident, can you believe that your nephew's three successive accidents were coincidences when they each happened just in time to prevent the sale of the property?"

Miss Columba put her head back against the door and said, "What's the good?"

Miss Silver looked at her with steady kindness. "I must remind you of the remaining members of your family. No owner will be safe until the murderer's identity is discovered."

Miss Columba straightened up and moved away. "The place belongs to Jack. He's in Malaya. Let sleeping dogs lie."

Miss Silver pressed her lips together. One Pilgrim had engaged her professional services, and she had failed to save his life. He had gone against her advice, but she felt that she owed him a debt. And a much heavier one to that Justice which she served with a single mind . . .

Also by Patricia Wentworth

THE CASE IS CLOSED

THE CLOCK STRIKES TWELVE

THE FINGERPRINT*

GREY MASK

THE LISTENING EYE*

LONESOME ROAD

THE WATERSPLASH

WICKED UNCLE

Published by

WARNER BOOKS   *forthcoming

PATRICIA WENTWORTH

PILGRIM'S REST

WARNER BOOKS

A Warner Communications Company

WARNER BOOKS EDITION

Copyright 1946 by Patricia Wentworth Turnbull
All rights reserved.

This Warner Books Edition is published by arrangement with J. B. Lippincott
Company, c/o Harper & Row, Publishers, Inc., 10 East 53rd Street, New York,
N.Y. 10022

Warner Books, Inc.
666 Fifth Avenue
New York, N.Y. 10103

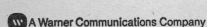 A Warner Communications Company

Printed in the United States of America

First Warner Books Printing: January, 1985

Reissued: May, 1988

10 9 8 7 6 5 4 3

Chapter One

Judy Elliot stepped off the moving staircase at Piccadilly Circus, and felt a hand under her elbow. As it was undoubtedly a male hand and she was not prepared to be picked up by something in the lonely-soldier line, she first quickened her pace, and when that didn't seem to be any good whisked round with a few refrigerated words upon her tongue.

They never got said. The keep your distance look melted into one of pleased recognition. She tilted her chin, gazed up at a tall young man in a dark blue suit and a discreetly chosen tie, and exclaimed, "Frank!"

Detective Sergeant Abbott gave a poor imitation of his usual rather cynical smile. He was in fact considerably handicapped by the behaviour of his heart, a perfectly sound organ but responding at the moment to a quite uncalled for access of emotion. When you haven't seen a girl for a year, when she hasn't answered your letters, and when you have convinced yourself that any slight interest you may have felt is now a thing of the past, it is extremely discomposing to find yourself behaving like a schoolboy in love. He couldn't even be sure that he had not changed colour, and, worst symptom of all, he was rapidly beginning to feel that, Judy being here, nothing else mattered.

He continued to smile, and she continued to tilt her chin, this being made necessary by the difference in their heights. The chin was a firm one, the face to which it belonged agreeable rather than pretty, the mouth wide and curving, the eyes indeterminate in colour but very expressive. They began at this moment to express surprise. What on earth Frank

Abbott thought he was doing, standing looking at her like that. . . . She pulled him by the arm and said,

"Wake up!"

He came to with a jerk. If anyone had told him he would make a public exhibition of himself like this, he would have laughed in the idiot's face. He found a tongue very little accustomed to being out of action, and said, "It's shock. You must make allowances. You were the last person on earth I expected to see."

The gaze became severe.

"Does that mean you thought you had hold of a perfectly strange girl's elbow, and found it was me?"

"No, it doesn't. I should get the sack from the Yard if I went about doing that sort of thing. Besides, not very subtle—I can do better than that when I give my mind to it. Judy, where have you been?"

"Oh, in the country. . . . We're blocking the traffic."

He took her by the arm and steered for a backwater.

"Well, here we are. Why didn't you answer my letters?" He didn't mean to say that, but it came out.

"Letters? I didn't get any."

He said, "I wrote. Where have you been?"

"Oh, here and there—with Aunt Cathy till she died, and then rather on the trek."

"Called up?"

"No. I've got Penny—she hasn't got anyone else."

"Penny?"

"My sister Nora's baby. She and John went in an air raid just after the last time I saw you. All right for them, but rotten for Penny."

He saw her face stiffen. She looked past him as he said, "I didn't know. I'm sorry. What can one say?"

"Nothing. I can talk about it all right—you needn't mind. And I've got Penny. She isn't quite four, and there isn't a single other relation who can take her, so I've got exemption. What about you?"

"They won't let me go."

"What rotten luck! Look here, I've got to fly and feed the child. We're staying with Isabel March, and she's lunching out, so I simply daren't be late. She said she'd have Penny whilst I shopped."

He kept hold of her arm. "Wait a minute—don't vanish till we've got something fixed. Will you dine with me?"

She shook her head.

"No—Isabel's out—there'd be no one in the flat. I can't leave Penny. And if you say what you were going to say, I'll never speak to you again."

There was a rather sardonic gleam in the light eyes as he said,

"Undoubtedly an angel child. I adore them!"

Judy burst out laughing.

"Don't they teach you to tell lies better than that at Scotland Yard?"

"They don't teach us to tell lies at all. We're all very high-toned. My Chief is an esteemed Chapel member. If your Isabel March is out, what about my dropping in to help look after Penny?"

"She'll be asleep. I could do an omelette—reconstructed egg, of course."

"What time?"

In spite of himself his voice was eager. Judy wondered why. They had been friendly, but no more. They had dined together, danced together. And then she had had to go back to poor old Aunt Cathy, and he hadn't written or anything. Only now he said he had. . . . She wondered about that. She wondered if he was one of the out-of-sight, out-of-mind kind, because if he was, she wasn't the right person to try it on. A year's silence, and then that eager voice. And it wasn't like him to be eager. She recalled an elegant young man with a rather blasé manner. He was still elegant—slim and tall, with very fair hair slicked back and mirror-smooth, and light blue eyes which had appeared to contemplate his fellow-beings with supercilious amusement, but which at the moment were fixed upon her in rather a disturbing manner.

She began to regret the omelette. Because what was the good of being disturbed? She wasn't going to have any time for young men, what with Penny and getting a job as a housemaid. She had a moment of wanting to back out—she had a moment when she would have liked to run away. And then the voice of common sense chipped in with one of its most insidious and fallacious remarks—"After all, it's only one evening—what does it matter?"

She gave Frank a smile of pure relief, said, "Half past seven—3 Raynes Court Buildings, Cheriton Street," and walked rapidly away.

When one is four years old going to bed is a very important ceremony. Miss Penny Fossett exacted the full rites. Any attempt at hurry, any scamping, merely resulted in a mellifluous "Do it again." Judy's attempts to maintain the upper hand were conscientious, but they didn't always come off. The way of the transgressor was, unfortunately, so very beguiling. At the very moment of Judy's screwing herself up to be severe the infant sinner would remark with a heart-piercing smile, "It loves its Judy," and fling damp throttling arms about her neck.

On this particular evening the bath had been a very lingering one. Isabel had unearthed an aged rubber duck from an attic in her mother's country house. It should, of course, have gone to salvage long ago, but had been overlooked, much to Penny's delight. When she could be torn away from it, there was not as much time left as Judy could have wished. Even if you are completely indifferent to a young man, you do like to have time to do the hair and give nature a helping hand with the face before he comes to supper. It is difficult to bathe the very young without becoming dishevelled. The old-fashioned Nanny could do it, but it is a rapidly dying art. Judy was hot and damp as she sat on the edge of her bed and held out her arms.

"Now Penny—prayers."

Miss Penelope Fossett was wearing pale blue pyjamas. Her dark hair curled artlessly about her enchanting head. She had little pink ears and rather a heart-shaped face. Her eyes were unbelievably blue, her lashes unbelievably long and black. The colour in her cheeks was pure and deep. She diffused warmth, moisture, and a smell of lavender soap as she kneeled up beside Judy, bowed her head upon her folded hands, and emitted a long penetrating "Moo!" If you laughed you were lost. Judy bit the inside of her lip, which sometimes helped.

"Penny! I said prayers!"

One blue eye opened, gazed at her, and shut again.

"It is saying its prayers. It's a moo-cow. That's the way they say them."

It took about a quarter of an hour to persuade Penny to be human again. Even then a last faint contumacious "Moo!" followed the final amen.

Judy turned a deaf ear, forbade further conversation, and went to tidy herself up in the bathroom. She had just come to the conclusion that she had never looked plainer in her life, when the front door bell rang and she had to go and let Frank Abbott in.

They made the omelette together in Isabel's minute kitchen. There is nothing like a homely, domestic job for breaking the ice. By the time he had laid the table, and she had called him an idiot for dropping the butter-dish, they might have been married for years. Over the omelette, which was very good and had all sorts of exciting scraps in it, Frank told her so. His naturally impudent tongue was his own again, but if he expected to raise a blush he was disappointed. Miss Elliott agreed with perfect calm.

"Yes, we might—only not so dull."

"It mightn't be dull with the right person."

Judy proffered tomato sauce.

"You mightn't think it was going to be until it was too late. I mean, we both like this sauce, but if we had to eat it at every meal for the next forty or fifty years we'd be bored stiff."

"My child, you make me shudder! I can assure you that I have at least thirty distinct flavours—like all the soup and jelly makers used to advertise, and you could always try mixing them if thirty wasn't enough. Besides, the brain is not completely stagnant—I can invent new ones. You've got it all wrong. People are dull because of something in themselves—a tendency to stew over old tea-leaves—keeping the windows tight shut to prevent any new ideas getting in—all that sort of thing. You have been warned!''

"Thank you." Words and tone were meek. Her eyes mocked him.

When she saw he was going to speak, she said with her best smile,

"How many girls have you said that to?"

"I've only just thought of it. It's their loss."

Something made her say a little more quickly than she meant to,

"We're going away tomorrow."

"*We?*"

"Penny and I."

"Where?"

With the feeling of having reached nice firm, safe ground, Judy could relax. The smile came out again, bringing with it a rather pleasant dimple.

"We're going to be a housemaid."

"*What!*"

"A housemaid. In a nice safe village because of Penny. Their total casualties up to date are one goat in an outlying field."

"Did you say a housemaid?"

"I did. And if you're going to say I can do better than that—which is what everybody does say—you haven't tried, and I have. If I hadn't got Penny I could get dozens of jobs—but if I hadn't got Penny I should be called up. And I have got Penny, so that's that. And I'm going to keep her, so that's another that. And when you've got all that straightened out you'll find like I did that the only job you can get with a child is a domestic one—and you can only get that because people are so desperate they'll do anything. Think how nice and appropriate it is, the policeman and the housemaid having supper together!"

Frank looked down his long nose and didn't laugh.

"Must you?"

Judy nodded.

"Yes, I must. I haven't a bean. Aunt Cathy was living on an annuity, though nobody knew it. By the time I'd got everything paid up there wasn't anything left. John Fossett had nothing but his pay, so there's nothing for Penny except a minute pension, and I want to save that up to pay for her going to school later on.''

Frank crumbled a piece of bread. What business had John and Nora Fossett to get killed in an air raid and leave Judy to fend for their brat? He said in an angry voice,

"Where are you going?''

Judy was feeling pleased with herself. She removed the bread and told him not to waste good food. Then she answered his question.

"It sounds rather nice. Penny and I are to live with the family because—well, I rather gather the cook and butler put all their feet down and said they wouldn't have us. There are two Miss Pilgrims and an invalid nephew, and the house is called Pilgrim's Rest. The village is Holt St. Agnes, and—'' She got no farther, because Frank rapped the table and said in the loudest voice she had ever heard him use,

"You can't go there!''

Judy became Miss Elliot. Whilst remaining only just across the table from him, her lifted eyebrows and the expression of the eyes beneath them indicated that he had been relegated to a considerable distance. In a tone of suitable coolness she enquired,

"Why not?''

Frank wasn't cool at all. The detached and indifferent manner which he affected no longer afforded him any protection. He looked very much taken aback as he said,

"Judy, you mustn't. I say, don't look at me like that! You can't go there.''

"Why can't I? Is there anything wrong with the Miss Pilgrims? One of them came up to town to see me—I thought she was nice. Do you know them?''

He nodded.

"That would be Miss Columba. She's all right—at least I suppose she is.'' He ran a hand back over his hair and pulled himself together. "Look here, Judy, I'd like to talk to you about this. You know you always said I'd got more cousins than anyone you'd ever heard of, and I suppose I have. Well, one lot lives just outside Holt St. Agnes, and I've known the Pilgrims all my life. Roger and I were at school together."

She said with a zip in her voice, "That probably wasn't his fault."

"Don't be a fool! I'm serious. I want you to listen. Roger is just home from the Middle East. He was taken prisoner by the Italians, escaped, put in some time in hospital, and is still on sick leave. I've just had a spot of leave after 'flu myself. I've been staying with my cousins at Holt St. Agnes, and I saw quite a lot of Roger." He paused and looked at her hard. "You can hold your tongue, can't you? What I'm telling you is what everyone in the village knows more or less, but I wouldn't want Roger to think I'd been handing it on. He's a nice chap, but he's a bit of a dim bulb, and he's in the devil of a flap. I wouldn't be talking about it to anyone else, but you oughtn't to go there."

Judy sat opposite him with her elbows on the table and her chin in her hands. Her cheeks were flushed and her eyes wary. She said,

"Why?"

He hesitated, a thing so unusual that it rattled him. The cool self-assurance to which he was accustomed had left him in the lurch. It was like coming into a house and finding the furniture gone. It rattled him. He found nothing better to say than,

"Things keep happening."

"What kind of things?"

This was the devil. The gap between what he could get into words and what he couldn't get into words was too wide. And behind that there was the horrid niggling thought that the gap had only become evident when he learned that it was Judy who was going to Pilgrim's Rest. If it had been anyone else, he wouldn't have bothered his head.

Judy repeated her question.

"What kind of things?"

He said, "Accidents—or perhaps not—Roger thinks not. The ceiling came down in his room—if he hadn't gone to sleep over a book downstairs he'd have been killed. Another room was burnt out, with him inside—the door jammed and he very nearly didn't get out in time."

Judy kept her eyes on his face.

"Who does the place belong to?"

"Him."

"Is he the invalid nephew?"

"No—that's Jerome. He's a cousin, a good bit older than Roger. Smashed up at Dunkirk. No money. They took him in—have a nurse for him. They're a very clannish family."

"Is he, or is Roger, well—a neurotic type? Would it be either of them playing tricks?"

"I don't know. It wouldn't be like either of them if they were normal. And both things might have been accidents. In the first case a tap had been left running and a sink had overflowed. That's what brought the ceiling down. In the second Roger went to sleep in front of a fire and the whole place littered with papers he'd been sorting. A spark may have jumped out of the fire."

Judy said, "Is that all?"

There was a little scorn in her voice. It got him on the raw. He said more than he had meant to say.

"Roger doesn't believe his father's death was an accident."

"Why doesn't he?"

Frank's shoulder jerked.

"Old Pilgrim went for a ride and never came back. They found him with a broken neck. The mare came home in a lather, and the old groom says there was a thorn under the saddle—but as they'd come down in a brier patch there's a perfectly believable explanation. Only that makes rather a lot of things to explain, don't you think? I don't want you to go there."

He saw her frown, but there was no anger in her eyes.

"It's not so easy, you know. Everyone says there are millions of jobs, but there aren't—not with Penny. Even now people don't want a child in the house—you'd think you were asking if you could bring a tiger. And then a lot of them seem to think I couldn't have Penny if she wasn't mine. When I tell them about Nora and John they get a kind of we've-heard-that-tale-before look. I was beginning to think I should have to go round with Nora's marriage lines and Penny's birth-certificate and even then they'd have gone on believing the worst, when I saw Miss Pilgrim's advertisement and answered it. And I liked her, and it's a nice safe village. And anyhow I couldn't back out at the last minute. We're going down there tomorrow. It's no good, Frank.''

He found himself accepting that. It laid a burden on his spirits.

Judy pushed back her chair and got up.

"Nice of you to care and all that." Her tone, casual again, indicated that the subject was now closed.

As they cleared away and washed up together, the sense of pull and strain was gone. Presently she was asking him about the people at Holt St. Agnes—about his cousins, and he was offering to write and tell them she was going to Pilgrim's Rest. And then,

"You'll like Lesley Freyne. She's right in the village, only a stone's throw from the Pilgrims. Both the houses are right on the village street. She's a good sort.''

"Who is she—one of your cousins?''

"No—the local heiress. Rather shy and not very young. Pots of money and a big house. She's got about twenty evacuees there. She was going to marry a cousin of the Pilgrims, but it never came off—''

He had nearly stumbled into telling her about Henry Clayton, but he caught himself in time. She would only think he was piling it on, and it was, of course, quite irrelevant. He changed the subject abruptly.

"If by any chance a Miss Silver turns up, either in the house or in the village, I'd like you to know that she's a very particular friend of mine.''

Judy gave him a bright smile.

"How nice. Do tell me all about her. Who is she?''

Frank was to all appearance himself again. His eye had a quizzical gleam, and his voice its negligent drawl as he replied,

"She is the one and only. I sit at her feet and adore. You will too, I expect.''

Judy felt this to be extremely unlikely, but she went on

smiling in an interested manner whilst Frank continued his panegyric.

"Her name is Maud—same as in Tennyson's poetry, which she fervently admires. If you so far forget yourself as to put an 'e' on to it, she will forgive you in time because she has a kind heart and very high principles, but it will take some doing."

"What are you talking about?"

"Maudie. I love her passionately. She used to be a governess, but now she is a private detective. She can't really be a contemporary of Lord Tennyson's, but she manages to produce that effect. I've told Roger to go and see her, so she may be coming down, and if she does, I shall feel a lot happier. Only you don't know anything, remember. She may be just an ordinary visitor taking a holiday in the village or anything, so not a word to a soul. But if she's there, you'll have someone to hold on to."

Judy swished water into the washing-up bowl and stuck her chin in the air.

Miss Silver was inclined to see the hand of Providence in trifles. Her first contact with the Pilgrim case occurred when she had just finished working out a new and elaborate stitch for the jumper which she intended for her niece Ethel's birthday. This she regarded as providential, for though she could, and did, knit her way serenely through all the complications which murder produces, she found it difficult to concentrate upon a really elaborate new pattern at the same time. Ethel Burkett's annual jumper provided sufficient mental exercise without being brought into competition with a criminal case.

She was considering her good fortune in having obtained this excellent pre-war wool. So soft—such a lovely shade of blue—and no coupons, since it had been produced from a box in the Vicarage attics by Miss Sophy Fell, who had pressed, positively pressed, it on her. And it had been very carefully put away with camphor, so it was as good as on the somewhat distant day when it had been spun.

She had all her stitches on the needles, and the pattern well fixed in her mind, when her front door bell rang and Emma

Meadows announced Major Pilgrim. She saw a slight, dark young man with a sallow complexion and a worried frown.

On his side Roger Pilgrim was at once reminded of his aunts. Not that Miss Silver resembled any of them in person, but she and her surroundings appeared to be of approximately the same vintage. His Aunt Millicent, who was as a matter of fact a great-aunt, possessed some curly walnut chairs which were the spit and image of those adorning Miss Silver's flat—waists, and bow legs, and tight upholstery—only the stuff on Aunt Milly's had once been green, whilst Miss Silver's were quite freshly covered in rather a bright shade of blue. Both ladies crowded every available inch of mantelshelf and table-top—Miss Silver's writing-table excluded—with photographs in archaic silver frames. His Aunt Tina had clung for years to very similar flowered wall-paper, and possessed at least two of the pictures which confronted him as he entered—*Bubbles* and *The Black Brunswicker*. But the frames of Aunt Tina's were brown, whilst these were of the shiny yellow maple so dear to the Victorian age.

Miss Silver herself added to the homely effect. His old Cousin Connie also wore her hair in a curled fringe after the fashion set by Queen Alexandra in the late years of the previous century. Aunt Collie's stockings were of a similar brand of black ribbed wool. For the rest, Miss Silver was herself—a little governessy person with neat features and a lot of grey-brown hair very strictly controlled by a net. It being three o'clock in the afternoon, she was wearing a pre-war dress of olive-green cashmere with a little boned lace front, very fresh and clean. A pair of pince-nez on a fine gold chain was looped up and fastened on the left side by a bar brooch set with pearls. She also wore a row of bog-oak beads ingeniously carved, and a large brooch of the same material in the shape of a rose, with an Irish pearl at its heart. Nothing could have felt less like a visit to a private detective.

Miss Silver, having shaken hands and indicated a chair, bestowed upon him the kind, impersonal smile with which she would in earlier days have welcomed a new and nervous pupil. Twenty years as a governess had set their mark upon her. In the most improbable surroundings she conjured up the safe, humdrum atmosphere of the schoolroom. Her voice preserved its note of mild but unquestioned authority. She said,

"What can I do for you, Major Pilgrim?"

He was facing the light. Not in uniform. A well-cut suit, not too new. He wore glasses—large round ones with tortoise-shell rims. Behind them his dark eyes had a worried look. Her own went to his hands, and saw them move restlessly on the shiny walnut carving which emerged from the padded arms of the Victorian chair.

She had to repeat her question, because he just sat there, fingering the smooth wood and frowning at the pattern on the bright blue carpet which had kept its colour so well. Reflecting with satisfaction that it looked as good as new, she said,

"Will you not tell me what I can do for you?"

She saw him start, glance at her quickly, and then away again. Whether people use words to convey their thoughts or to conceal them, there is one thing very difficult to conceal from a practised observer. In that momentary glance Miss Silver had seen that thing quite plainly. It was the look you may see in the eyes of a horse about to shy. She thought this young man was reluctant to face whatever it was that had brought him here. He was not the first. A great many people had brought their fears, their faults, and their follies into this room, hoping for they hardly knew what, and then sat nervous and tongue-tied until she helped them out. She smiled encouragingly at Roger Pilgrim, and addressed him very much as if he had been ten years old.

"Something is troubling you. You will feel better when you have told me what it is. Perhaps you might begin by telling me who gave you my address."

This undoubtedly came as a relief. He removed his gaze from the multi-coloured roses, peonies, and acanthus leaves with which the carpet was festooned, and said,

"Oh, it was Frank—Frank Abbott."

Miss Silver's smile became warmer and less impersonal.

"Sergeant Abbott is a great friend of mine. Have you known him for long?"

"Well, as a matter of fact, we were at school together.

He's a bit older, but our families knew each other. He comes down to stay with some cousins near us. As a matter of fact, he was there last week-end having a spot of leave after 'flu, and I got talking to him. Frank's a pretty sound fellow—though you wouldn't think it to look at him, if you know what I mean.'' He gave a short nervous laugh. ''Seems awfully funny, somebody you've been at school with being a policeman. Detective Sergeant Abbott! You know, we used to call him Fug at school. He used to put on masses of hair-fug. I remember his having a lot which fairly stank of White Rose, and the maths master going round smelling us all till he found out who it was, and sending Fug to wash his head.''

While recounting this anecdote he looked a little happier, but the worried frown returned as he concluded.

''He told me I'd better come and see you. He says you're a marvel. But I don't see what anyone can really do. You see there isn't any evidence—Fug said so himself. He said there was nothing the police could take any notice of. You see, I put it up to him because of his being at Scotland Yard, but he said there really wasn't anything they would do about it, and he advised me to come to you. Only I don't suppose it's any use.''

Miss Silver's needles clicked briskly. She had the new pattern well in hand. She coughed and said,

''You do not expect me to reply to that, do you? If you will tell me what you seem to have told Sergeant Abbott, I may be able to give you an opinion. Pray proceed.''

Roger Pilgrim proceeded. This was the voice of authority. He blurted out, ''I think someone's trying to kill me,'' and immediately thought how damnfool silly it sounded.

Miss Silver said, ''Dear me!'' And then, ''What makes you think so?''

He stared at her. There she sat, the picture of a mild old maid, looking at him across her knitting. He might have been saying he thought it was going to rain. He kicked himself for having come. She probably thought he was a neurotic ass. Perhaps he was a neurotic ass. He frowned at the carpet and said,

"What's the good of my telling you? When I put it into words it sounds idiotic."

Miss Silver coughed.

"Whatever it is, it is certainly worrying you. If there was no cause for your worry, you would be glad to have this proved to you, would you not? If, on the other hand, there is a cause, it is a matter of some importance that it should be removed. What makes you think that someone is trying to kill you?"

He looked up with an air of arrested attention.

"Well, I thought they were."

Miss Silver coughed and said "They?" on an enquiring note. She was knitting very fast in the continental fashion, her hands low in her lap, her eyes on her visitor.

"Oh, well—that's just a way of speaking. I haven't an idea who it is."

"I think it would be better if you were to tell me what has happened. Something must have happened."

He nodded emphatically.

"You've said it! The things happened—you can't get away from that. Lumps of plaster aren't just imagination, and no more is a lot of burnt ash where there used to be papers and a carpet."

Miss Silver said, "Dear me!" And then, "Pray begin at the beginning and tell me all about these incidents."

He was sitting forward in his chair now, looking at her.

"The bother is I don't know where to begin."

Miss Silver coughed.

"At the beginning, Major Pilgrim."

The eyes behind the glasses met hers in a worried look.

"Well, as a matter of fact that's just what beats me—I don't know where it begins. You see, it's not only me, it's my father. I was out in the Middle East when my father died—I haven't been home very long. And of course, as Pug says, there's no evidence. But I ask you, why should a quiet beast that he'd ridden every day for the last ten years suddenly go mad and bolt with him? She'd never done such a thing in her life. When she came back all of a lather they went out to look for him, and found him with a broken neck. The old groom says she'd a thorn under the saddle—says somebody must have put it there. The trouble is it wasn't the only one. She hadn't thrown him, you see—they'd come down together, and the place was just a tangle of wild roses and brambles. But what William said, and what I say is, what would make her bolt? And we both got the same answer—only it isn't evidence."

"What reason had anyone to wish your father dead?"

"Ah—there you have me! There wasn't any reason—not any *reason*."

The heavily accented word invited a question. Miss Silver obliged.

"You speak as if there was something which was not a reason?"

"Well, as a matter of fact that's just about the size of it. Mind you, I don't believe in that sort of thing myself, but if you were to ask William—that's the groom I was talking about—or any of the other old people in the village, they'd say it was because he was going to sell the place."

"And there is a superstition about such a contingency?"

The word appeared to puzzle him. He frowned, and then got there.

"Oh, yes—I see what you mean. Well, as a matter of fact there is. The place has been in the family donkey's years. I don't set a lot of store by that sort of thing myself—a bit out of date, if you know what I mean. No good trying to live in the past and hang on to all the things your ancestors grabbed—is there? I mean, what's the good? We haven't any money, and if I fancied an heiress, she probably wouldn't fancy me. So when my father wrote and said he was going to sell I told him that as far as I was concerned, he could get on with it—only as a matter of fact he never got the letter. But people in villages are very superstitious."

"What form does this superstition take, Major Pilgrim?"

"Well, as a matter of fact it's a rhyme. Some ass had it cut into the stone over the fireplace in the hall, so it's always there—under everyone's nose, so to speak."

Miss Silver coughed.

"What does it say?"

"It's all rubbish of course—made up round our name and

the name of the house. We're Pilgrims, the house is Pilgrim's Rest. And the rhyme says:

> 'If Pilgrim fare upon the Pilgrims' Way,
> And leave his Rest, he'll find nor rest nor stay.
> Stay Pilgrim in thy Rest, or thou shalt find
> Ill luck before, Death but one pace behind.' ''

He gave a short nervous laugh.

"A lot of nonsense, but I should think everyone in the village believes that's why the mare bolted and my father broke his neck."

Miss Silver continued to knit.

"Superstitions are extremely tenacious. After your father's death, Major Pilgrim, were the negotiations for the sale carried on?"

"Well, as a matter of fact they weren't. You see, by that time I'd managed to get taken prisoner. I was in a prisoners of war camp in Italy, and nothing more happened. Then when Musso got the sack I escaped. I was in hospital for a bit, and then I got home. The chap who wanted to buy the place bobbed up again, and I thought I'd play. That's when the ceiling came down on me."

Miss Silver coughed.

"Literally—or metaphorically?"

Seeing that he was a little out of his depth, she amended her question.

"Do you mean that the ceiling really came down?"

That emphatic nod again.

"I should just about think it did! Rather a spot ceiling too—nymphs, and garlands, and all that sort of thing. It's not the best bedroom—that's next door—but the eighteenth-century chap who put in the ceiling there had it carried on into his dressing-room. He cribbed it from some Italian palace, and it's the sort of thing people come and look at. Well, about a month ago my particular lot came down all over where I'd have been if I had been in bed, which I would have been if I hadn't gone to sleep over a poisonously dull book in the study."

"Dear me! Why did it come down?"

"Because there was a leak from one of the water-pipes and the nymphs and whatnots had all got wringing wet. They weighed quite enough to start with, and the water brought them down like a cartload of bricks. If I'd been in that bed I'd have been dead—there isn't any doubt about that."

"A very providential escape. I think you mentioned another incident?"

He nodded.

"A week ago. There's a sort of small room my father used to keep his papers in. Odd sort of place. Pigeon-holes right up to the ceiling, all crammed with papers. Well, I'd been getting on with going through them a bit at a time, and last Tuesday afternoon I'd had a good old worry at them. Round about half past six I had a drink, and the next thing I knew I couldn't keep my eyes open. I sat down in a chair by the fire and went to sleep. I must have been dead to the world, because I didn't wake up till the whole place was in a blaze. I don't know what started it. It could have been a spark from the fire—wood throws them out—and there was a pretty fair litter of papers, one of them might have caught. But what made me go off to sleep like that, and why didn't I wake up? I'm a pretty light sleeper, you know."

Miss Silver said, "What do you mean?"

The frowning gaze met hers.

"I think someone doped me and set light to the papers," said Roger Pilgrim.

Chapter Two

Miss Silver laid down her knitting, balancing it carefully on the arm of her chair, after which she got up and, crossing over to the writing-table, seated herself there, all without hurry. When she had opened a drawer and taken out an exercise-book with a bright green cover she addressed herself to Roger Pilgrim.

"Perhaps you will come over here—it will be more convenient. I should like to take some notes."

By the time he had settled himself in an upright chair which faced her across the table she was waiting for him, the exercise-book laid open before her and a neatly pointed pencil in her hand. Her manner, though perfectly kind, was brisk and businesslike as she said,

"If these two incidents were deliberate attempts upon your life, you are certainly in need of advice and protection. But I would like to know a little more. You spoke of a leaky pipe. I suppose that you had it examined. Was there any sign of its having been tampered with?"

He had an embarrassed look.

"Well, as a matter of fact it wasn't a pipe—it was a tap."

Her look reproved him.

"Accuracy is of the very first importance, Major Pilgrim."

He pulled off his glasses and began to polish them with a dark blue handkerchief. Without them his eyes had a defenceless look. They avoided hers.

"Yes—that's just it. We thought it must be a pipe, but there wasn't anything wrong with the pipes. As a matter of fact there wasn't any water laid on upstairs until my father put it in, so the plumbing is fairly modern. On the attic floor they turned a dressing-room into a bathroom and cut a bit off to make a housemaid's cupboard with a sink. When the ceiling came down, the tap over this sink was found running. Someone had left the plug in, so of course it had overflowed. The trouble is, I don't think that would account for my ceiling coming down. The cupboard is not directly over it, for one thing, and I don't think there'd have been enough water, for another. I've thought about it a lot. There's a loose board in the room right over mine. The room hasn't been used for years. Suppose someone bunged up the sink and left the tap running to make it look as if the water came from there, and then helped out by sloshing a few buckets of water under that board—it would have brought the ceiling down all right. What do you think about that?"

Miss Silver nodded slowly.

"What is the distance from the sink to the edge of your ceiling?"

"Something like eight or nine feet."

"Was there water under the boards all that way?"

"Well, that's just it—there was. Some, you know, but not an awful lot. The passage ceiling underneath didn't come down. And mind you, the ceiling that did—the one in my room—would sop up quite a lot of water—all those heavy mouldings, and the nymphs and things."

"Quite so." She coughed. "Of what does the staff at Pilgrim's Rest consist?"

"Well, there's only Robbins and his wife that sleep in. They've been there ever since I can remember. There's a village girl of about fifteen who comes in by the day. She might have left the tap running. But she goes away at six, and Mrs. Robbins says she drew water from it at ten o'clock herself when she and Robbins went up to bed. And she says she's never left a tap running in her life, and would she be likely to begin now?"

Miss Silver made a note—"Robbins to bed at ten o'clock." Then she asked,

"What time did the ceiling come down?"

"About one o'clock. It made no end of a row—woke me up."

Miss Silver repeated a remark she had already made.

"You had a most providential escape. You believe that your life was attempted. I can see that you are quite sincere in this belief. May I ask who it is that you suspect?"

He replaced his glasses and looked her straight in the face.

"I haven't the slightest idea."

"Have you any enemies?"

"Not that I know about."

"What motive do you suggest?"

He looked away again.

"Well, there's that business about selling the house. My father starts to sell it, and a quiet old mare he'd ridden for years bolts with him and breaks his neck. I start to sell it, and a ceiling that's been there for a hundred and sixty years or so comes down across my bed, and a room where I'm sorting papers is burned out whilst I'm too dead asleep to do anything about it.''

Miss Silver looked at him gravely. "You were indeed fortunate to escape. You have not told me how you did so.''

"Well, as a matter of fact it was my trouser-leg catching that brought me around. I had come in from outside, and my old waterproof was hanging over the back of a chair. I put it over my head and got to the door. You couldn't see across the room for smoke—all the wooden pigeon-holing had caught. And when I got to the door I couldn't get it open. You know, I've an idea that it was locked. The key was there quite handy on the outside, so that I could leave the papers and lock up when I got through.''

"Dear me! What did you do?''

"I broke the window and got out that way. I got William and his grandson from the stables, and we put the fire out. Most of the papers were burned—which was a pity, but it might have been worse. The room is in the oldest part of the house, and the walls behind the pigeon-holing are stone, so the fire wouldn't spread.''

"A most fortunate circumstance. Major Pilgrim—you say that to the best of your belief the door was locked. I presume that you verified this.''

"Well, as a matter of fact by the time the fire was out it wasn't. But there it is—I couldn't open it when it wanted opening, and in the end I don't know who did open it, because by that time practically everyone in the house was rallying around. Anyone might have unlocked it, but no one seems to remember whether they did or not.''

"In fact anyone in the house may have locked it, anyone may have unlocked it, or it may never have been locked at all?''

Roger Pilgrim looked at his feet.

"That's about the size of it," he said. "But why wouldn't it open—can you tell me that?''

Miss Silver changed the subject.

"Now, Major Pilgrim, will you give me the names of everyone who was in the house on these two occasions—the name and just a short description.''

He had picked up a half sheet of writing-paper from the table. His hands folded and refolded it, the fingers as tense as if they were about some matter of life and death. He kept his eyes on the twisting paper, but Miss Silver doubted whether he saw it. He said in a dragging voice,

"Well—I don't know, you know—"

Miss Silver coughed. Her pencil tapped the table.

"You are not married?"

"Oh, no."

"Engaged?"

"Well—as a matter of fact—no, I'm not engaged."

He received a bright smile.

"I see—I am premature. But you have an attachment. Was the lady in the house at the time of either of these incidents?"

"Oh, no."

"In the neighbourhood?"

"Oh, no."

"Then let us return to those who were in the house. Will you give me the names?"

"Well, there are my aunts—my father's sisters, but a good bit older. My grandfather was married twice—they belonged to the first family. There were four of them, all girls. These two didn't marry. They have always lived at Pilgrim's Rest."

"Their names?"

"Aunt Collie—short for Columba. And Aunt Netta—short for Janetta."

Miss Silver wrote in the exercise-book, "Miss Columba Pilgrim—Miss Janetta Pilgrim."

"And now a little about them."

"Well, Aunt Collie's large, and Aunt Netta's small. Aunt Collie's mad on gardening. I don't know what we'd do without her, because of course there's no labour to be had. She and old Pell just keep things going. Aunt Netta doesn't do anything except embroidery. She's making new needlework covers for all the chairs—she's been at it for thirty years or so. Shocking waste of time, but she's by way of being an invalid, so I suppose it's a good thing for her to have something like that."

Miss Silver wrote in the exercise-book. When she had finished she looked up and said, "Pray go on."

"Well, there's my cousin, Jerome Pilgrim. He got pretty badly smashed up at Dunkirk. He has to have a nurse. We're lucky to have been able to keep her. She's very good with him, and she keeps an eye on Aunt Netta too."

"Her name?"

"Oh, Day—Miss Lona Day."

Miss Silver wrote down, "Jerome Pilgrim—Lona Day," and enquired,

"What age is your cousin?"

"Jerome? Oh, about thirty-eight—thirty-nine. He's Captain Pilgrim, if you want to put that down. He was a barrister before the war—rather mildly, if you know what I mean. And he wrote thrillers—not at all bad. But he hasn't done anythng since Dunkirk—too smashed up, poor chap."

"Is he confined to his bed?"

He stared.

"Jerome? Oh, no. He gets about—except when he has a bad turn. It's his head chiefly. They used to say he'd get all right, but he doesn't, you know."

Miss Silver coughed.

"Major Pilgrim, I am obliged to ask you—is your cousin at all mentally unbalanced?"

The stare was repeated.

"Jerome? Oh, good lord no! I mean—no of course he isn't, poor chap."

Miss Silver left it at that. If at this stage of the proceedings it occurred to her that an explanation of the incidents narrated by Roger Pilgrim might not be far to seek, she had a constitutional caution which warned her against accepting too easy a solution. She contented herself with underlining Captain Jerome Pilgrim's name, and enquired,

"Are those all the inmates of Pilgrim's Rest?"

Roger disliked the word inmates. Coming on the top of being asked whether poor old Jerome was off his head, it produced a definitely irritated feeling. He had found it a relief to talk. Now he began to wish he hadn't come. It was in a slightly sulky voice that he replied,

"No—there's Miss Elliot, and the little girl."

He met an encouraging look and a questioning "Yes?" He explained.

"She's come down to help in the house. One of the village girls who came in has been called up, and the other is only fifteen."

"And what age is Miss Elliot?"

"Oh, quite young. Her name's Judy. About twenty-two, I should think. She isn't called up because of the little girl. It's her sister's and there isn't anyone else to look after it. The father and mother were killed in an air raid."

Miss Silver inclined her head.

"A tragic bereavement."

She wrote, "Miss Judy Elliot," and paused with suspended pencil for the name of the little girl.

"Oh, Penny Fossett. She's about three. And they couldn't have had anything to do with what's been happening, because they've only just come."

"I see. Major Pilgrim—who would succeed to your property if you were to meet with a fatal accident?"

He looked startled. Then his frown deepened.

"Oh, my brother Jack. But we don't know whether he's alive or not. He was in hospital in Singapore the last we heard of him, just before the Japs walked in. And of course we hope he's all right, but we can't tell."

"So that if either of those accidents had had a fatal result, the sale of the property would have been indefinitely postponed?"

"I suppose it would. As a matter of fact it couldn't be sold as long as there was no proof one way or another about Jack."

"And if there was proof of your brother's death—who would inherit then?"

"Oh, Jerome."

There was quite a pause. When she thought it had lasted long enough Miss Silver said in a serious voice,

"What do you wish me to do? If I am to help you, it will be necessary for me to be on the spot. I could either come down openly as an enquiry agent, or, which would be preferable, as an ordinary visitor. Do you think it would be possible to confide in one of your aunts? Because if so, I could be paying a visit in the character of an old friend—perhaps an old schoolfellow."

He said in a doubtful voice,

"I might tell Aunt Collie. Not Aunt Netta—she'd get in a flap. Or I might tell Lona—she could say you were her aunt or something."

Miss Silver glanced at her list of names.

"Miss Lona Day—the nurse? No, I do not think that would be desirable. It would be better to confide in Miss Columba. People who spend their time gardening are as a rule very reliable. The qualities of industry, patience and perseverance are fostered, and they usually have calm and steady nerves. I do not think that you gave me Miss Day's age."

"Lona? Didn't I? Well, as a matter of fact I don't know it. She'd be somewhere over thirty, you know. She's an awfully good nurse, and I don't know what we'd do without her. Now I come to think of it, she must be nearer forty than thirty, because there was something said about her age when she came. Three years ago it would be, because it wasn't very long before all that business about Henry."

Miss Silver coughed and enquired,

"Who is Henry?"

Judy had come to Pilgrim's Rest in the pouring rain. It is not the best way to arrive, or to see a house for the first time. The old hired car which had met them at Ledlington stopped halfway down the village street. It was about the wettest street she had ever seen, because not only were there gallons of water falling on it from the low grey sky, but quite a sizable little stream ran down the left-hand side in a paved channel bridged at intervals to give access to the houses which lay beyond, each with its own front garden and paved or gravelled path.

The car stopped on the right, and she saw the rain running in cascades over what looked like a conservatory. When the old driver opened the door of the car she discovered that it was a glazed passage about fifteen feet long leading from the street to the house. Of the house itself she had only a vague impression. For one thing, there was a high brick wall on either side of the entrance. It looked big and old-fashioned and there were a lot of windows. She wondered if she would have to clean them.

And then the door of the glass passage was opening, and she jumped Penny across the narrow wet pavement on to old, dry cocoanut matting. The passage was paved with small red and black tiles, with the cocoanut matting running down the middle. A row of staging on either side supported some sparse and disagreeable plants. She was to discover that they were a source of controversy between Miss Columba and her sister—Miss Netta insisting that they should be retained because they had always had plants there, and Miss Collie asseverating that you couldn't expect any self-respecting plant to put up with the draught in that horrible passage, and that if Miss Netta wanted to keep them there she could look after them herself. At the time, Judy was taken up with paying the driver, taking charge of the hand-luggage inseparable from travelling with a child, and controlling Penny, who was thrilled to the core.

It was the butler who had opened the door, an elderly man with a disapproving face. Whether it was always like that, or whether he thought it as well that Judy should know straight away how he and Mrs. Robbins felt about a young lady housemaid with a child of four, she had no means of knowing. There was, however, no sign of softening when Penny put out a small polite hand and said, "How do you do?" in her very best social manner.

They came into a large square hall with rooms opening off it on either side and a staircase going up in the background. The house felt big and cold though it wasn't really a cold day. When she sorted out her impressions afterwards, that is what they amounted to—rain, and a big, cold house, and Robbins' unwelcoming face.

The sorting out took place, as it generally does, at bedtime. She and Penny had a nice room, only one floor up, which was a great relief to her mind, because she would have hated to leave Penny all by herself at the top of the house. Their room was quite near the stairs, and farther along there was the invalid cousin, and his nurse, and a bathroom. She and Penny didn't use it. They went through a door and half way down a crooked stair, and when you got there, the floor was all uneven and the roof very low, and the bath was enormous, with a wide mahogany surround. Penny found it all very thrilling.

But their room was quite modern, with twin beds enamelled white, which was a surprise, because the house rather suggested gloomy four-posters. Judy lay on a rather hard mattress and told herself that it wasn't too bad at all; that everything would feel better when the rain had stopped and the sun came out; that it was idiotic to suppose it wouldn't come out, because it always did in the end; and doubly, trebly idiotic, to let anything Frank Abbott said make the slightest difference to her feelings about Pilgrim's Rest.

She began to think about the people there. Miss Columba coming into the hall to meet them. Rather a shock after only seeing her in town, large and quite normally covered up in a fur coat and a felt hat. In sprawling birdseye tweeds she looked immense, with an orange sweater up to her double chin and thick curly grey hair cut almost as short as a man's. Perfectly enormous hands and feet, and even less to say for herself than at their previous meeting. But quite nice and kind—the sort of kindness that expects to be taken for granted, and takes you for granted too. Very difficult to connect her as a sister with Miss Janetta, sitting in the sofa corner working at a tambour frame with a small frail white hand which looked as if it had never in its life done anything more practical than embroidery. The one thing that she and Miss Collie had in common was the curl in their hair, but Miss Netta's was silver-white where Miss Collie's was iron-grey, and she wore it in the most elaborate rolls, and curls, and twirls. And not one of them looking as if it could get out of place if it tried. Judy had wondered how long they took to do, and could make an approximate guess when she was informed that Miss Netta's room could never be done till twelve o'clock, as she breakfasted in bed, and did not leave it until then—"I'm a sad invalid. I'm afraid I give a great deal of trouble."

Judy thought she didn't look in the least ill, with those blue eyes and pink cheeks, but of course you never could tell. Some of the colour was make-up, and very well done. She suspected that her personal appearance was one of Miss Netta's preoccupations, the other two being her embroidery and her health.

Roger Pilgrim—she had sat through a meal with him, but they hadn't exchanged a word except the bare conventional "How do you do?" If Miss Janetta didn't look ill, Roger certainly did. And nervous. His hand shook when he lifted his glass, his eyes looked here and there, he jumped when a door banged. Having come in late for the meal, he disappeared as soon as it was over, with a hasty "I'll go and have a cigarette with Jerome." When she came to think of it Judy couldn't remember that he had spoken at all between his "How do you do?" to her and this excuse to get out of the room.

The invalid cousin's name naturally brought Miss Day into her mind. Lona—that's what they all called her—the nurse who looked after Captain Pilgrim and Miss Netta. She didn't dress like a nurse, because Captain Pilgrim hated things that rustled and Miss Netta found the uniform inartistic. So there was Miss Day with a skirt of russet tweed and a soft yellow jumper. Not very young, but she had a good figure, and the jumper showed it off. Not goodlooking exactly—a peaked, pale face, greenish hazel eyes, and a lot of chestnut hair— rather good hair. There was some likeness—something odd and elusive—Judy couldn't place it. It stayed in her mind in the irritating niggling way that sort of thing does. But she was quite sure she had never seen Lona Day before—she would have remembered her if she had. Something warm and interested in her manner. She seemed really to care about Penny, and about Nora and John. It wasn't Judy who mentioned them, it was Miss Janetta. Lona Day hadn't said a word, but Judy felt as if she cared. She had talked very nicely about Captain Pilgrim.

"I'm afraid his room is going to be rather tiresome for you. You will have to do it whilst he is in the bathroom, but that will give you quite half an hour, because he shaves there as well as having his bath. He wouldn't shave for a long time because of the scar, but I am so glad he has begun now. He's so sensitive about the disfigurement, and it's so bad for him, poor fellow."

"Doesn't he come down at all?"

"Oh, yes, he does as a rule—on his good days. But it really is an ordeal for him to meet a stranger, and he's dreadfully afraid of frightening your little Penny. What a perfectly lovely child she is. I don't wonder you feel you can't part with her. And so good!"

The last of all this was the best. Penny was being the authentic angel child, and she had gone down in the most miraculous way. It was too good to last, but just as well to begin with a buttered side. For this evening at least, Penny had done all the things which even the Victorian child was supposed to do—had said "Yes, please," and "No, thank you," had dropped no crumb on the floor, spilled no drip on the table, and had reserved for the privacy of the bath an enthusiastic appreciation of Miss Columba.

"Wouldn't she make a lovely big yelephant!"

With a sleepy giggle Judy drifted out of waking thought.

Chapter Three

The sun shone next day. Penny could be loosed in the garden whilst Judy coped with the housework. There was going to be quite enough of it—she could see that. Early morning tea to all the bedrooms, but she didn't have to collect the trays. The child from the village did that. Her name was Gloria Pell, and old Pell the gardener was her grandfather. Gloria had red hair, and a free and impudent tongue when out of earshot of the Robbinses, who had somehow managed to inspire her with awe. Judy had her till eleven o'clock, when she descended to the kitchen to be at Mrs. Robbins' beck and call. She came at eight, and stayed until six.

This first day she was being uppish and superior and showing Judy how, but friendly underneath.

"It's not a bad place if you don't get across Mr. Robbins. He's a one, he is—and Mrs. Robbins too. But she's a lovely cook. My mum says it's a opportunity, and I've got to watch and see how she does everything. My mum says there's going to be good money in cooking. My Auntie Ethel, she cooks for one of these British Restaurants, and she says they're going to be all the thing. But I dunno. My Auntie Mabel says my hair 'ud be just right for me to go in for the hairdressing line—waves up lovely with a curler or two, only Mrs. Robbins makes me brush it flat when I come of a morning. A shame, I call it. I bet she couldn't get her hair to curl, not if she took the kitchen poker to it."

The house was big and rambling. Behind the Victorian glazed passage was an eighteenth-century façade, and behind that a perfect rabbit-warren of rooms on different levels, with steps going up and steps coming down, and passages all over the place. A lot of the rooms were empty. Judy said to herself, "The housemaid's nightmare!" But it fascinated her all the same. One fairly level corridor ran right and left from the top of the stairs.

Gloria, full of importance, pointed out the room where the ceiling had fallen.

"It's in ever such a mess, but I can't show you, because Mr. Roger's locked the door and taken away the key. He's moved in next door. This is the best bedroom, on the other side of the one where the ceiling's down. Mr. Pilgrim's room it was. And the ceiling is all the same as the one that came down. I shouldn't wonder if it wasn't any too safe either. Too heavy by half, my mum says, with all those dancing girls and bunches of flowers—and not too decent, she says. She used to be under-housemaid here before she married my dad. And look at the staff they kept then! Mr. and Mrs. Robbins were here same as they are now—evergreens my mum calls them. And there was a kitchen-maid, and a house-parlour under Mr. Robbins, and a head housemaid, and my mum, and a woman to scrub, and a boy for the boots and knives."

Judy contemplated the big room, and felt glad she would not have to do it every day. There were acres of old-fashioned Brussels carpet and a great deal of monumental Victorian furniture. But the bed was much older—a huge eighteenth-century four-poster, stripped of its curtains now, but with what looked like the original valance showing just how heavy and gloomy they must have been. The colour had gone away to a rusty brown, but where the pleats shielded it from the light there were streaks of the old deep red. The walls had a flowered paper—rose-garlands tied up with blue ribands, but there were so many pictures that they only appeared in bits. Most of the pictures were portraits. Mr. Pilgrim had obviously liked to have his family around him.

Gloria, very full of herself, did showman.

"That's Mr. Roger when he was a baby—they didn't ever think he'd live. And that's Mrs. Pilgrim—she died when he was a week old. And that's Miss Janetta and Miss Columba, took together when they was presented at Court. And that's Mrs. Clayton—Miss Mary Pilgrim that was."

Judy turned from a thin, gawky Miss Columba and a quite recognizable Miss Janetta, both in white satin, to the portrait of a handsome smiling young woman with a baby on her knee.

Gloria dropped her voice, but went on at full speed.

"She died quite young. That's Mr. Henry Clayton on her lap. And that's him grown up. My mum says he was the handsomest young gentleman you could see when that was took."

Judy looked at the portrait of Henry Clayton. The name meant nothing to her. She had never heard it before. No shadow of the time when she was to hear it again and again reached out to touch her. She saw a lively, handsome young man of six or seven and twenty. He had his mother's features, the dark eyes of her family, and an air of assured charm that was his own. She was aware of Gloria slipping away to the door, shutting it, and coming back again.

"The queerest start there ever was, his going off like that."

"Did he go off?"

Gloria screwed up her eyes and widened her mouth in a most expressive grimace.

"Didn't he just! And he wasn't so young neither. That picture was took a long time before—he didn't go off no more than about three years ago. He was going to be married to Miss Lesley Freyne. Lots of money she'd got, and they did say that was why he was marrying her. Anyway he come down here for the wedding, but it never come off. My mum says she wasn't surprised—not about its being broke off, you know. But nobody knows what come of him. Three days before the wedding, and he went off and nobody's never seen nor heard of him since. My mum says he did ought to be ashamed of himself, serving Miss Lesley the way he did. Everyone likes Miss Lesley ever so, and if she wasn't pretty, well, he'd knowed that all along, and if he wasn't in love with her, he knowed that too, and he didn't ought to have gone so far—coming down for the wedding and all! My mum says she don't wonder he couldn't show his face here after the way he served Miss Lesley. But don't you say I said nothing about it, because if Mrs. Robbins knowed she'd give me what for."

She edged towards the door and opened it cautiously, as if she expected to find Mrs. Robbins with an ear to the keyhole. Confronted by an empty corridor, she giggled and resumed her narrative.

"Those two rooms opposite is the Miss Pilgrims'. This one's Miss Netta's—and it takes her all the morning to dress, so you can't ever get in to do it till after twelve. The other door's their bathroom. There's another one at the end of the passage past the stairs. That's Mr. Jerome's room next to it—and you can't get in there except when he's in the bathroom." She gave Judy an impudent sideways grin. "Pretty old bag of tricks, isn't it? And that's Miss Day's room opposite so she can go in to him if he gets one of his bad turns. It's in the night he gets them. Something awful, they say. I wouldn't sleep here, not for love nor money, and my mum wouldn't let me neither. Shouts and calls out fit to curdle you, poor gentleman. I wouldn't like to be you, sleeping so near."

Judy thought it was time to apply the brake.

"How do you know, if you don't sleep in?"

Gloria tossed her head. The red unruly mop flew out.

"Nor wouldn't!" she said. "Not if they was to go down on their bended knees! But Ivy, the other girl that was here, the one that's been called up to go in a factory, she slept in till she couldn't bear it no longer, and then my mum give her a bed, and we'd come and go together. Ever such a nice girl she was. But of course you'd never think it to look at Mr. Jerome. He's ever so quiet to look at, only he don't like you to look at him, because of his face. My mum says he didn't ought to be given way to about it. It isn't nothing to be ashamed of, she says, and he did ought to be roused up and got to come off of it—that's what my mum says."

Judy had a feeling that she was going to hear more than she wanted to about Gloria's mum. It was a relief when she departed kitchenwards. But oh, what a lot of cleaning there was to be done, and what a little time there was going to be to do it in!

When she heard the click of the door along the passage and saw out of the tail of her eye something large and male in a dressing-gown limp over to the bathroom, she went hurriedly in to do the room.

Rooms are interesting. They tell you a lot about the people who live in them. This one told her something about the Pilgrims. Because it was, she thought, the nicest room in the house, and only nice people would give the nicest room in the house to a more or less penniless cousin who had been landed on them as a permanent invalid. It had two windows looking over the garden, and a deep alcove nearly all glass, so that as long as the sun was out at all there would be some of it in this room. She stood looking out, and saw a garden with high brick walls. Most of it seemed to be paved, with round, square, and rectangular beds in which dwarf conifers made a green contrast with the brown winter twigs of what she thought were flowering shrubs. There were snowdrops in bloom, and all manner of bulby things coming up. All the walls were covered with neatly trained fruit trees, with here and there the stark spread shoots of a climbing rose. The end wall was pierced by a really beautiful pair of wrought-iron gates leading to a second walled garden beyond. She was to discover that there were four of these gardens, one behind the other, each larger and less formal than the last.

She turned back to the room and looked at it between curtains gay with flowers. There were a couple of deep, comfortable chairs, and a spacious sofa, as well as the bed, which had a most expensive and up-to-date spring mattress. There were bookshelves against the walls, books piled on the bedside table, a radio set—everything, in fact, that kindness could suggest to soften an invalid's lot.

As Judy got on with her work she felt pleased about this. She thought slightingly about Frank Abbott, who had tried to put spokes in the wheel and stop her coming down to such nice people. These feelings were confirmed when she presently ran out into the garden to see how Penny was getting on and found her playing ecstatically on a sand-heap. She had a trowel and a lot of three-inch pots provided by old Pell, and she was turning out rows and rows and rows of lovely castle puddings and decorating them with white pebbles and scarlet berries, while Miss Collie, vast in navy slacks and a fisherman's jersey, sieved earth into seed-boxes and sowed her early onions. The sun shone, and a great ramshackle greenhouse kept off the wind.

The sun shone for two days. Roger Pilgrim went away up to town. Penny played in the garden. Judy worked harder than she had ever done in her life. Then it poured with rain. Penny had to stay indoors. Judy gave her a little dustpan and brush, and a duster. But when Gloria departed downstairs Penny's interest in house-work waned. She came and stood in front of Judy and turned a commanding gaze upon her.

"It's bored of being a little girl. It's a lion—it's a very fierce, stamping lion. Make it a tail to go swish, swish!"

Judy pinned on the duster, and for about half an hour all went miraculously well. The lion swished, and growled, and pounced. She got Jerome Pilgrim's room done, so that was off her mind, and managed to get Penny to the far end of the corridor before he came out of the bathroom.

A few minutes later Miss Janetta called her, and she found herself involved in looking for a ring which had fallen and rolled. Miss Netta, in a pale blue dressing-gown, continued to arrange her elaborate curls, and to say at intervals, "I can't think where it's gone," or, "It must be somewhere." By the time Judy had found it and emerged into the passage she was hot and dusty, and Penny was nowhere to be seen—not in the corridor—not in their bedroom—not in any of the other rooms whose doors she opened as she passed them. With a feeling of horror she realized that the last door on the left was open—the door of Captain Pilgrim's room. If the little toad had gone in there—

She had. Before she reached it Judy could hear the growling noise which meant that Penny was still being a lion. She looked round the edge of the half-open door and saw the duster tail being vigorously swished, whilst Penny proclaimed in the hoarsest tone she could manage, "It's a very fierce lion. It can roar and it can bite. It's the most fierce lion in the world."

Jerome Pilgrim sat forward in his chair. He wore a camelshair dressing-gown, and he looked very large. One side of his face was handsome still, but drawn and haggard. The other, partly screened by a lifted hand, showed a long puckered scar which ran from temple to chin. The eyes which looked from those hollow sockets were dark and moody. The hair above the frowning brows was almost black except for a long white streak which carried on the line of the scar.

Penny stopped halfway through a growl, came a step nearer, and said in an interested tone,

"Did something bite your face? Was it a lion?"

The deep, rather harsh voice said.

"Something like that. You'd better run away."

Penny advanced another step.

"It's not a fierce lion any more. It's a kind lion. It won't bite. Does it hurt where the bad lion bit you?"

"Sometimes."

Penny said, "Poor—" in a cooing voice. And then, "Didn't they kiss the place to make it well?"

Judy heard him laugh. It wasn't a merry sound.

"Well, no—they didn't."

"Silly people!" Penny's voice was full of scorn. She tugged at the screening hand and stood on tiptoe. A soft, wet kiss was planted solemnly upon the scarred cheek.

Jerome Pilgrim sat up with a jerk as Judy came round the door. She said in the most matter-of-fact voice she could manage, "I'm so sorry, Captain Pilgrim—Miss Janetta called me and she got away. She isn't really used to being in somebody else's house yet. Come along, Penny!"

As she spoke, his hand had gone up to his cheek. Penny tugged it down again.

"Not come—stay. Man tell story—'bout lion—"

"Penny!"

Judy got a frown, Jerome Pilgrim an enchanting smile.

"It wants a story. 'Bout a fierce pouncy lion."

Judy could see him slipping. She thought it would frightfully good for him to take Penny off her hands whilst she finished the rooms. She said in a brisk, friendly way,

"She's love it if you would—and I'd get on about twice as fast. But not if it would be a bother—"

There was a spark of bitter amusement in the dark eyes.

"She gets her way a good deal, doesn't she? But you'd better take her away—I don't want to give her bad dreams."

He wasn't prepared for the bluntness with which she came back at him.

"Don't be stupid! Why should you give her dreams?"

If the words were blunt, she had a friendly smile and a friendly voice. A pleasant-looking young thing—nice brown hair, nice teeth, blue overall—looked at him as if he was a human being and not an object of pity. His hand had dropped. He said,

"Well, I'm not very pretty—am I?"

He thought she looked surprised.

"Because you've got a scar? What difference does it make? Men don't have to bother about their complexions. As for Penny—she kissed you, didn't she? Will you really take her off my hands for a bit? It would be awfully kind. But mind you turn her out if she's too much for you or anything like that. I shall be doing your bathroom, and then Miss Janetta's room."

She went away without really giving him time to answer, leaving the door as she had found it. She left the bathroom door open too. As she cleaned the bath and tidied up, snatches of *Androcles and the Lion* came to her—snatches of Penny in comment, argument, appreciation. The story was undoubtedly going down well.

When she collected her, Penny's eyes were like stars. Jerome received the throttling embrace which was her highest tribute, and the departure was a reluctant one.

To the surprise of the family, Jerome came down to lunch.

Chapter Four

"I am going down to Holt St. Agnes tomorrow," said Miss Silver. "But before I go I should like to ask you some questions. I am very glad that you are able to afford me the opportunity of doing so."

The curtains were drawn in her cosy sitting-room. She wore a figured silk dress, bottle-green with a sort of Morse code of multi-coloured dots and dashes, which had been her last summer's best, and over it a short black velvet coatee which was one of the veterans of her wardrobe. In his more impudent moments Frank Abbott had indulged in speculation as to whether it did not date from before the last great war. He sat in front of the fire on a padded stool with the same curly walnut legs as Miss Silver's chair. Hands clasped about his knees, he turned and permitted himself to smile.

"We do get off occasionally, you know. As Lord Tennyson has truly remarked, 'The leisured hour, how sweet a thing it is.'"

Miss Silver coughed.

"I do not recall the passage."

As Master Frank had just made it up, this was not surprising. He preserved the smile, and said without a blush,

"One of my favourites. What did you want to ask me?"

To pull Maudie's leg was an awful joy. The thing he was never sure about was, did she know that he was pulling it? Sometimes he had a horrid suspicion that she did. He gazed at her ingenuously and said,

"Anything I can do—"

Miss Silver knitted in silence for a moment. She had made a very good start on Ethel's birthday jumper, but she had come to a place where it was necessary to count her stitches. Her lips moved, the needles clicked. Then she said.

"You can tell me more about the Pilgrim family. Major Pilgrim was in so nervous a state that I did not wish to give him the feeling that he was being cross-examined. That is one of the things I wanted to ask you about—has he always been of a neurotic temperament?"

"No, I shouldn't say he had. He wasn't supposed to be strong, but he grew out of that. He's just been through a pretty gruelling experience, you know—Western Desert—prison camp—escape—hospital—his father's death—uncertainty about his brother—I suppose he told you they'd no news of him since Singapore. And then all this ceiling-falling and room-burning business. I don't think you can be surprised if he's jumpy."

"No, indeed, poor young man. I hope it may be possible to relieve his mind. He left me in a state of some uncertainty, but I have had a note from him since, asking me to go down there tomorrow. I told him that it would be as well if I could appear as an ordinary visitor, and he informs me that he has confided in Miss Columba Pilgrim, and that she agrees with my suggestion. I am, in fact, to be an old schoolfellow. This is made possible by the fact that Miss Columba went away to boarding school, whereas Miss Janetta, who was considered delicate, remained at home and shared in the studies of the Vicar's daughters, who had an admirable governess. One of the things I wished to ask you was whether Miss Columba can be relied upon to be perfectly discreet."

Frank Abbott laughed.

"She says so little at any time that the chances of her saying one word too much are, I should say, practically nil. She's good solid stuff, you know, but she's always taken her own way and had her own thoughts. Don't ask me what they are, because nobody but Miss Columba knows."

Miss Silver counted again for a moment before she said.

"What is your opinion of the invalid cousin, Jerome Pilgrim?"

Frank Abbott's face settled into gravity.

"Jerome? He was one of the best. He's a good bit older than Roger and I. Let me see—I'm twenty-nine, and Roger's a couple of years younger—Jerome must be forty-one or forty-two. We looked up to him like anything. You know the way schoolboys do. Then I hardly saw him for years—you know how it is, one gets off on another line—until—well, something happened that brought us together again, and by that time the poor chap was a wreck. Not too good, seeing him like that."

Miss Silver looked at him very directly.

"Frank, you know these people, you know all the circumstances. Do you think Jerome Pilgrim is responsible for what has been happening?"

"Not unless he's off his head. I mean, the Jerome Pilgrim I knew was quite incapable of anything that wasn't straight. But after a knock on the head like he had—well, you know—"

"Is he considered to be mentally affected by his wound?"

"No, he isn't. The doctors hoped he'd get all right I gather the position is this. He shrinks from going out because he thinks he's worse disfigured than he is—imagines he gives everyone a turn—that sort of thing. The answer to that is, he ought to be encouraged to go out and get over it. Well, various people have encouraged him—my cousins, Lesley Freyne, myself. And what happens? Every time he does the least extra, there's the most unfortunate reaction. He starts having nightmares again, shouts the house down in the middle of the night, and scares everybody into fits. So the doctors say let him alone, keep him quiet, don't force anything. And there you are! They're lucky in the nurse they've got—she seems to understand him."

"Miss Lona Day?"

"Yes. They're all devoted to her."

"How long has she been with him?"

"Three years? . . . Yes, it must be quite that, because she was there when Henry Clayton went."

Miss Silver rested her knitting on her knee and said,

"Yes. I would like you to tell me about that."

"About Henry Clayton?" He sounded a little surprised.

"If you please, Frank."

"Well, it's ancient history—three years ago. But it's really quite up your street. No connection with what's going on now of course, but odd enough to be intriguing. Henry Clayton was a first cousin—may be still for all I know—of Roger and Jerome. His mother was a sister of Miss Collie and Miss Netta. He was about the same age as Jerome, and he'd been a bit of a rolling stone—been all sorts of things—done a spot of farming, a spot of prospecting, a spot of journalism. When the war broke out he landed in the Ministry of Information— don't ask me why. A very agreeable chap, very good-looking, always had lots of friends, generally stone broke. Well, some time towards the end of the phony war he got engaged to Lesley Freyne. Owing to the general landslide that summer they weren't getting down to being married until early in '41. To tell you the honest truth, the impression in Holt St. Agnes was that Henry wasn't any too keen. I don't know if anyone's told you about Lesley. She's got a good figure and a heart of gold, but she's no glamour-girl, and Henry had a reputation for liking them glamorous. On the other hand, she had, and still has, pots of money, and I suppose Henry thought he could do with some of it. As Tennyson says, 'Don't ee marry for money, but go where money is.' "

There was a note of reproof in Miss Silver's voice as she remarked,

"Words put into the mouth of a cross-grained old farmer, Frank, can hardly be considered to express Lord Tennyson's own sentiments."

He hastened to placate her.

"As you say. He leaves the court without a stain on his character. Let me go on telling you about Henry. We approach the climax. Three days before the wedding Henry Clayton had a tiff with Lesley Freyne. No one knows what it was about. I call it a tiff because that's what Lesley called it. She said it wasn't serious, it wasn't a quarrel. I got all this first-hand, because the Yard was called in, Henry being domiciled in London and in the Ministry of Information, and they sent me down because I knew the place and the people."

Miss Silver said, "Quite so."

Hands still clasped about his knees, looking not at her but down into the fire, Frank went on.

"Well, this tiff having taken place some time in the afternoon, nothing else seems to have happened until ten-thirty PM, when Robbins, the butler, was locking up for the night. They were early-to-bedders at Pilgrim's Rest, the ladies at ten, and the old man at ten-fifteen—Roger's father was alive then, you know. Robbins thought they had all gone up, but when he came to the study door he could hear Henry Clayton at the telephone. He wrapped it up pretty, but actually he stood there and listened. And he heard Henry say, 'No, Lesley, of course not. Darling, you couldn't think a thing like that! Look here, I'll come round.' There was a pause whilst she said something, and then he went on, 'Oh, no—it's only half past ten.' Then he hung up and came out into the hall, only just giving Robbins time to get away from the door. Lesley Freyne corroborated this account, and said Henry rang to make up their disagreement, her remark in the pause being that it was too late for him to come round. Well, Henry, having reached the hall, told Robbins he was going to see Miss Freyne, and added, 'I shan't be long, but don't stay up for me—I'll take the key and put up the chain when I come in.' After which he walked out of the house just as he was."

Miss Silver's needles clicked.

"In evening-dress?"

"No. There were still a good many air-raid alarms going, and the men were sticking to ordinary clothes. Henry was wearing a dark blue town suit. It was a mild evening, and Lesley's house isn't more than fifty yards down the street. He put the front door key into his pocket and went out. Lesley Freyne was waiting for him. When she left the telephone she went to a window which overlooked the street. It was a clear moonlight night. Pilgrim's Rest was in plain view. It was rather an odd entrance, a sort of glass passage leading from the front door to the village street. She saw Henry come out of this passage and begin to walk towards her, and she drew back from the window because she didn't want him to see that she was looking out for him. She let the curtain fall between her and the glass and crossed over to the other side of the room. Minutes went by. She had told him that she would leave the front door open so that he could just walk in. He didn't come. When she couldn't bear it any longer she went back to the window. The street was quite bright, and clear, and empty."

He slewed round and looked up in her face.

"Well, there you are! Henry Clayton was seen leaving Pilgrim's Rest, but he never arrived at St Agnes' Lodge, and from that day to this he's never been seen or heard of."

"My dear Frank!"

"I told you it was a queer start. He wasn't missed until the morning. When he was, of course the obvious conclusion was that he had jibbed at the post. No one seems to have thought that he was very much in love with Lesley, and everyone concluded that he had just backed out. If it hadn't been for the war, I expect the Yard would have thought so too. Masses of people disappear every year, but it isn't so easy in wartime. Henry wasn't a boy, he was nearly forty—and he'd a government job. You can't walk out on your job in the middle of a war without landing in very serious trouble. There are identity-cards, ration-cards—it isn't all that easy to disappear. I went down to Holt St. Agnes and did my stuff. Family very upset. Lesley—well, I'm fond of her, and I don't mind saying I'd have liked five minutes alone with Henry. She didn't make any fuss. She was simple, she was dignified, but she was taking it hard."

Miss Silver coughed.

"How long was she away from the window after she saw Mr. Clayton coming down the street towards her?"

"She says not more than four minutes. She went over to the fire, and there is a clock on the mantelpiece. She says she was watching the time."

"You say the distance between the houses is about fifty yards. Is there any side street or lane?"

"No, there isn't. The wall of Pilgrim's Rest covers half the distance. It is too high to climb. There is an entrance to the garage and stables, but it was locked. After the wall comes a branch of the County Bank, closed for the duration, two or three shops, and then the wall of St. Agnes' Lodge. All the way on the other side there are village houses, standing back from the street, with strips of garden in front. If Henry had wanted to do a bunk he could, of course, have made off that way. But why should he go blundering through a cottage garden into a lot of plough-land in the opposite direction from the line of rail? And why should he do a bunk on a winter's night, however mild—it was February, but I count that winter— bareheaded, in a lounge suit, without so much as a scarf, and no luggage? Everything he had brought down to Pilgrim's Rest was accounted for. It's a bit much to swallow, don't you think? Unless he had a real, genuine black out—didn't know who he was or where he was, but just walked away into the blue."

"He may have been picked up by a car."

Frank nodded.

"He must have been. But no car passed through Holt St. Agnes while Lesley was waiting for him. She was on the listen and she couldn't have missed it."

"No." Miss Silver agreed. "She would certainly have heard a car if one had passed then. But it might not have been then. Have you thought of that? Mr. Clayton started out to see Miss Freyne. Suppose he thought better of it and turned back. He may have gone back into the house and remained there for some time. Some mental conflict would surely precede so grave a step as an abrupt departure on the eve of his marriage—"

Frank was shaking his head.

"He didn't come back into the house. Robbins wasn't easy about leaving him to lock up. He's been there since Henry and Jerome were schoolboys, and you know how it is with an old servant like that—you never really grow up. He didn't trust Mr. Henry, not with the wedding coming on and all and Mr. Pilgrim so particular about the locking up, so he just went through to tell Mrs. Robbins he'd be late, and then he came back to the hall and waited there."

"How long did he wait?"

"He heard the clock strike twelve, and then he must have fallen asleep, because the next thing he knew it was striking six. And Henry Clayton hadn't come back."

Miss Silver directed a searching look upon him.

"Robbins had been asleep for six hours. How, then, did he know that Mr. Clayton had not returned?"

"Because before sitting down to wait for him he had put up the chain on the door."

"Why did he do that?"

Frank laughed.

"Well, he displayed a certain reticence when I put that question to him myself. I deduced that he wasn't at all sure of being able to keep awake, and he wouldn't have liked Henry to catch him napping, so he put up the chain. You can't get round it—Henry didn't come back into the house."

Miss Silver coughed.

"He could have come back whilst Robbins was speaking to his wife, could he not?"

Frank stared.

"I suppose he could. But why should he? He had rung Lesley up of his own free will, the suggestion to go round and see her was of his own making, and he had only just left the house. Why should he come back? Or if he did come back, when and how did he leave again? The chain was up on the front door—he couldn't have gone out that way. There's a door at the back of the house, and a side door from the kitchen premises to the stable yard. Robbins was pressed about these doors. They were both locked, and keys in the locks. All the ground floor windows have old-fashioned wooden shutters secured by an iron bar. Robbins swears they were all closed and barred when he went round to open up in the morning. I suppose Henry might have dropped from a first-floor window. But, good lord, why should he, and risk breaking a leg, when he could have walked down by the back stairs and out by the kitchen way? Even then, he'd got to get off the premises. There's a ten-foot wall all round the place, and every single gate locked on the inside. I'm twelve years younger than Henry, and an inch taller and a couple of stone lighter, and I'd be very sorry to climb that wall. Besides, he could have got past Robbins without waking him if he'd liked, and out by the front door—only then the chain wouldn't have been up. No, it doesn't make sense—he never came back into the house. The door from the glazed passage into the street was just as he left it when he went out, you know—unlocked, with the key sticking on the inside.''

Miss Silver knitted for a few moments in silence. Then she said,

''What do you think happened to him, Frank?''

''Well, he was a rolling stone—I told you that. I think he started out to see Lesley, and then he had a come-over of some sort. Remember they'd quarrelled. If they made it up now, he'd be in for life. Perhaps he saw his last chance slipping. Perhaps he thought he was selling himself for a mess of pottage. Perhaps he thought he'd just cut and run, and did it—a last dash for freedom, so to speak. Suppose he did that without any plan—managed to thumb a lift. Remember it was bright moonlight.''

''Yes?'' said Miss Silver in a gently interrogatory manner. ''And what then?''

''Well, he wouldn't be the first man who pitched a tale and enlisted under somebody else's name. I've been over it hundreds of times, and I think that's what must have happened. He didn't get away by train—that's certain. There are two stations he might have reached by walking—Burshot and Ledlington. At Burshot he'd have been recognized, and at either place he'd have been sufficiently conspicuous to be noticed—without hat, scarf, or overcoat.''

''And nobody saw him?''

"He's never been seen or heard of again."

The room was quiet for a time. It did not seem long to either of them. Frank Abbott broke the silence by saying,

"I haven't known you for seven years, have I? But if I don't put something on this fire, it will go out."

Miss Silver smiled in rather an absent manner and said,

"Pray do so."

She watched him being dexterous with some reluctant embers and a shovelful of coal. Chief Detective Inspector Lamb had once remarked in her presence that if Frank was good for nothing else, he could always manage to get a fire going. Which was his way of counteracting what he considered to be a tendency to wind in the head.

When the fire was producing small but hopeful flames, she said, "There are still a few questions I should like to ask, and if you do not mind, I should like to take some notes."

She laid down her knitting, went over to the writing-table, and opened the shiny green exercise-book which lay ready upon the blotting-pad.

Frank Abbott got up from his stool and took up a position half sitting, half leaning, against the far corner of the table.

"Well, what can I do for you?"

"You can tell me who was in the house when Mr. Clayton disappeared."

He gave her the names, ticking them off on his fingers.

"Mr. Pilgrim—Miss Columba—Miss Janetta—Roger—"

She stopped him with a cough.

"You did not mention him before."

"Didn't I? Oh, well he was there—seven days' leave. Jack was abroad out east, so he wasn't.... Where was I?" He ticked off the fourth finger of his left hand—"Roger," and went on to the fifth—"Jerome—Lona Day—Henry himself—and the staff."

She wrote down the names and looked up at him.

"Of what did the staff consist?"

"At that time? Let me see.... Mr. and Mrs. Robbins—two

young village girls, Ivy Rush and Maggie Pell—that's the lot. But Maggie and Ivy didn't sleep in, so they're a wash-out."

Miss Silver wrote that down.

"And who were in the house when Mr. Pilgrim met with his fatal accident?"

"The same as before—but not Roger. He was in the Middle East being taken prisoner about then."

"And who is in the house now?"

He cocked an eyebrow, and thought, "Roger must have told her that. What's she up to?" Aloud he replied.

"Same lot again plus Roger and minus the two girls, who have both been called up. Maggie's younger sister has taken her place. Their grandfather, old Pell, is gardener at Pilgrim's Rest—been there since the year one."

"And the other girl has been replaced by Miss Judy Elliot?"

Looking up to ask this question, she observed a slight change in his expression. It was so slight that with anyone else it would have passed unnoticed. It did, however, prepare Miss Silver for the fact that his voice as he answered her was also not quite as usual, the difference being hard to define.

He said, "Oh, yes." And then, "She's a friend of mine, you know. But I had nothing to do with her going there—in fact, I did my best to stop her. She's got a child tagging along—her sister's. I don't like their being there—I don't like it a bit. That's one reason why I'm so glad you're going down."

It wasn't the slightest good—he was giving himself away right and left. Maudie could see through him like a pane of glass.

Whatever she saw, Miss Silver showed no consciousness of its being anything unusual. The friendly attention of her manner was unchanged as she said,

"There should not be any risk for them."

He leaned towards her with a hand on the table.

"Look here, what are you driving at with these three lists? You're not trying to make out that Henry's disappearance has anything to do with Roger's bonnetful of bees?"

Miss Silver gave her slight habitual cough.

"My dear Frank, in the last three years a number of unusual things have happened at Pilgrim's Rest. Mr. Henry Clayton disappeared on the eve of his wedding. Mr. Pilgrim met with a fatal accident which his groom and his son believed not to have been an accident at all. And his son is now convinced that two serious attempts have been made upon his own life. I do not assert that these things are connected, but so strange a series of coincidences would certainly seem to call for careful investigation. There is just one thing more I wished to ask you. When Mr. Henry Clayton disappeared, was he known to have any money with him?"

Frank straightened up.

"Well, yes, I ought to have told you about that. It's one of the strongest reasons for supposing that he was doing a bolt. Mr. Pilgrim had given him a cheque for fifty pounds as a wedding-present. Henry asked if he could have it in notes because he would need the cash for his honeymoon. Everyone in the family knew that old Pilgrim kept money in the house. Well, when Henry asked him if he could have the cash he took back the cheque and tore it up. Roger told me about it—he was there. Said his father went off upstairs and came back with four ten-pound notes and two fivers, and Henry got out his wallet and put them away."

"Was anyone else present?"

"Robbins came in with some wood for the fire whilst Henry was putting the notes away. He said he saw Mr. Henry putting his wallet away in an inside pocket, but he didn't know why he had had it out, and he didn't think anything more about it."

"What about the notes, Frank—were any of them traced?"

He lifted a hand and let it fall again.

"We couldn't get the numbers. The Pilgrims own a lot of farm property, and the old man collected the rents himself. He used to ride around, have a bit of a friendly chat, come home with the cash, and stuff it away anywhere. Didn't think much of banks—liked to have his money where he could put his hands on it. Roger tells me they found over seven hundred pounds in the house after he died, most of it in a tin box under the bed. Lord knows how long he'd had the notes he gave Henry, or where he got them.''

When, presently, after this, Frank Abbott took his leave he got as far as the first step into the hall and then came back. After all, what was the odds? If Maudie knew, she knew. He might just as well have the smooth with the rough. He said in his most detached manner,

"By the way, you could trust Judy Elliot. She's got a head on her shoulders and she'd be good at a pinch. As a matter of fact, I've told her about you. She knows you may be coming down.''

Miss Silver looked right through him. That at least was his impression—a very probing glance which reproved, admonished, and, a good deal to his relief, condoned. She said,

"My dear Frank! I trust that she will be discreet.''

Chapter Five

Miss Columba announced Miss Silver's forthcoming arrival at the evening meal which everyone except Miss Janetta and Robbins now called supper. That is to say, in reply to Roger's jerky "When are you expecting your friend Miss Silver?'' she produced the single word "Tomorrow.''

There was immediately a slight domestic stir. Lona Day looked up as if she were going to speak, and then down again. Miss Netta turned upon her sister with a flounce of heliotrope silk.

"Your friend Miss Silver? I've never heard of her. Who is she?''

It was Roger who supplied the answer.

"An old schoolfellow. I met her in town. She wanted to get down into the country for a bit, so I asked her here.'' He crumbled a bit of bread with a nervous hand, whilst Judy pricked up her ears, and thought what wasteful creatures men were.

"Schoolfellow?'' said Miss Netta in an exasperated voice.

"My dear Roger! Collie, who is this person, and why haven't I ever heard of her?"

Miss Columba continued to eat fish in a perfectly collected manner. In contrast to her sister's bright rustling silk she herself wore a voluminous garment of tobacco-coloured woollen material which had once been an afternoon dress. It was still warm, and nothing would have induced her to part with it. She said,

"I suppose she would be about my age. She has been a governess."

After which she went on eating fish.

Later, in the morning-room, used instead of the big drawing-room because it was so much easier to warm, Lona Day said to Judy what she had stopped herself saying at the table.

"I do wish he hadn't asked anyone else down just now. Of course I can't say anything—or at least I don't like to. I don't know Roger so well as the rest of the family, but it isn't—no, it really isn't good for Captain Pilgrim."

Judy thought, "How odd—she says she doesn't know Roger, but she calls him by his name, and she talks about Jerome as Captain Pilgrim. If there's anyone in the world she must know inside out, it's *him*. Of course he's older than Roger, and so is she. I wonder how old she is—thirty-fivish? She ought always to wear black velvet."

Here she had to repress a giggle at the idea of all the things a nurse has to do. It petered out, because the likeness which had bothered her on her first evening came sharply to her mind, and this time she caught it. Lona Day in a long black velvet housecoat, with her auburn hair taken loosely back off her forehead, bore a quite undeniable resemblance to the portraits of Mary Queen of Scots. There was the look in the eyes, the look that charmed. There was the warm and winning way. Of course, she ought to have had a ruff, and one of those entrancing little caps, or a Scots bonnet with a feather at the side. Judy found the idea so beguiling that she lost everything except Lona's voice flowing on in a rich undertone.

When she came to, Miss Day was saying,

"I know he likes to have her, and I hate to deprive him of

the least pleasure, but I can't help feeling anxious. You do understand, don't you?''

Judy hadn't the faintest idea what she was talking about, and hoped for a gleam of light. It came.

''She is such a darling child, but I do feel perhaps it would be wiser if you could keep her out of his room.''

''But, Miss Day, he loves having her, and honestly, I think it is doing him good.''

''I know. But he really does have to be kept very quiet. Those stories he tells her—I'm afraid of the effect it may have on him. You see, he used to write. I'm afraid of his wanting to start doing it again.''

''Why shouldn't he? I should have thought it would be a very good thing.''

Lona shook her head.

''I'm afraid not—too exciting. That is what we have to avoid at any cost—he mustn't get excited.''

Judy felt a queer sort of antagonism rising in her. How could it do Jerome Pilgrim any harm to make up stories for a child of four? She thought, ''They've all got into a regular fuss about him. I should think the most of what's the matter with him now is being nearly bored to death. I *won't* stop Penny if he wants her.''

As if Lona Day was aware of what was passing in her mind, she smiled rather sadly and said,

''You think it's nonsense, don't you? I suppose that's natural. But we are all so fond of him, and so sorry—we have all tried so hard to help him. And of course you don't know how much care he needs. If you were to see him in one of his attacks you would understand—but I hope you never will.''

Judy felt as if a cold finger had touched her spine. She was being warned. She was being warned about Penny.

As if she had spoken the name aloud, Lona said,

''Don't leave her alone with him, my dear.''

Then she got up and went over to sit by Miss Janetta.

Miss Silver came down next day, arriving in time for tea, at which she appeared in indoor dress, her hair neat under its net, her feet in beaded slippers, her knitting-bag upon her arm. She might have been in the house for weeks. Avoiding the difficult question of Christian names by the use of an occasional "My dear," she further placated Miss Columba by addressing to her only such remarks as were in no need of an answer. For the rest, she found something to say to everyone else, and when tea was over won Miss Janetta's heart by her interest in the current chair-cover. The interest was perfectly genuine. She could, and did, admire the pattern, the colour-scheme, the small fine stitches, the pink and blue roses on the ground of pastel grey. Very charming—very charming indeed. Really most beautiful work.

With Miss Day **she** conversed upon other topics. A nurse has such an interesting life. Such opportunities for studying character. And sometimes for travel. Had Miss Day travelled at all?... Oh, in the East? How very, very interesting! China perhaps?... No? India?... How intensely interesting! Such a wonderful country.

"I have not had the opportunity of travelling myself. The scholastic profession is, to that extent, rather limiting."

"Do you still teach?"

Miss Silver gave her slight cough.

"No, I have retired."

Jerome Pilgrim kept his room that afternoon. When Judy came down to supper she found her feet halting and reluctant. The farther they took her from Penny, the more clearly did Lona Day's words come echoing back in the empty spaces of her mind—"Don't leave her alone with him, my dear."

"Don't leave her alone—" But she *was* leaving Penny alone, and just along at the end of the passage was the door behind which Jerome Pilgrim sat in his big chair. She knew quite well by now just how he would look, sitting there, his head propped on his hand, staring into the fire. Suppose he really wasn't sane. Suppose he was dangerous. Suppose—no, she couldn't even suppose that he would hurt Penny. But... Her feet stopped of their own accord, and she found that she was turning round and going back. Frank hadn't wanted her to come here—Frank had begged her not to come. And she had been obstinate about it.

She had almost reached her own door, when the door at the end of the passage opened and Jerome came out in a dark suit, with the rubber-shod stick he used about the house. As she stood uncertain and a little afraid, he called out to her in a friendly manner,

"Are you going down? Then we can go together."

Judy had a change of mood. Her fear of a moment ago seemed monstrous. She felt so much ashamed of it that she made her voice extra warm as she said,

"Oh, how nice! Are you coming to supper?"

She went to meet him, and kept pace with him along the corridor.

"Lona's furious," he said. "She'd like to lock me in and take the key. She'll come down presently draped in sweet reproach. She's marvellous at registering the emotions. She's wasted as a nurse of course—she ought to be at Hollywood."

Judy said cautiously, "She's attractive—"

He nodded.

"Oh, very. And a most excellent nurse—I owe her a lot. But one likes to escape once in a way, and if you must know, I'm dying to see Aunt Collie's school friend. What is she like?"

Judy looked over her shoulder and said,

"Ssh! She's got the room next mine."

He actually laughed.

"Couple of conspirators—aren't we? Is she a dragon?"

They had begun to negotiate the stairs. Jerome had to take his time. Judy thought, "He's quite easy with me now—I might have been here for years. He'd get used to seeing people—I'm sure he would. It can't be right to keep him shut away. He's *friendly*. You can feel it when he comes out of his hole." She said with a little laugh,

"Oh, no, not a dragon at all—prim and Victorian, like the people in Aunty Cathy's nineteenth-century books. I was brought up on them. She makes you feel like schoolroom tea." She paused, and added with a warmth that surprised herself, "She's *nice*."

At supper Jerome actually talked. Miss Columba, delighted to see him, found herself a good deal embarrassed by the interest he displayed in the school-days which she was presumed to have shared. Judy, tickled, could not help admiring the dexterity displayed by Miss Silver.

"To tell you the truth, Captain Pilgrim, those days seem now so very far away—quite like a dream, or something one has read about in a book. They do not, if you know what I mean, seem to be at all actual. Your aunt will, I am sure, bear me out. I could not myself give you the names of half a dozen of my contemporaries at school, yet I recall the personalities of many more, and am aware of the manner in which each of them affected me."

She had caught his attention. He said musingly,

"Names are just a label. They're nothing—like clothes, to be changed. Individuality is what counts. That goes on."

She gave him one of her really charming smiles.

" 'A rose by any other name would smell as sweet.' "

His interest deepened. There was something in the look and the quality of the smile which enabled her to get away with about the most hackneyed quotation in the whole range of literature. He was conscious of annoyance when Miss Janetta said fretfully,

"There really ought to be a law against people calling their children after film stars. Lesley Freyne has two Glorias amongst her evacuees. It's bad enough of the Pells, but when it comes to three Glorias in one village!"

Miss Silver said brightly, "I heard of some people called White who had their son christened Only Fancy Henry. So it made Only Fancy Henry White. Not very considerate to mark a child out in that way. Names present a great many pitfalls. There are, of course, such charming ones for girls." She smiled at Miss Columba. "Your name, for instance—most unusual and attractive. And your sister's too. But when it comes to boys, I must own to a preference for what is solid and plain—William, George, Edward, Henry—all good names, and all, I am informed, quite out of fashion at present."

Miss Columba looked up from a baked apple.

"My father's name was Henry."

Miss Silver gave her the look with which she might have encouraged a diffident or tongue-tied child and said,

"An excellent name. Has it been passed on to the present generation?"

There was one of those pauses. Roger muttered something that sounded like "Yes—a cousin," and Miss Janetta began in a hurry to deplore the prevalence of Peters.

"I've nothing against the name, but there really are too many of them."

Miss Silver agreed.

They went on talking about names.

As they talked, Miss Silver's eyes went from one to another, seeing all that was on the surface and searching for what might lie beneath. When Robbins came and went she watched him too. Such a secretive face—but a well-trained manservant will look like that for no reason at all. In his own way a goodlooking man—straight regular features and an upright carriage. Perhaps off duty and in his own quarters he could relax and be off guard. The word kept coming back to her. He was on guard. Over what? It might be his professional good manners, his dignity as an old family servant, or it might be something else. She felt a good deal of interest in Robbins.

Miss Columba conducted her school friend all round the house next morning. She did it with an air of gloom, because it is impossible to take anyone over an interesting old house without more conversation that she cared about. It was also an exceptionally good day for the garden and she wished to put in a row of early peas. Pell said it was too soon, but she didn't intend to let him down her. If the weather was to change over night, it would give him a very unfair advantage, and he would certainly make the most of it. She knew her duty, and she did it without a protest, but certainly not in any spirit of cheerfulness, and she wore her gardening slacks and fisherman's jersey so as to be ready to go out and confront Pell at the first possible moment.

The house had three stories, and they began at the top. In her capacity as showman Miss Columba was obliged to talk. As a matter of fact, once the ice was broken and she had made up her mind to it, the house was the one topic upon which she could, if she chose, find words. She would not be prodigal of them, but she could produce enough to serve the purpose in hand.

As they emerged upon the top landing, she said,

"The hall used to run right up to here. It was sealed over in the early eighteenth century to make the rooms below. These used to be one large garret. They were partitioned off at the same time."

Miss Silver looked about her with the bright interest of a bird who hopes to breakfast on the early worm. The ceilings were low, the rooms small. There were a great many of them, and none in use except the largest, which was apparently occupied by the Robbinses. Mrs. Robbins came out of it as they passed.

Miss Columba said, "Good-morning. I am showing Miss Silver the house," and added, "Mrs. Robbins has been with us for a great many years—how many is it, Lizzie?"

"Thirty years." The tone was colourless, the pale lips hardly moved. The hollow eyes looked once at the visitor and then away.

Miss Silver saw a tall, gaunt woman, very sallow and melancholy-looking, in a dark wrapper with a clean apron tied over it. She went down the stairs and out of sight.

Miss Columba led the way along a passage to the housemaid's cupboard and the sink which was said to have overflowed and brought the ceiling down below. But not immediately below. Miss Silver was able to confirm Roger Pilgrim's statement on this point when she had been taken into the empty attic over the room with the fallen ceiling. The water would have had quite a distance to travel—ten or twelve feet. The boards which had been taken up were still loose. Miss Silver lifted them and observed what lay beneath. There had been water there. It had dried out, but the marks remained. The water had run in a narrow channel between the sink and the middle of the attic floor. Water had run and left its mark plainly to be traced on the joists and plaster under the floor. But what had made it spread out and form a pool when it came to the middle of the attic? At this point the narrow track became a wide, dark patch smelling of dust and mould, and still extremely wet. All the boards in the middle of the floor had been lifted here, and the window set open, but the damp had not dried out.

Miss Columba stood by in silence until her guest turned away.

When Miss Silver spoke, it was of Mrs. Robbins.

"Thirty years is a long time to be in the same family. She looks ill—"

"It is just her look."

"And unhappy—"

"She has looked like that for a long time."

Miss Silver coughed.

"May I enquire since when?"

"They had trouble. It was before the war."

"What kind of trouble? Pray do not think me intrusive."

"It has nothing to do with what has happened since. They lost their daughter, a pretty, clever girl."

"She died?"

Miss Columba was frowning.

"No—she got into trouble and ran away. They couldn't trace her. They felt it very much."

"Who was the man?"

"They never knew."

Miss Columba led the way resolutely to the next floor, where she unlocked the door of what had been Roger's room and displayed a great mass of fallen plaster.

The geography of the house was extremely confusing. Besides the main staircase there were three others, steep, narrow, and winding. By one of these they presently descended to a passage which led back into the hall by a door beneath the stairs.

Miss Silver looked up at the massive stone chimney-breast. Everywhere else the walls were panelled, but the great chimney stood out in bare grey stone. Across it, deeply carved, ran the lettering of the verse which Roger Pilgrim had repeated:

"If Pilgrim fare upon the Pilgrims' Way
And leave his Rest, he'll find nor rest nor stay.

*Stay Pilgrim in thy Rest, or thou shalt find
Ill luck before, Death but one pace behind.''*

Miss Columba said gruffly,

"Superstitious stuff. Some people believe in it."

Then, turning abruptly, she walked toward the entrance and threw open the door nearest to it on the right. It was the dining-room, the same gloomy apartment in which they took their meals—door masked by a heavy screen, furniture all in the heavy Victorian style, two windows with an excellent view of a dark shrubbery and the high wall which screened the street, and two more at the end of the room more or less blocked by creepers but affording an occasional glimpse of huge old cypresses. Not an inspiriting room, and certainly not of any historical interest. Such of the walls as were not obscured by the towering furniture had been covered by a wallpaper once dark red but now almost indistinguishable from the surrounding wood. Upon this background two large trophies of arms were displayed, comprising pistols, rapiers and daggers in variety.

Miss Columba opened a door which lurked in the shadow of an immense mahogany sideboard. Here they were in a stone passage again. Miss Columba pursued it until she came to a locked door. Diving into the pocket of her slacks, she produced the key and opened it. As soon as she did so the smell of burnt wood came out to mingle with the smell of damp which had caused Miss Silver to reflect upon the unfortunate fact that old houses really were deplorably unhygienic.

"This is where the fire was," said Miss Columba.

For once it really was not necessary for her to speak at all. Of the wooden pigeon-holes which had once covered the walls only some charred pieces remained, but the walls, of the same stone as the passage, stood firm. The floor had been swept, the furniture removed. The place stood empty except for the smell of fire. Miss Silver permitted herself to say, "Dear me!" After which Miss Columba locked the door and turned back.

A cross passage ran off in the direction of the kitchen premises. Just beyond it she opened another door and said,

"The lift room."

It was square and quite unfurnished—bare stone walls and a bare stone floor, except where an old-fashioned hand-worked lift bulged out from the left-hand side. There was no window.

Miss Columba explained.

"This is the oldest part of the house. There was a spiral staircase going up to the next floor and down to the cellars. My father had it removed and the lift put in after he broke his hip in the hunting field. It comes up just beyond the bedroom you are in, and he had it made to go right down to the cellars because he had some very fine wine, and he liked to be able to go down and look at it."

"You have extensive cellars?"

"Oh, yes. That's what keeps the house so dry. They are very old."

"This is not the only entrance, I suppose?"

"No—there is a stair in the kitchen wing."

They proceeded there, returning by way of the dining-room to the hall, and leaving it again by yet another long stone passage.

The kitchen premises were as large and inconvenient as is usual in old houses. There were innumerable rooms, many of them not in use, or devoted to mere collections of lumber. The kitchen itself spoke of the time when hospitality meant endless courses. Ghosts of the enormous meals of other days presented themselves to the imagination—dinner-parties where two kinds of soup were followed by a practically endless procession of fish, entrée, roast, birds, two kinds of sweets, a savoury, an ice, and finally dessert. After more than four years of war the ghosts had a somewhat shamefaced air. Miss Silver gazed at the range, and thought how large and inconvenient it was, and what a lot of work all these stone floors must make.

They came out of the kitchen and branched into another passage. Miss Columba opened a door and switched on the light.

"This is the way to the cellars. Do you wish to see them?"

If she hoped that Miss Silver would say no, she was

disappointed. With a slight deepening of gloom she led the way down what was evidently a very old stair, the treads worn down and hollowed by generations of Pilgrims and their butlers visiting and tending that centre of hospitality, the wine-cellar.

"My grandfather was said to have some of the finest madeira in England," said Miss Columba. "All these cellars on the left were full in his day, but now there is only the one with any stock in it. I believe there is still a bottle or two of the Napoleon brandy. Roger should really go through the cellar-book with Robbins—it has not been checked up since his father died. But I can't get him to take an interest. He likes a whisky and soda, but he always says he doesn't know one kind of wine from another. I am a teetotaller, but my father had a very find palate."

As this was by far the longest speech she had heard Miss Columba make, Miss Silver was able to assess the importance of the wine-cellar as established by family tradition.

She was presently shown where the lift came down, and the hand-trolley was pointed out by means of which the wine could be transported without being handled or disturbed.

"It can be wheeled into the lift. You see, old wine must never be shaken. My father had these rubber-tyred wheels substituted for the old hard ones."

The cellars were certainly very extensive. They branched off right and left from a central hall, the roof supported by pillars. Before the days of electric light it must have been unpleasantly dark. Even now there were heavily shadowed corners and a passage or two that rambled away into gloom. The air was still and warm, and the whole place wonderfully dry. Farther in, several of the cellars appeared to be full of discarded furniture. Others were piled with trunks and packing-cases.

"We have all Jerome's things here, and my other nephew's too."

"Mr. Clayton?"

There was a little silence before Miss Columba said, "Yes." She continued without any pause. "And of course my nephew Jack's things. He is Roger's brother. We have had no news of him since he was taken prisoner at Singapore." Voice and manner set Henry Clayton aside from questioning.

They came to the end of the cellars and turned. There was something about the stillness, the warmth and dryness of the air, that was oppressive. If they stood still and did not talk, there was no sound at all. In any house, in any place above the ground, there are at all times of the day and night so many small unnoticed sounds which blend with one another and are not distinguished or distinguishable—they are part of the background against which thought passes into action. But under the earth that background is blotted out—there are only ourselves, and silence comes too near.

Both ladies were conscious of relief as they mounted the steps and came out into the very moderate daylight of the kitchen premises. Miss Columba switched off the light and shut the door. After which they completed their tour of the house by visiting a large, cold, double drawing-room with all the furniture in dust-sheets. Six long windows were framed in pale brocade. They looked upon the paved garden. Warmed and peopled, the room might easily have been charming. Now it too suggested ghosts—elegant, faded drawing-room ghosts, doing a little vague haunting in their best clothes, nothing more alarming about them than the slight frail melancholy of an old-fashioned water-colour drawing. There were four heads in this style upon one of the walls. Perhaps Miss Silver recognized Janetta Pilgrim's scarcely altered profile, perhaps she was only guessing. She stopped in front of the four oval frames and admired.

"Very charming—very charming indeed. Your sister? And yourself? And the other two? You had two married sisters, I believe."

Miss Columba said, "Yes."

Miss Silver pursued her enquiries.

"Mrs. Clayton? And—?"

"My sisters Mary and Henrietta. Henrietta married a distant cousin. Jerome is her son."

"Very charming indeed. Such delicate work."

The four young girls in their white muslin and pink and blue ribbons gazed serenely on the room. Even in this restrained medium the young Columba looked solid and rather sulky. But Mary, who was to be Mrs. Clayton, bloomed like a rose. Perhaps the pink ribbons helped, perhaps she had been pleased with them. Her dark eyes smiled, and so did her rosy mouth.

There remained only the study, a moderate-sized room, book-lined and smelling of wood-fire and tobacco, with a faint undercurrent of dry rot. The books, handsomely bound editions of an earlier day, were obviously in dignified retirement—Thackeray, Dickens, Charles Reade, Oliver Wendell Holmes, Jorrocks, and, surprisingly, the entire works of Mrs. Henry Wood. All had the air of having fallen asleep upon the shelves a generation or two ago.

It was pleasant to return to the morning-room, which faced the dining-room across the hall and was of the same date. Furnished in Miss Janetta's taste, Miss Silver approved it as bright and comfortable. True, its front windows also faced the wall, but there was less shrubbery, so the effect was not so dark, and the two side windows looked south-east and admitted all the sun. There was a blue cineraria in a pink china pot, and a pink cineraria in a blue china pot; curtains, carpets, and chintzes in variation upon these two themes; a large sofa for Miss Janetta, and a number of extremely comfortable chairs. When Miss Columba observed that her nephew Roger was standing by the far window looking out, she shut the door on Miss Silver and hastened to do battle with Pell about the peas.

With a slight preliminary cough Miss Silver addressed a rather unpromising back.

"I should be very glad of a word with you, Major Pilgrim."

He turned round with so much of a start that it seemed he must have been unaware of the opening and shutting of the door. Miss Silver, advancing to meet him, admired the pink cineraria.

"Really most charming. Such a sweet shade. Miss Columba is a most successful gardener. She tells me these plants do not require heat, only protection from the frost."

He said in a worried voice, "You wanted to speak to me?"

"Yes, indeed—a most fortunate opportunity."

Roger did not appear to share this view. His voice sounded uneasy as he said, "What is it?"

Miss Silver had a reassuring smile for him.

"Just a little information which I hope you will be able to give me. I think we will remain here by the window. It will then seem quite natural that we should break off our conversation and move back into the room if anyone should come in." She continued in a conversational style. "You have really a most interesting house—very interesting indeed. Miss Columba has just been taking me round it. I was deeply interested. No, thank you," as he pushed forward a chair, "it will be better if we remain standing. The view from this window must be very pleasant in summer. Those are lilacs over there, are they not—and a very fine laburnum. It must be very delightful indeed when they are all in bloom together." Here she coughed and went on with no real change of voice. "Pray will you tell me whether you have taken my advice?"

He gave a nervous start.

"I don't know what you mean."

"I think you do. Before you left me the other day I advised you to return home and inform your household that you had no present intention of proceeding with the sale of your property. Did you do this?"

"No, I didn't." Then, as she made a faint sound of regret, he burst out, "How can I? I'm more or less committed, and the place will have to go soon anyhow. It's too expensive to run. Look at the house—you've just been over it. It wants the sort of staff people used to have and nobody's ever going to get again. They're all at me to keep it, but why should I? And after what's happened here I don't want to. I'd like to get clear of it and have a place I can run on my income. I don't like big houses, and I don't like old houses. I want something clean and new that doesn't need an army of servants to look after it. I'm selling!"

Miss Silver appeared to approve these sentiments. It was, indeed, her considered opinion that old houses, though of interest to the sight-seer, were by no means comfortable to live in. Recollections of dry-rot, neglected plumbing, a deficiency of modern amenities, and a tendency to rats, arose in her mind and rendered her tone sympathetic as she replied,

"You have every right to do so. I merely suggested that you should for the moment employ a subterfuge."

He looked at her so blankly that, as on a previous occasion, she obliged with a translation.

"My advice was that you should allow your household to think that you had given up the idea of selling. You could, I imagine, ask the intending purchaser to give you a little time."

He looked at her in a wretched kind of way.

"You mean I'm to tell lies about it. I'm no good at it." He might have been confessing to being bad at sums.

Miss Silver coughed.

"It is very advisable, in view of your own safety."

He repeated his former remark.

"I'm no good at it."

"I am sorry about that. And now, Major Pilgrim, I would like to ask you a few questions about the Robbinses. I know that they have been here for thirty years. I want to know whether they have, or whether they think they have, any grounds for a grudge against you, or against your family."

He was certainly discomposed, but there might have been more than one reason for that—surprise, offence, or just mere nervousness. What he said was,

"Why should they have?"

Miss Silver coughed.

"I do not know. I should like to be informed. Are you aware of any such grudge?"

He said, "No," but might as well have left it unsaid, there was so little conviction in his tone. He may have been aware of this himself, for he followed it up with a vexed "What made you think of anything like that?"

"I have to think of motives, Major Pilgrim. You have told me that you think your life has been attempted. There must be a motive behind that. Neither you nor I can afford to say of anyone in his house that he or she is to be beyond suspicion or above enquiry. I believe the Robbinses had a daughter—"

"Mabel? How could she have anything to do with it? She's been dead for years."

"Miss Columba did not say that."

"What did she say?"

"That the girl had got into trouble and run away, and her parents had been unable to trace her."

He turned and stared out into the garden.

"Well, that's true. And as it happened before the war, I can't see any reason for digging it up now."

Miss Silver gave a slight reproving cough.

"We are looking for a motive. If you do not wish to give me the information for which I am asking, I can no doubt obtain it elsewhere, but I would rather not do so."

He said in an irritable voice,

"There isn't the slightest necessity—I'll tell you anything you want to know. It's just that I don't see why it's got to be dug up. She used to be here in the house, you know. She was a jolly little kid. They sent her away to school, and she passed all sorts of examinations and got a very good job in Ledlington—lived there with an aunt and came back here for week-ends. Then all of a sudden they found out—the Robbinses found out, or the aunt, I think it was the aunt—that she was going to have a child, and she ran away. I was up in Scotland with my regiment, and I didn't hear about it till afterwards. It was in the summer of '39, just before the war. The Robbinses were frightfully cut up. They tried to find her, but they couldn't. That's as far as Aunt Collie knows."

"But there is something more? You said she was dead."

He nodded. Now that he had got going he seemed to have lost his reluctance. He said,

"Yes. It was in the blitz—January '41. I'd been down on leave. Robbins told me he'd heard that Mabel was in London. He said he was going to see her. We travelled up together. I had to go to the War Office, so I was staying with a chap I knew. There was a raid in the late afternoon. Getting on for midnight Robbins walked in looking ghastly, poor chap, and told me Mabel was dead. The baby was killed right out, but she lived to be taken to hospital, and he saw her there. He said he would have to tell his wife, but he didn't want anyone else to know. He said they'd got over it and lived it down as much as they ever could, and it would rake it all up again. I could see his point. I said I thought my father ought to know, and he agreed with that, but we didn't tell anyone else. I hope you won't tell anyone. It would be very rough luck on the Robbinses if it was raked all up again now.''

Miss Silver looked at him gravely and said,

"I hope it may not be necessary to speak of it. But since you have told me so much, will you tell me who was responsible for Mabel Robbins's disgrace?"

"I don't know."

"Do the Robbinses know?"

He gave her the same answer—"I don't know."

"Major Pilgrim, suspicion is not knowledge. Have you, or have they, no suspicion in the matter? It is not pleasant to have to ask you such a question, but I must do so. Had the Robbinses any reason to suspect a member of your family, or did they suspect anyone without perhaps having a reason at all? I do not suggest that there was a reason, but I must know whether such a suspicion existed."

He turned a horrified face to her.

"What are you driving at? If you think—"

She put up a hand.

"Pray, Major Pilgrim—I think you must give me an answer. I will put my question again, and more plainly. Did the Robbinses suspect anyone?"

"I tell you I don't know!"

"Did they suspect you?"

He swung round with an angry stare.

"Would they have stayed on if they had?"

She coughed.

"Perhaps—perhaps not. Did they suspect Mr. Jerome Pilgrim?"

"Why should they?"

"I do not know. Did they suspect Mr. Henry Clayton?"

Roger Pilgrim turned round and walked out of the room.

By three o'clock that afternoon the house was settling into silence. It was the Robbinses' afternoon off. Lunch being at one, they could just get through in time to catch the Ledlington bus at two forty-five. Judy watched them depart, he in a black overcoat and bowler, she also in black, with a formidable trimmed hat which might once have had coloured flowers on it but was now given over to a waste of rusty ribbon bows and three dejected ostrich tips.

They were hardly out of sight, when Lona Day followed them in a fur coat and a bright green turban. She too was going to Ledlington. Jerome Pilgrim liked his books changed at least once a week, and she had shopping of her own to do as well.

Roger Pilgrim had gone for a ride, Miss Columba was in the greenhouse, Miss Janetta and Penny were resting, Miss Silver writing letters, and Gloria finishing the pots and pans in the scullery, when a tall woman walked down the street and rang the bell at Pilgrim's Rest.

Judy knew who it must be before she opened the door. She saw good brown tweeds and a dark brown country hat. Between the brim and the coat collar a line of dark hair, a strong, well-modelled brow, and good grey eyes—in spite of which Lesley Freyne was a plain woman. The face was square, rather high on the cheek-bones, rather heavy in the jaw, and the mouth too wide, too full. But when she spoke there was something that was attractive—a deep musical note in the voice, an honest, friendly look in the eyes.

"I think you must be Judy Elliot. I am Lesley Freyne. I have been wanting to meet you. Frank Abbott wrote and told me you were going to be a near neighbour."

Judy took her to the morning-room, where they talked about Frank, about Penny, about Miss Freyne's evacuees, reduced now to a mere ten.

"Nearly all little ones, and such dear children. I wonder if you would like to let your little Penny join them in the mornings. We have a little nursery school. Miss Brown who is helping me has all her certificates. I thought perhaps it would be a help to feel that she was off your hands and out of mischief whilst you were busy, and it would be company for her."

Judy found herself accepting with so much relief that the

feeling startled her. When they had talked a little more Lesley said,

"I should like to go up and see Jerome. He doesn't sleep in the afternoon, does he?"

Judy said, "I don't know." And then, "You know so much more about them all than I do. Frank said I could talk to you if I needed anyone to talk to—"

She hadn't meant to say any of this. It was trance-like.

Lesley Freyne said, "And do you?"

Judy's colour rose.

"I think I do. It's all—I don't know what Frank told you, but he didn't want me to come down here."

"No—I can understand that."

Judy faced her resolutely. It was quite horribly difficult to say, but she meant to get it said.

"It doesn't matter about me. It's Penny—is there any real reason why Penny shouldn't be here?"

Heaviness closed down over Lesley's face. Her words came heavily too.

"I—don't—know—"

Judy made herself go on.

"Do you mind if I ask you something? I mustn't take any risks about Penny. She has taken a very great fancy to Captain Pilgrim. She goes in every morning when I'm doing the rooms round there. They talk, and he tells her stories."

Leslie Freyne's face had lighted up.

"How very good for him!"

"That's what I thought. But Miss Day wants me to stop Penny going in. She says it's too exciting for him, and he mustn't be excited. She says the stories he tells Penny might set him off wanting to write again. It sounds nonsense to me. I mean I think it would be a very good thing if he did start doing anything that would take him out of himself."

Lesley's face was grave and controlled as she said,

"It isn't easy to go against the nurse who is responsible for a case."

Fear pricked Judy on.

"Miss Freyne, will you tell me the truth? About Penny— Miss Day said, 'Don't leave her alone with him.' I want to know why she said that. I want to know if there's any reason. Please, *please*, won't you tell me?''

The strong, deep colour came up under Lesley Freyne's brown skin. She set her jaw and kept her mouth shut for a full half minute before she said,

"Jerome would *never* hurt a child.''

Reassurance and comfort flowed in on Judy. She cried out,

"That's what I feel—but I wanted to hear you say it. He wouldn't—would he?''

Lesley said, "No.'' And then, "I don't know what is going on here. There's something. There was that ceiling, and the burnt-out room, and there have been other things as well. I don't think it's a house for a child, Judy. That's one of the things I came here to say if you gave me an opportunity. Frank's Miss Silver is down here, isn't she—perhaps I shall see her before I go. He believes she may be able to clear things up. I only hope he is right. But meanwhile why not let Penny come to me on a visit? We could say that it was to give you a chance of settling down and catching up with some of the work.'' She smiled suddenly and delightfully. "And it would all be perfectly true, because I expect everything is simply inches deep in dust since Ivy went. Gloria isn't a bad child, but she couldn't begin to get through with the work on her own. Now, what do you say?''

Judy didn't know what to say. She had never liked anyone better on a short acquaintance, but it was too sudden—too soon. Perhaps Lesley saw all this in her face, for she said very kindly,

"You'd like to think it over, wouldn't you? Don't feel you've got to give an answer at all. Bring her round about half past nine for the morning's play, and I'll send her back in time for lunch. Then you'll see how she likes it, and if you want her to come on a visit you need only bring her along. And now I'll go up and see Jerome.''

Jerome Pilgrim was in his chair with a writing-pad on his knee and a pencil in his hand. He looked up with so much pleasure when Judy said, "Miss Freyne is here to see you,'' that she went away wondering why he should not have this pleasure more often. That the occasions for it were few and far between seemed clear from his words as Lesley came in.

"I thought you had forgotten me. It's weeks since you've been in."

Miss Freyne stayed to tea, and brought Jerome down with her. It was very evident that the whole family liked her. Roger's moody brow smoothed out as he greeted her with a "Hullo, Lesley!" Miss Janetta and Miss Columba kissed her with affection. She was introduced to Miss Silver, and created the best possible impression by saying presently that she had always admired Tennyson and felt sure that he would some day come back into his own. After which the tea-party became pleasant and cosy to the last degree. Penny behaved as every fond relation hopes its child will behave when strangers are present. She ate tidily and perseveringly, managed her cup with elegance, and only spoke when spoken to.

Lona Day, coming in when tea was nearly over, expressed her own pleasure at the comfortable scene.

"It's turning so cold outside. I've been thinking of this warm room and a nice hot cup of tea for the last half hour." As she slipped into a chair by Judy, who had made room for her, she went on in a lowered voice, "How nice that Miss Freyne was able to come in. I was worried about Captain Pilgrim being alone, but if she was with him he wouldn't be dull. Only he must go upstairs and rest between tea and supper, or he won't sleep tonight. He loves to see his friends, but I'm afraid he pays for it afterwards."

She threw him a troubled glance. Then, with a sudden bright smile, she began to talk about her shopping. Judy thought she looked tired and strained. She wondered, and not for the first time, whether a nurse staying on year after year with a private patient didn't become overanxious, overconcentrated. She thought Miss Day might be the better off for a change, and so might Captain Pilgrim.

Chapter Six

Judy was a long time getting to sleep that night. There were all sorts of things in her mind, walking up and down there, talking in whispers, talking aloud, arguing with each other, and coming to no conclusion at all. She became so much provoked by them that she arrived at the point of wishing with all her heart that she had taken Frank Abbott's advice. She found this so humiliating that it produced a reaction upon whose tide she presently drifted into sleep.

It seemed like only a moment, but actually it must have been nearly two hours later when she waked up to a dreadful clamour of sound. She had never heard a man's scream before, but she heard it now as she tumbled out of bed and ran to the door. The corridor was in darkness. The scream had died on the shaken air, but there was a dreadful groaning broken by sharp cries.

She ran as she was, in her night-gown, to the switch that controlled the passage light, feeling her way along the wall. As the light came on, a door opened behind her and Miss Silver emerged in a crimson flannel dressing-gown adorned with hand-made crochet and tied about her waist with a woolly cord, her hair neat and unruffled, her expression interested but calm. Judy was so glad to see her that she could have cried. She said,

"What is it? What's happening?"

And with that Jerome Pilgrim's door was flung violently open, and in the same moment the dreadful groaning stopped. Jerome stood on the threshold, his pyjama coat torn open, his hands groping until they caught the door-posts. As he stood there, breathing like a man who has run up hill and staring at the light with wild unseeing eyes, Miss Silver put a hand on Judy's arm.

"Go back and put on your dressing-gown, my dear, and stay with Penny. I will come back."

For the life of her Judy could get no farther than the door of her room. Penny hadn't moved—thank God for that. She stood there and watched Jerome Pilgrim and Miss Silver's brisk advance. But before she could reach him Lona Day came out of the room opposite. She was in a dressing-gown too, her auburn hair loose about her neck, but she was very much the nurse as she laid a hand upon his arm and said,

"Why, you've been dreaming again, Captain Pilgrim. Come along back to bed, and I'll give you something to settle you down. Look—you've disturbed Miss Silver!"

The staring eyes turned as if with an effort, a shaking voice said, "So—sorry." Shaking hands dragged at the open jacket. With Lona's hand on his arm he went stumbling back into his room and the door was shut.

Miss Silver stood where she was for a minute, and then came slowly back. Passing her own door, she came to Judy's and shook a reproving head.

"My dear, your dressing-gown—pray put it on. Shall we wake Penny if I come in?"

"Oh, no—nothing wakes her. I'll put on the bedside light. It's screened on her side."

She was shivering as she slipped into her dressing-gown.

"Most imprudent," said Miss Silver. "You should have put it on at once. I am afraid you have been a good deal startled. I think Miss Day will probably look in as soon as she can leave her patient. I imagine this is one of the attacks of which we have heard. Most distressing. But I do not think there is any real cause for alarm. Captain Pilgrim has had a bad nightmare. When we first saw him he was not fully awake, but when Miss Day told him he had disturbed me he made a very pathetic attempt to apologise. He also became aware that his clothing was disordered and tried to set it to rights. The ability to recover self-control in this manner is evidence of sanity. I think you should not allow yourself to feel alarmed."

It was no good. Everything in Judy shook, and went on

shaking. She said things to herself like "Despicable worm!" but they didn't seem to produce any result. Aloud she said,

"It was horrible. I shan't be able to stay—I can't keep Penny here. Miss Freyne offered to have her—I'll take her round tomorrow. Suppose she had waked up, or suppose I'd been downstairs—"

Miss Silver laid a hand upon her knee.

"Since she did not wake, and you were not downstairs, it is very foolish to suppose anything of the sort. Ah—that I think is Miss Day!" She got up and went to the door. "Ah, yes—pray come in. I hope that all is well. Rather a startling experience, but quickly over. So kind of you to come and reassure us."

Lona Day came floating in. No greater contrast to Miss Silver could have been imagined. Leaf-green draperies flattered the white skin and red-brown hair. She had the warm pallor which goes with that touch of red hair and eyes. Seen like this, she was younger, softer, and, to every sense, in deep concern.

"Judy, I'm so sorry. I'm afraid it was very startling. Perhaps I ought to have warned you—and Miss Silver—but that seems like expecting him to have an attack, and we always hope each one will be the last. He hasn't had one—oh, for weeks—let me see—oh—"

She broke off in so much dismay that Miss Silver enquired,

"You were going to say something about the last attack?"

She had a distressed look.

"Only that it was just after the last time Miss Freyne was here." There were tears in her eyes. "There—I suppose I oughtn't to have said it. But what am I to do? They are all so fond of her—she's such a great friend, and he likes seeing her. But it's no good pretending. There's something about her that upsets him. Not at the time, but afterwards—like this. It happens nearly every time she comes. And look at the position it puts me in. It really isn't fair."

Miss Silver gazed at her with mild enquiry.

"May I ask you a professional question? Is there any danger in these attacks—not to Captain Pilgrim himself, but to others?"

Lona stopped on her way to the door and said vehemently, "Oh, no, no, *no!* How can you think such a thing?"

No one referred to the incident next day, yet it was obvious that it was on everybody's mind. Miss Columba looked glum beyond words, and when Judy told her that she was letting Penny go on a visit to Lesley Freyne she came out with "Quite a good plan," and had no more to say.

Penny was enchanted. She packed an imaginary suit-case with blankets and a pillow for her latest "pretend," a baby bear called Bruno—"Only he's not 'xactly a baby, because he can talk. You can hear how nice he talks, can't you, Judy? He says we'll come every day and play with J'rome and Judy. He loves J'rome because he gifted him to me—and he gifted me his 'tacha case, and his blanket and his pillow. Wasn't it *kind* of him? Bruno and me think it was very kind."

Judy came back with a light step. Penny, joyfully absorbed by the evacuees, had not even turned her head to see her go. She would be perfectly happy and perfectly, perfectly safe. Nothing else mattered. It restored her self-respect quite a lot to realize that, now Penny was out of it, she wasn't afraid any more. She was quite ready to go in and do Jerome Pilgrim's room, but it appeared that she wasn't going to be allowed to. Lona Day took the things out of her hands and practically shut the door in her face. Quite unreasonably, Judy's temper flamed. She shut her mouth on the words she wanted to say, but her eyes were much too bright.

Lona was very nice about it afterwards.

"I can't let anyone in today. He must be kept absolutely quiet. Please don't feel it's anything to do with you. I'm just afraid of his talking about it—wanting to apologise for having disturbed you—that kind of thing. You do understand, don't you, Judy?"

Judy felt that she had made a fool of herself.

There was an uncomfortable, prickly sort of feeling in the house. Mrs. Robbins looked as if she had been crying. Gloria, chattering in the bathroom which Judy shared with Miss Silver, supplied the reason.

"It's her daughter's birthday. Turned out a real bad girl,

Mabel Robbins did. Got too big for her boots, my mum says, getting scholarships, and passing examinations, and thinking herself somebody. I tell you what—she had lovely hair— nearest thing to black you ever saw. Curled natural, with a lovely wave across the front—never had to have it permed nor nothing. And ever such big dark blue eyes. But she was a bad girl, and she come to a bad end. Only nobody never knew who the fellow was. Must have been someone she met in Ledlington, my mum says. Mrs. Robbins was all broke up about it. And look here, I'll tell you something—she and Mr. Robbins, they've been having words. I was a bit early and I heard them. 'It's her birthday,' she says, and of course I knew who she meant. 'Anyone's got to cry sometimes,' she says. And Mr. Robbins says, 'Crying won't bring her back,' and she says, 'Don't talk so cruel!' And he says, 'It's nothing to what I'd *do* if I was to get the chance!' What do you think of that?''

Judy said, ''I think you'd better get on with those taps— they're a disgrace,'' and felt that she should have said it before.

As she went out of the door she almost ran into Miss Silver, who was standing there with a packet of soap-flakes in one hand and half a dozen handkerchiefs in the other. Judy wondered how long she had been there.

It was at lunch that the general discomfort came to a head. Miss Janetta was fretful to a degree, complained that she could not eat sausages, enquired whether cabbage was the only vegetable which the garden produced, and complained that there was a draught somewhere.

''Are you sure there is nothing open, Robbins? The least crack affects me. Please see if all the fastenings are firm.''

Miss Columba kept her eyes on her plate. Miss Silver enquired innocently whether fish was obtainable from Ledlington, but it appeared that she could have introduced no more unfortunate subject. With a high laugh Miss Janetta replied,

''Oh, yes, we can get it—we do get it. But how often is it bad? That, I think, is the point.''

''We had some very nice fish last week,'' said Lona Day, in a voice that was meant to be soothing.

It did not, unfortunately, soothe Miss Janetta, who tossed her head until the piled-up curls were quivering.

"My dear Lona! Well, of course it all depends on what you call nice. Tastes differ of course, but I was brought up to consider that fish should be *fresh*. That may be all a mistake, but I was brought up that way, and I am afraid I can't change now. I would be glad to, but I don't see my way to it."

Roger Pilgrim had been eating in silence. Now, as Robbins came back from the farther windows, Roger straightened, and said with a note of nervous anger in his voice,

"If it's a change you want, Aunt Netta, we'll all be having one quite soon, and I can't say I'm sorry. There's been quite enough dilly-dallying over selling the place—I've had too much of it. I'm taking Champion's offer, and I'm going to have the sale pushed through as quickly as it can be done. And if you want my opinion, I should say it would be the best thing for all of us."

Everyone appeared to be struck silent and motionless. Miss Columba had not looked up. Lona Day leaned forward, her lips parted, her eyes on Roger Pilgrim's face. Robbins, halfway down the room, had halted there, his dark face set, his hands and arms quite stiff, like artificial limbs. Miss Janetta's face worked. She cried out,

"No, no—you don't mean it! Oh, Roger, you can't!" and with that caught her breath and began a low hysterical sobbing very painful to watch.

Roger Pilgrim did not stay to watch it. He said a little too loudly, "I meant every word I said!" and with that pushed back his chair and went out of the room and out of the house. They heard the front door bang.

Miss Janetta was crying into her table-napkin and dabbing her tears. Lona Day got up to go to her. Miss Columba lifted her eyes for the first time and looked at her sister.

"Don't be a fool, Netta!" she said.

That evening between six and seven o'clock Roger Pilgrim fell from one of the attic windows to the paved garden below and was taken up dead.

Chapter Seven

Dr. Daly came out of the room and shut the door, his cheerful face drawn into lines of appropriate gravity.

"Well, it's a bad business," he said,—"and nothing I or any other doctor could have done for him if we'd been here when he fell. Pitched on his right shoulder and broke his neck, by the look of it. You'll need to notify the police."

Miss Columba looked him full in the face and said, "Why?"

"There's no need for you to worry about it—it's just the law. When there's a fatal accident the police must be notified, and it'll be for the Coroner to say whether there's to be an inquest. I'd do it for you myself, but I think I had better look in on Captain Jerome. Perhaps this lady—I didn't catch the name—"

Miss Columba spoke it heavily—"Miss Silver."

Dr. Daly turned to her, and saw with relief an elder person with a composed manner and an intelligent eye.

"Just ring up Ledlington and ask for the police station. Tell them what's happened—that will be all you need to do. I'll go along to my patient. But tell me first—does he know?"

"Miss Day was obliged to tell him."

He allowed himself to look more cheerful.

"Ah—Miss Day—what would he do without her, poor fellow? You're in luck to have her—great luck, with the war where it is and all."

He moved off along the passage with Miss Columba.

Miss Silver went down to the study and put through a call to Ledlington police station.

"I should like to speak to the Superintendent."

A bass voice appearing to demur, she repeated the words with firmness. "I wish to speak to the Superintendent. You will inform him that it is Miss Silver."

A good many years before, Randall March and his sisters had received their early education in a schoolroom dominated by a younger but no less efficient Miss Silver. Now well in the running for a Chief Constableship, he would no more have disregarded her summons than he would have done in those far-off days. She had kept in affectionate touch with his family, and in the past few years they had been thrown together in circumstances which had enhanced his early respect. In the case of the Poisoned Caterpillars he freely admitted she had saved his life. She awaited him, therefore, with considerable confidence.

"Miss Silver?"

"Yes, Randall. I am staying in the neighbourhood. At Holt St. Agnes. I have something to report to you in your official capacity. Do you know the Pilgrims at all?"

"I know of them. I used to know Jerome."

Miss Silver said gravely,

"Roger Pilgrim is dead. He fell from one of the attic windows about half an hour ago. I am staying in the house. Dr. Daly asked me to ring you up."

He had made some exclamation. Now he said,

"Bad business. I'll send Dawson over at once."

Miss Silver coughed.

"My dear Randall, I said that I was staying here. I should be much obliged if you would come over yourself."

At the other end of the line Randall March sat up and took notice. He knew his Miss Silver tolerably well. If she wanted him to come over, he would certainly have to go. She had summoned him before, but never on a fool's errand. He resigned himself and said without any perceptible pause,

"All right, I'll be over."

Miss Silver said, "Thank you," replaced the receiver, and turned to see that Miss Columba had entered the room. She was in her gardening clothes—boots mired well over the uppers, earth under her nails, a smear of mud on her cheek, the grey curls wild. She might have been a figure of fun, but she was not. The heavy face had its own dignity, the eyes their own courage. She set her back against the door as a man might have done, and waited for Miss Silver to come to her before she spoke.

"It was an accident."

Miss Silver met her look with one as steady.

"Do you think so?"

"It was an accident."

"That will be for the police to say."

There was no expression at all upon Miss Columba's face. She said,

"My nephew engaged you. He is dead. Your engagement is over. I should like you to go as soon as possible."

Miss Silver showed no offence. She said,

"Are you sure that you wish me to go?"

"What can you do now? He's dead."

"Others are living."

"He thought you could help him. He's dead."

"He would not take my advice. I begged him yesterday to let it be known that he was proceeding no farther with the sale of the property. You know how completely he disregarded that advice."

The courage in Miss Columba's eyes never wavered. She said,

"That's all over. He's dead. It was an accident."

Miss Silver shook her head.

"You do not think so, and nor do I. Let us be honest with each other. We are quite alone. I should be glad if you will listen to what I have to say."

"You can say it."

"You said just now that it was over, but that is not true. Two people have died violently, perhaps three. Are there to be more deaths? If you can believe that your brother's death was an accident, can you believe in the three successive accidents which befell your nephew? Either of the first two might have proved fatal. The third has done so. If you can believe that all these things were accidents, can you accept the coincidence of their happening in each case just in time to prevent the sale of the property?"

Miss Columba drew a long, slow breath. There was not

enough sound in it for a groan, but it had the effect of one. She put her head back against the door and said,

"What's the good?"

Miss Silver looked at her with steady kindness.

"I must remind you of the remaining members of your family. You have a nephew who is a prisoner in Japanese hands. I understand that the estate now devolves upon him. If he survives to come home, and wishes to sell, is he to be the victim of another *accident?* If he does not survive, the estate will pass to Captain Jerome Pilgrim. If he decides to sell, is he to pay the same penalty?"

Not a muscle of Miss Columba's face moved. Something flickered in her eyes. It was gone again in a flash. She said in a sort of deep mutter,

"It's not that—how can it be that?"

"What other motive is there? Do you know of any?"

There was a negative movement of the head with its blown grey curls.

Miss Silver said very firmly,

"Someone is determined to prevent the sale of this property. No owner will be safe until this person's identity is discovered."

Miss Columba straightened up and moved away from the door. She said gruffly,

"The place belongs to Jack. He's in Malaya. Let sleeping dogs lie."

She went out of the room and up the stair.

Miss Silver pressed her lips together and reflected upon the shortcomings of her own sex. She would not have admitted these shortcomings to Chief Inspector Lamb, or to Superintendent March. She thought very highly of women, and hoped to be able to think more highly yet, but to credit them with any abstract passion for justice was beyond her.

She considered it probable that she would have to leave Pilgrim's Rest with her work there only half done, and it went very much against the grain. Roger Pilgrim had engaged her professional services, and she had failed to save his life. He had gone against her advice, but she felt that she owed him a debt. And a much heavier one to that Justice which she served with a single mind.

* * *

Randall March had been in the house for well over an hour before he asked to see Miss Silver. It was no part of his plan to advertize an intimacy, nor did he wish to be presented with her opinions before he had had the opportunity to acquire some of his own. The study having been placed at his disposal, he sat there at the writing-table which had been used by at least three generations of Pilgrims, and looked, against a background of olive-green curtains and walls lined with unread books, much more like a country gentleman than a police officer. He might have been in the Army. The overhead light shone down on a tall, well set-up figure, good features, clear blue eyes, and naturally fair hair burned brown.

He got up to meet Miss Silver as she came in. She had a knitting-bag on her arm, and she wore an expression of gravity until she took his hand and smiled at him. Even in the presence of murder she retained the social amenities.

"My dear Randall! I hope you are well."

No one could have looked at him and doubted it, but he produced a suitable reply. "And your mother? I hope she has quite recovered from the cold she had before Christmas?"

"Oh, yes, quite, thank you."

"And dear Margaret and Isabel? I hope you have good news of them?"

She had never allowed herself to have favourites in the schoolroom. The "dear" in front of his sisters' names marked this unswerving impartiality. She would not have found it necessary to say "Dear Randall" if she had been speaking to Isabel or Margaret. She may have admitted to herself that the blue-eyed, fair-haired little boy with the angelic smile and a talent amounting to genius for resisting instruction was dearer to her than the two docile and intelligent little girls, but she would certainly never have admitted as much to anyone else. And so successfully had she overcome the little boy's resistance that here he was, in his early forties, on the brink of becoming a Chief Constable. Even the presence of death in the house could not prevent her beaming upon him as he informed her that Margaret was in Cairo, her husband in Italy, and that Isabel had just recieved a commission in the A.T.S.

These preliminaries over, he gave her a chair and returned to his own, looking at her across the table and thinking how little she had changed—how little she ever changed. From fringe net to beaded shoes she remained intact and unique, a stable factor in a dissolving age.

Over Ethel Burkett's jumper her needles began to click. Thirty-five years slid away. It might have been the same jumper, the same needles, the authentic Miss Silver of his childhood.

"My dear Randall, you are not attending."

She hadn't really said it, but at any moment she might. He hastened to forestall her by speaking himself.

"Well? What are you going to tell me?"

"What do you know already, Randall?"

He picked up one of the papers on the blotting-pad.

"Here it is, as far as I can make it out. Roger Pilgrim rode in the afternoon, came in late to tea, and hardly spoke to anyone. Somewhere before half past five he went up to this attic room to go through his father's papers. I gather that they had been damaged in a fire about ten days ago, and what had been saved had been taken up to this empty room to be gone through. There were a couple of tin boxes more or less intact, and a lot of partly burned stuff from a bureau or a nest of drawers. Somewhere about half past five Robbins answered the door and let in Miss Lesley Freyne. She said Roger was expecting her and went straight up to the attic. She seems to be very intimate with the family. Isn't there something I ought to remember about her?"

Miss Silver coughed.

"She was engaged to Henry Clayton. You will remember that he disappeared on the eve of their wedding."

"Of course! Did they ever find out what had happened to him?"

She stopped knitting for a moment, let her eyes meet his, and said,

"No, Randall."

He thought to himself, "I'm meant to make a note of that." The needles were clicking again. He said,

"How people crop up! I remember the case. But the Yard

was handling it—Henry being in the Ministry of Information and properly their pigeon. Frank Abbott was on it, wasn't he?"

"Yes."

"Well, to get back to Miss Freyne. It looks as if she was the last person to see Roger alive. She says he rang her up and asked her to come over because he thought she might be able to help him out over some of the damaged papers. His father was very fond of her and used to talk things over with her. She says they were sorting papers there for about three quarters of an hour. Then she looked at her watch, saw it was a quarter past six, and said she must go home and help put the children to bed—she's got her house full of evacuees. She came downstairs and let herself out without seeing anyone to speak to. But as she crossed the bedroom corridor to the head of the stairs, she says Miss Day came out of Jerome's room and into her own. They didn't speak, and it's the length of the corridor away. Miss Day says she was backwards and forwards between her own room and Jerome's because he had had a bad turn during the night, and she never saw Miss Freyne. You may call that para one. Now we come to para two. Miss Judy Elliot says she was in the bathroom off the back stairs, washing out some things in the hand-basin. The door was half open, and she saw Robbins go up the stairs to the attic floor. Unfortunately she doesn't know what time it was, except that it was after six, and before a quarter to seven, because the light was still good. Her feeling is that it was before half past six, but she is really very uncertain. Robbins says it was only just after six, and that he went up to his room for a handkerchief. He says he wasn't there five minutes, and that Miss Elliot didn't hear him come down because there's another stair and he used that. He says he doesn't know why—he just did."

Miss Silver coughed.

"There are four staircases from this floor to the next, and two to the attic floor. It is extremely confusing and makes a great deal of work."

Randall March agreed.

"It makes it impossible to check what Robbins says. Mrs.

Robbins corroborates him, but of course she would—says he was only away a few minutes. The daily girl had gone home. Of course there's not the slightest reason to suspect the Robbinses of anything. Thirty years service is a character in itself.''

Miss Silver looked up.

''A great many things may happen in thirty years,'' she said.

He returned her look with one half startled, half protesting.

''And what do you mean by that?''

''I will tell you presently. Pray proceed.''

''Robbins says that Miss Freyne was still there when he was in his room, which is next door to the attic where the papers were being sorted. I asked him how he knew, and he said he could hear the voices. I said, 'You could hear people talking, but how do you know that one of them was Miss Freyne? It might have been somebody else.' He said it was Miss Freyne, because his window was open and he had to lean out to shut it—it's one of those casements, as you know. He says the next-door window was still open and he could see Miss Freyne. She was sitting on the window-seat with her back to him, and Roger was standing by her. He says he heard her say, 'Oh, Roger, you can't do it—you mustn't!' and then he shut his window and came downstairs. I asked Miss Freyne what about it, and she said yes, Roger told her he was going to sell, and she felt very upset about it. She doesn't remember exactly what she said, but it would be something like that. I asked her why the window was open, and she said Roger had an oil stove up there and they got hot. You do, you know, when you're sorting things. I asked her if there was any quarrel, and she said oh no, of course not. And I asked her how soon after this she came away, and she said almost at once. Which to some extent corroborates Robbins, because she originally said she left at a quarter past six, and Robbins says it was ten past when he went up to his room. The trouble is that we don't know the actual time of the fall. Nobody seems to have heard anything. And that's odd.''

Miss Silver's needles clicked.

''It is not as strange as it appears. The bedrooms which

look out upon the garden are old Mr. Pilgrim's and the one which Roger used to occupy, neither of which is in use, the one into which Roger had moved, and on the other side of the stairs an empty room and the one occupied by Captain Jerome Pilgrim. On the ground floor there are the two unused drawing-rooms and the study. Miss Day's room and the one I am occupying, Miss Elliot's and the two Miss Pilgrims' rooms, all look towards the street."

He nodded.

"Yes, I have seen the rooms. Jerome should have heard something, but I understand that he had the wireless going. Even so, you would have thought—" He broke off with a frown, looked down at the paper in his hand, and went on again. "Pell found him when he went to lock the gates just before seven. Daly says he might have been dead half an hour or three quarters when he saw him, which was at five minutes past seven, as he happened to be in and had only to walk about a hundred yards down the street when Miss Columba's call came through. You see how fluid it leaves the time. According to Robbins, Roger was alive and talking to Miss Freyne at ten minutes past six. According to Miss Freyne, he was alive when she looked at her watch and left him at a quarter past. I pressed Daly as to whether he might have been dead before that, and he said it was a thing nobody could swear to one way or the other. He doesn't think he'd been dead for more than three quarters of an hour, but—he might have been. If it was suicide it probably happened as soon as Miss Freyne had gone. I don't mind telling you that's what I'm inclined to think. Daly said he was in a very nervy state. He had screwed himself up to selling the place against a good deal of opposition from the family. What Miss Freyne said about it was the last straw. He waited until she was gone and threw himself out."

"No, Randall, it was not suicide," Miss Silver said.

"You sound very sure about it."

"I feel very sure about it."

"Why?"

"He did not want to die. He wanted to sell this place, get away from it, and live in a small modern house. He was not engaged, but he had an attachment. He looked forward to marrying and settling down. I feel quite sure that it was not suicide."

"Accident then. Those windows come down to within a few inches of the floor—that window-seat affair is only a low step up. It would be easy enough to over-balance if he had any kind of a turn."

Miss Silver shook her head again and said,

"No."

He looked at her with good-tempered exasperation.

"Then I suppose you are going to tell me just what happened."

She rested her hands upon the now voluminous mass of Ethel's jumper and said gravely,

"No, I cannot do that. But it was mruder, Randall. Roger Pilgrim was murdered."

Chapter Eight

There was one of those silences which are not noticed because thought talks so loudly. Murder is a word to which no amount of use can quite accustom us. The voice of blood calling from the earth must always be a dreadful voice, and one before which all others fall to silence.

Randall March broke this one, his voice dry and official as he said,

"What proof have you that it was murder?"

Miss Silver picked up her needles and began to knit again very composedly. She said,

"I have no proof. But I have a good many interesting things to tell you. To begin with, I am here in my profession-al capacity because Roger Pilgrim believed that two attempts had been made upon his life."

"What were they?"

She told him very succinctly.

"You can go and look at the two rooms for yourself. The

fallen ceiling was attributed to an overflowing sink, the burnt-out room to a spark from the wood fire setting light to the papers which Roger Pilgrim had been sorting. In the first case, the sink is twelve feet away on the other side of a passage the ceiling of which did not come down, and I shall be greatly surprised if you do not agree with me that the amount of wet still traceable under the floor of the room immediately over Roger's points to water having been deliberately applied there. In the second case, Roger was convinced that he had been drugged. He fell heavily asleep after taking a small whisky and soda, and awoke to find the room blazing and, as he declared to me, the door locked on the outside. He said he had been keeping the key there because of having these confidential papers spread about. It was his habit, apparently, to lock the room as he went out. By the time the fire had been got under, he told me, the door had been unlocked again. But he couldn't get out that way. He had to break a window."

"Did you believe that his life had been attempted?"

She was knitting rapidly.

"I kept an open mind. There was no real evidence, as Frank Abbott told him."

"Abbott?"

"They were at school together. Frank has relatives in the neighbourhood. He advised Roger to come and see me."

Randall March said abruptly,

"What would the motive be?"

"To prevent him from selling the property."

"What!"

"He was about to do so. In similar circumstances his father also met with a fatal accident."

Miss Silver frowned upon an exclamation which she considered profane. In a reproving voice she informed him of what the old groom William had told Roger about the presence of a thorn under his father's saddle.

"I cannot tell you whether it was true or not. I can only tell you that Roger believed it. I did not think it wise to question William, but you will be able to do so."

Randall March sat forward with his elbows on the table.

"My dear Miss Silver, are you seriously asking me to believe that two people have been murdered in order to prevent the sale of this estate?"

"It is what I believe, Randall."

"But why? Good heavens—you want a motive for that sort of thing! Who had one? The next heir is Jack Pilgrim, who has been out of the country for the last four years—and why should anyone murder Mr. Pilgrim and Roger to put Jack in?"

Miss Silver coughed.

"To prevent the estate from being sold."

"But why   why   *why?*"

Miss Silver leaned towards him and said,

"In order to answer that we shall have to go back three years."

"Three years?"

"Yes, Randall—to the disappearance of Henry Clayton."

He looked astonished, then quite definitely on his guard.

"Are you going to explain that?"

"Yes. And I will ask you to listen to me with an open mind."

"I hope I should always do that."

She inclined her head in acquiescence. After which she led off briskly, sitting up straight and knitting extremely fast.

"I must remind you of the statements made at the time by Robbins and Miss Lesley Freyne. They were, in that order and on their own showing, the last two people to see Henry Clayton. He was staying at Pilgrim's Rest, being, as you probably know, a nephew of Mr. Pilgrim, and therefore first cousin to Roger and Captain Jerome, who were also in the house. It was about seven months after Dunkirk where Captain Pilgrim had been wounded, and about three months after he had been allowed to leave the military hospital where he had been treated and come here under the charge of Miss Lona Day, who was already at Pilgrim's Rest, having nursed Miss Janetta through a tolerably severe illness. Henry Clayton, as you know, was employed in the Ministry of Information in

London. He had come down to be married to Miss Freyne, and the wedding was only three days off. On the day of his disappearance he received fifty pounds as a wedding present from his uncle. He asked to have it in cash as he intended to use it for his honeymoon. Mr. Pilgrim was in the habit of keeping fairly large sums in the house—he collected his own rents, and did not bank them. There was no record of the numbers of the notes given to Mr. Clayton.''

Randall March smiled a little grimly.

"That makes it so nice and easy—doesn't it?"

Miss Silver coughed with a hint of reproach.

"None of it is easy, Randall. Let me proceed. It is not in dispute that Mr. Clayton and Miss Freyne had some disagreement during the afternoon. According to her it was not of a serious nature. Robbins states that at about half past ten that night he heard Henry Clayton at the telephone making an appointment with Miss Freyne, the words, as repeated to me by Frank Abbott, being 'No, Lesley of course not! Darling, you couldn't think a thing like that!' After which he suggested coming round, and when she evidently demurred he remarked that it was only half past ten. He told Robbins he was going round to see Miss Freyne, and said that he would not be long, but not to sit up for him—he would take the key and put up the chain when he came in. He then walked out of the house just as he was, in a dark lounge suit without hat, coat, or scarf. And according to Robbins that was the last he saw of him.''

"And what exactly do you mean by that?"

Miss Silver coughed.

"For the moment I should prefer to continue. Robbins said in his statement that he did not like to leave Mr. Henry to lock up, as Mr. Pilgrim was very particular. He went through to the kitchen to tell his wife that he might be late, and then came back to the hall, where he put up the chain on the door and sat down to wait. He heard the clock strike twelve, and nothing more until it waked him by striking six.''

"How long was he away talking to his wife?"

"I do not know. Frank thought a few minutes only. The

least time would be five minutes, I should think. Now we come to Miss Freyne's statement.''

March said,

''I remember that. She was watching for him, and saw him come out of the house and walk a bit along. Then she came away from the window because she didn't want him to know that she was looking out for him. You know, that rather got under my skin.''

Miss Silver's needles clicked.

''One touch of nature makes the whole world kin,'' she observed.

''As you say. That was the last anyone saw of Henry Clayton. And now where do we go from there?''

The tempo of the busy needles slackened. She said slowly,

''We have the statements of two people here. If one of them was not telling the truth, the disappearance of Henry Clayton would be less mysterious. Or they might both be telling the truth, and yet not all the truth. Miss Freyne may have seen Mr. Clayton leave the house as she described, but that may not have been the last she saw of him. The quarrel between them may have been more serious than she was willing to admit. Instead of a reconciliation there may have been a complete breach. I do not incline to this view, because it does not explain the two subsequent deaths, but if you believe these to have been accidental you may perhaps entertain it.''

March nodded.

''Well, as a matter of fact I've always had an idea that something of that sort must have happened. By all accounts Clayton was a bit of a rolling stone, and if he'd had a slap in the face like being turned down on the eve of the wedding he might just have gone off into the blue and enlisted or something.''

''I do not think so. To continue. I would like to put a hypothetical case. Mr. Clayton has been seen to leave Pilgrim's Rest, and then someone comes down the glass passage to the street door and calls him back. He re-enters the house and is taken into the dining-room, which is the first room on the left as you come in. It is a modern room, but immediately behind it lies a much older part of the house. A door leads from the dining-room into a flagged passage. In this passage Henry Clayton receives a fatal wound. I do not think that firearms would be used. There are two very striking trophies of weapons in the dining-room, comprising a number of swords and daggers. One of these could have been employed. There is a lift going down from the flagged passage to the cellars almost immediately opposite the door from the dining-room. The body could be taken down in it and conveyed to any part of the cellars upon the very convenient wine-trolley.''

"Are you serious?''

"Very serious indeed. But it is, of course, a hypothetical case.''

"But—the motive . . . My dear Miss Silver, I suppose you mean Robbins. What motive could Robbins have had?''

She replied soberly.

"There may have been a very strong motive. His daughter had got into trouble and run away. About a month before the disappearance of Henry Clayton, Robbins found out that she was in London and went up to see her. She and her child were killed that night in an air raid, but Robbins saw her in hospital before she died. If she told him that it was Henry Clayton who had seduced her, Robbins would have a motive.''

"Who told you all this?''

"Roger Pilgrim. He said that only he and his father knew about Mabel's death. The Robbinses didn't wish it known. Robbins said they had suffered enough and didn't want it all raked up again.''

"Did Roger tell you that Henry Clayton was the girl's lover?''

"No, Randall. But Mabel Robbins was brought up in this house. She was given a good education and had an excellent post in Ledlington. She was here for week-ends and for holidays. She was not known to have any special man friend. I asked Roger Pilgrim whether Robbins suspected anyone in this house. He was very nervous and upset. I asked if Robbins suspected him, or Captain Jerome, and he said No . . . very angrily. I asked if Robbins suspected Henry Clayton, and he walked out of the room.''

"Oh, he did, did he? Well, well!" He looked at her with his mouth pursed up as if he was going to whistle. Perhaps he would have liked to—perhaps the click of the needles restrained him. After a moment he nodded and said, "That's a pretty lot of rabbits to bring out of your hypothetical hat. What do you expect me to do with them?"

She shifted the mass of wool in her lap.

"I should like you to make a thorough search of the cellars under this house."

"You said you were serious—"

"Certainly, Randall."

"You have presented me with a hypothetical case which offers an ingenious theory. You won't claim to have produced any evidence in support of it. Do you expect me to apply for a search-warrant in a three-year-old case which I didn't even handle, without any evidence?"

"No search-warrant would be necessary if you had Miss Columba's permission."

He allowed a faint sarcasm to flavour his tone as he enquired,

"Do you suppose that she would give it?"

"I do not know."

March laughed.

"And you consider yourself a judge of character! Even to my humble powers of observation Miss Columba appears anxious for one thing, and one thing only—'Let the finger of discretion be placed upon the lip of silence!'"

Receiving no reply, he leaned back in his chair and contemplated Miss Silver and the situation. After a little while he said,

"Look here, if anyone but you had put this up to me, I shouldn't have any difficulty in knowing what to say. As it's you, I'm going to tell you how I'm placed, and then ask you again just how strongly you feel. Colonel Hammersley, the Chief Constable of the county, is retiring at the end of the month. I have been given some tolerably strong hints that the Committee would give my candidature a very favourable reception. I don't pretend to be indifferent to the prospect, but if meanwhile I were to raise a groundless scandal about people like the Pilgrims who've been here ever since the ark unloaded on Ararat, the Committee might very well have a change of heart.''

Miss Silver quoted again, in French this time but with a very patriotic accent:

" 'Fais ce que doit, advienne que pourra.' ''

He gave a short laugh.

"Do what's right and blow the consequences! That's admirable! But you will have to convince me of where the right lies before I reach the point of letting my professional prospects go down the drain.''

She gave a gentle cough.

"You will have to convince yourself, Randall. I have nothing more to say.''

Randall March was not called upon either to strain his conscience or to jeopardize his prospects. The truth of the homely proverb which asserts that it never rains but it pours was once more exemplified. An hour after a silent party had breakfast next day Miss Columba was called to the telephone by Robbins.

"It is a telegram, madam. I began to take it, but I thought—perhaps you would prefer—''

She got up and went out without a word.

Ten minutes passed before she returned. With no discernible change in face or voice, she addressed the only other occupant of the morning-room, Miss Silver.

"It was a telegram from the War Office about my nephew Jack. They have proof of his death.''

Miss Silver's condolences were all that a kind heart and good manners dictate, yet to both women they seemed only what is taken for granted on these occasions. Beneath the conventions, beneath Miss Columba's affection and grief for a nephew so long removed that his death could hardly be felt as something new, there was a compelling urgency. It brought words to Miss Columba's unwilling lips.

"Jerome—'' she said, her eyes on Miss Silver's face. "Did you mean what you said yesterday? Is he in danger?''

"Not immediately. Not unless he should wish to sell the house."

Miss Columba dropped her voice to a gruff whisper.

"He will have to sell—two lots of death-duties—he hasn't any money—"

It was easy to see where her affections centred. For the two dead nephews she felt a reasonable grief. A possible danger to Jerome brought the sweat to her forehead and a dumb anguish to her eyes.

It was with this look of distress fastened upon Miss Silver's face that she said,

"I asked you to go. Things have changed. Now I ask you to stay."

Miss Silver returned the look with one in which firmness and kindness were blended.

"My commission was from your nephew Roger. Are you now asking me to accept one from yourself?"

"Yes."

"You must realize that I do not know in what direction my enquiry may lead. I cannot guarantee that the result will please you."

Still in that gruff whisper, Miss Columba said,

"Find out what's been happening. Keep Jerome safe."

Miss Silver said gravely,

"I will do my best. Superintendent March is a very good man—he also will do his best. But you must help us both. He may wish to search the house. It will be pleasanter and more private if you will give him leave to do so instead of obliging him to apply for a warrant."

Miss Columba said, "Keep Jerome safe," and walked out of the room.

Half an hour later she was giving Randall March a free hand to go where he liked and search where he pleased. After which she disappeared into the garden, where she showed Pell such a frowning face that the customary grumble died in his throat and he allowed her for once in a way to do as she wished with the early peas. Later he told William that they would all be frosted, and they had a very comfortable heart-to-heart talk about the interferingness of women.

The search began at two o'clock. When the last of the heavy-booted men had gone clumping down the old worn cellar steps, Miss Silver came along the passage and pushed open the kitchen door. She had a cup in her hand and an expression of innocent enquiry on her face. If these were meant to provide her with an excuse for what might be considered an intrusion, they were not required, for the movement of the door and her own soft footfall went unregarded. And for a very good reason. Mrs. Robbins was standing over the range stirring something in a saucepan and sobbing convulsively, whilst her husband, with his back to her and to the room, was contemplating the flagstones of the yard upon which the kitchen window looked. Without turning his head he said harshly and in the tone of a man who is repeating what he has said before,

"Have done, Lizzie! What good do you think you're doing?"

To which Mrs. Robbins replied, "I wish I was dead!"

Miss Silver stepped back into the passage and remained there. The sobbing went on.

Presently Lizzie Robbins said in a tone of despair,

"I don't know what we're coming to—I don't indeed!" And then, "If there's any more to come, I'll give up, for I can't stand it. First Mr. Henry, and then Mr. Pilgrim, and now Mr. Roger and Mr. Jack—it's like there was a curse on the house!"

He said, "Don't talk stupid, Lizzie!" and she flared up at him, sobbing all the time.

"It's stupid to be fond of people, and you can throw it up at me as much as you like, for it's no fault of yours. You've been a hard, cruel husband, Alfred, and you was a hard, cruel father to our poor girl that's gone, or she wouldn't never have run away and hid herself like she did when she was in trouble."

He made a sharp sound at that, but she went on without giving him time to speak.

"I suppose you'll say you loved her, and I suppose you did in your own way, but it was all because you took a pride in her pretty looks, and her cleverness, and the credit she did you. But that's not loving, Alfred, it's just pride, and it comes to have a fall, the same as it says in the Proverbs. And you wouldn't have her back here to be buried—and it's a thing I shan't never get over, your letting her and her baby lie among strangers because it'd hurt your pride to bring them here where they belonged.''

He said, ''Lizzie!'' And then, ''That's not true, and you've no call to say it! Maybe I've done more than what you know—maybe I've done more than you'd have done yourself. There's different ways of showing what you think of people.''

She said with a gush of tears,

''You forgot her birthday!''

A door banged at the end of the passage. Footsteps could be heard coming nearer. Regretfully, Miss Silver turned back, and presently met Gloria in her outdoor things.

She advanced the cup.

''I wonder if I could have a little boiling water. If it wouldn't be a trouble. I don't quite like to go into the kitchen—but if you—''

Gloria said, ''Righty-ho!''—an expression which cost Miss Silver an inward shudder.

She took the cup, ran off with it, and brought it back full.

''Ever such a row going on in there,'' she confided. ''What's the good of getting married if you're going to quarrel like that? The p'lice in the house—that's what's upsetting them. He takes it out on her, and she takes it out on him. My mum's proper upset, I can tell you. But there's something exciting about it too, and I'd just as soon it wasn't my afternoon off. Now if I'd wanted to get out early, ten to one I wouldn't have been let, but just because there's something going on everyone's at me. Mr. Robbins, and Miss Columba, and Mrs. Robbins are all for getting me out of the way. My mum won't half be surprised to see me so early.''

She clattered off down the passage and out by the back door, which she shut with a hearty bang.

Miss Silver, after emptying the cup down the pantry sink and leaving it on the drip-board, went across the hall to the study, where she set the door ajar and awaited developments. The time seemed long, the house was silent. Miss Janetta had declared herself quite prostrated, and Miss Day, with a much more demanding invalid than Captain Pilgrim on her hands, could be supposed to have those hands too full to allow of her coming downstairs. Where everyone else was, Miss Silver had no idea, but she had no desire for company.

When the silence was broken by the sound of tramping feet, she went out into the hall.

Randall March met her there, took her back into the study, and shut the door.

"Well," he said—"you were right."

"My dear Randall—how very shocking!"

It was perfectly genuine. It was not in her to feel complacency or triumph. She was most seriously and genuinely shocked.

He nodded.

"In the far cellar, behind those piled-up chairs. There's a door to an inner cellar. The body was there, doubled up in a tin trunk. I suppose there's no doubt that it is Henry Clayton."

They stood looking at each other.

"Very shocking indeed," said Miss Silver.

Randall March looked grim.

"Your hypothetical case has materialized. I take it your reconstruction just about fits the facts. Someone called Clayton back, invented a reason for getting him into the lift passage, and murdered him there. Subsequent proceedings as outlined by you. I'm collecting the knives out of those trophies and having the lift floor scraped—there may be some traces. The floor is, fortunately, bare board, but three years—" He threw up a hand, and then went on in a different tone. "I shall suggest to the Chief Constable that the Yard be asked to send Abbott down to represent them. They'll want to be in at the death, and he was on the original enquiry into Clayton's disappearance. There shouldn't be any difficulty about fixing it up. And now I must get going on the telephone."

Chapter Nine

Judy Elliot heard the trampling feet and stood a moment on the back stair by the bathroom door. A word came up to her here and there, and her hair rose on her head. Something had happened—something more. The words told her that, but they didn't tell her what it was. She was left with a sense of horror and apprehension much greater than would have been produced by actual knowledge. Because as soon as you know a thing you can bring your reason to bear upon it, but the unknown takes you back to the cowering savage terrified by all the things he cannot understand.

The trampling ceased. She went down a few steps, and met Mrs. Robbins on the last of the stairs with a face as white as lard. They had hardly spoken before—no more than a good-morning here and there. The Robbinses hadn't wanted her, and they made it felt. But now, with Mrs. Robbins holding to the rail and staring as if she had seen a ghost, Judy ran to her.

"What's the matter—has anything happened?"

A hand came out and clutched her. She could feel the cold of it right through her overall.

"Mrs. Robbins—what is it? You're ill!"

There was a faint movement of the head that said, "No." The cold clutch persisted. The white lips moved.

"They've found Mr. Henry—"

Something like a small piece of ice slid down Judy's spine. She hadn't been a week at Pilgrim's Rest without hearing from Gloria how Henry Clayton had walked out of this house on the eve of his wedding and never been heard of again. But that was three years ago. She couldn't get her voice to work. When she forced it, it didn't sound like hers at all. It said,

"He went away—"

Mrs. Robbins moved her head again, and whispered,

"He were in the cellar all the time—he were dead and buried in an old tin trunk. And Alfred says it fare to serve him right. But I don't care what he done, I wouldn't want him buried thataway, not him nor no one, I don't care what they done. But Alfred says it fare to serve him right."

Judy was shocked through and through. The woman's look, the terrible whispering voice, conveyed a sense of horror. The country accent, the turn of words, the manner of their delivery all took her back to something simple, primitive, and dreadful. She didn't know what to say.

Mrs. Robbins let go of her arm with a shudder and went on up the stairs. Judy heard the slow fall of her climbing feet, the heavy clap of a door on the attic floor. Her own knees were shaking when she came out on the corridor by her room. It was in her mind to go in there and pull herself together. People were murdered every day—you read about them in the papers. It wasn't sense to go cold and sick inside and feel as if your legs were dangling loose like one of those jointed dolls which are threaded up on elastic and go limp when it begins to wear, just because Henry Clayton had been murdered three years ago.

As she stood there outside her own door, something twanged in her mind like a string being plucked on a fiddle, and something said in a small, clear voice with an edge to it, "Henry Clayton three years ago—and Roger Pilgrim yesterday. So the murderer is still in the house—and who will it be tomorrow?"

The red carpet down the middle of the corridor went all fuzzy at the edges and seemed to tilt. She put out her hand and caught at the door post to stop herself sliding down the tilt which would land her in Jerome Pilgrim's bathroom. And just as she thought about that, and how surprised Lona Day would be, his bedroom door opened and he stood beckoning to her.

She remembered that she was a housemaid, and the floor got back into the straight. He had his finger on his lips, so she didn't speak, only walked rather carefully down the middle of the red carpet until she reached him, when he put a hand on her arm, pulled her in, and shut the door.

"What's going on?"

What was a poor housemaid to do? If she'd known that telling lies to a nervous invalid was part of the job she'd have seen everyone at Jericho before she took it, because she never had been and never would be the slightest use at telling lies. Something in her got up and screamed with rage. Why should she have to tell lies? And what good did they do anyhow? Jerome would have to know.

He had his stick in his hand, but he wasn't leaning on it. A faint smile moved his lips. He said in an encouraging voice,

"Stop thinking up a good convincing lie and tell me the truth—it's much more your line. Lona will give me all the soothing syrup I need, so get on with it before she comes in and throws you out on your ear. Why this influx of policemen?"

"How did you know?"

"I looked out of my Aunt Columba's window and saw them arrive. What did they want?"

Judy gave up.

"They've been searching the house."

"Not this part of it." He limped over to his chair and sat on the arm. "Did March produce a search-warrant—or did Aunt Columba give him leave?"

"I think Miss Columba said he could."

"Well, where did they search?"

When Judy said, "The cellars," she had that sick feeling again. She got to the other chair and sat down on the edge of it.

Jerome Pilgrim looked at her white face and said,

"Find anything?"

Judy nodded, because she had a horrid feeling that if she tried to speak she would probably begin to cry. She saw Jerome's hand clench on the stick.

"I suppose they found Henry."

She nodded again.

He did not speak for what seemed like quite a long time. Then he got up and began to take off his dressing-gown.

Judy got up too.

"What are you going to do?"

He was dressed except for the jacket of his suit. He reached for it now.

"I'm going down to see March, and I don't want to have any argument with Lona about it. Give me a hand—there's a good child. You'll find a coat and a cap and muffler in the wardrobe. Just take them along to the hall, and see that no one gets them whilst I'm talking to March. I may have to go out."

She said *"Out?"* in such a tone of surprise that he almost smiled again.

"I'm not dead and buried," he said. And then, "Someone has got to tell Lesley Freyne, and I think it's my job."

Randall March hung up the telephone receiver and looked up as Jerome Pilgrim came into the room. When he saw who it was he pushed back his chair and went to meet him. For a moment the official manner fell away. He said,

"My dear fellow!" And then, "Look here, are you sure you're up to this?"

"Yes—but I'll have a chair."

He got down on to it and took a moment.

March said, "Do you object to Miss Silver being present? I don't know if you know that she is a private detective, and that Roger—"

Jerome put up a hand.

"Yes—he told me. She had better stay. I hear you've been searching the cellars."

"Yes."

"Well—I hear you've found Henry."

"Yes."

"Will you tell me about it?"

March told him.

Jerome said, "Then it was murder. He was murdered."

"Yes."

"How?"

"We'll know more about that after the post-mortem. The indications are that he was stabbed in the back. There's a slit in the stuff of the coat. The clothes are pretty well preserved.

There's no weapon present. Now may I ask who told you we had found him?''

Jerome was sitting forward in the chair, his elbow on the table, his chin in his hand. He said,

"Judy Elliot."

"And who told her?"

"I don't know. You'd better ask her. She's in the hall."

March went to the door, opened it, and called, "Miss Elliot!" She came in, holding Jerome's outdoor things. March took them away from her and went and sat down at the table. A little to his left, in the prim Victorian chair which might have come out of her own flat, Miss Silver was knitting.

Judy didn't know what to make of it. She supposed there was something she oughtn't to have done. She stood waiting to find out what it was. The nice-looking policeman had offered her a chair, but she didn't feel like sitting down. You feel taller and more important when you are standing.

"Miss Elliot—Captain Pilgrim says you told him that Mr. Clayton's body had been discovered in the cellars. How did you know?"

She told them about meeting Mrs. Robbins on the back stairs—"And she said, 'They've found Mr. Henry.'"

"Was that all she said?"

They were all looking at her. The sick feeling had begun to come back. She shook her head because it was easier than talking.

"Will you tell me just what she said?"

Now she would have to speak. She found Mrs. Robbins' words, one, and two, and three at a time. It was dreadfully difficult to say them.

"'Buried in an old tin trunk. And Alfred says it fare to serve him right.'"

"Are you sure she said that?"

Judy nodded.

"Yes—she said it again at the end. She said she didn't care what he'd done, she wouldn't want him buried like that. She went on saying it, and at the end she said again, 'But Alfred says it fare to serve him right.'" She looked at March, her eyes suddenly dark and distressed. "I went on upstairs. I was feeling—very upset. Captain Pilgrim saw me. He asked me—what was going on."

Jerome lifted his head.

"Oh, leave the child alone! She was looking green, and I dug it out of her. She didn't want to tell, but you could hardly expect me not to know that something was going on. I'm not deaf, and your constabulary are heavy on their feet." He got up. "Thank you—that's all I wanted to know at present. We can talk again when I come back. I'm going to see Miss Freyne now."

The thing hung in suspense for a moment. Then March let it go. He dropped the official manner to say,

"You're sure you're up to it?"

"Yes, thank you. My coat, Judy. You can come along, and see Penny."

They went out together.

Miss Silver continued to knit. Randall March turned to her with an exasperated expression.

"Well?"

"I do not know that I have anything to say, Randall."

"I couldn't very well stop him going to see Miss Freyne."

"No."

"What did you think of Robbins as reported by Mrs. Robbins via Judy Elliot?"

Miss Silver coughed.

"I think that Judy repeated what she heard. The turn of the words is unusual. She was repeating what she had heard Mrs. Robbins say."

"Yes."

Judy and Jerome Pilgrim made their way down the glass passage and came out into the street. It was so many months since he had set foot outside that everything had a strangeness. When you haven't seen things for a long time you see them new. There were grey clouds with rifts of blue between. There was a light air that came against the face with a touch of damp in it. The winter had been dry and the runnel of water on the other side of the street had fallen low. On any other errand his mind would have been filled with these impressions and a hundred more, but now it was like looking at everything through a darkened glass.

They had gone about half the length to the stable gate, when there were running footsteps behind them. Lona Day came up, flushed and distressed.

"Oh, Captain Pilgrim!"

He stood leaning on his stick.

"Please go back, Lona. I am going to see Miss Freyne. I shan't be long."

She stared at him.

"I saw you out of Miss Janetta's window. I simply couldn't believe my eyes. You are not fit for this. Please, *please* come back! Judy, you shouldn't have let him—it was very, very wrong of you."

"Leave Judy out of it, please. It has nothing to do with her, and I shall be obliged if you will stop making a scene in the street. I shan't be long." He began to walk on again.

After a moment Lona turned and went back to the house. It certainly wouldn't do any good to have a scene in the street. She looked about her in a smiling, easy way. You never knew who might be looking out of cottage windows. There was enough for the village to talk about without giving them any more. All anyone need think was that she had run after him with a message.

Lesley Freyne looked up in surprise as the door opened and her elderly maid announced,

"Captain Pilgrim—"

She came to meet him with both hands out.

"Jerome, my dear—how delightful!"

He had left his outdoor things in the hall. He leaned his stick against a chair and took her outstretched hands.

"Let's sit down, Les—here, on the sofa." Then, when they were seated and her expression had changed to one of grave enquiry, "My dear, I've come to tell you something."

Her colour failed a little.

"What is it, Jerome? Miss Columba rang me up about Jack."

"It isn't Jack, my dear."

He was still holding her hands. She felt him press them strongly. She said quite low,

"Then it's Henry—"

"Yes."

She drew her hands away, looked down at them, and said, "He's dead."

"Yes, my dear."

A minute went by before she spoke again.

"Will you tell me?"

"Les, he's been dead a long time."

"How long?"

"Three years."

She looked up at him then and caught her breath.

"Since that night?"

"Yes."

"How?"

"Les, you're so awfully brave—"

She said, "Tell me."

"He was murdered. They think stabbed."

"Oh—" It was just a long, shaken breath.

"They've found his body. March had the cellars searched. He was there—in the little cellar at the far end, behind the furniture."

He took her hands again, and she let him hold them.

"All this time—" she said. "Oh, Jerome!"

There was a long pause. Before either of them moved to end it a knock came at the door. Lesley got up and went to it. Jerome heard her speaking in a quiet, ordinary voice. He couldn't hear who spoke to her, or what was said, only Lesley's voice making its quiet answer,

"No, I can't come just now. I have Captain Pilgrim here. . . . Tell her she mustn't do that. It would disappoint me very much. Tell her to remember what she promised."

She shut the door and came back to him.

"Jerome—who did it?"

"I don't know."

"Who would have done it? I can't think. I don't seem to be able to think or to feel. It's—it's such a shock. It doesn't seem possible. I thought he was dead—I've thought that for a long time now—but I never thought of this."

"My poor dear!"

She looked at him steadily.

"No—don't be too sorry for me. It isn't like that. I want to tell you—I wasn't going to marry him."

"You weren't?"

"No. Something happened—it doesn't matter now. I felt I couldn't go on. If he had come to see me that night, I should have told him so. But he didn't come."

"Does anyone else know this?"

"No."

"Then I should keep it like that."

"I'll see. I won't say anything if I can help it. But they'll ask questions. I won't lie about it."

"You told them before that the disagreement between you wasn't a serious one."

"It wasn't—in itself. And then something happened—I felt I couldn't go on. When Henry rang up and said he was coming round to see me I made up my mind to break our engagement. Then when he disappeared and it was all so public I thought what was the good of making it any worse. It wasn't as if I had actually broken with Henry—he didn't even know I was going to, so it didn't account for his going. It was just in my own mind. I've never told anyone but you."

Chapter Ten

Frank Abbott came down next day. He was closeted with March and Miss Silver for half an hour, after which Robbins was sent for. He came in looking very much as usual. Features so marked and a complexion so sallow do not readily give a man's feelings away.

Frank had his notebook ready, and wrote in it as the questioning went on.

"You know that a body was found in the cellars yesterday?"

"Yes, sir."

"Do you know whose body it was?"

"I suppose, sir, that it would be Mr. Henry." He cleared his throat. "It was a great shock to us all."

"What makes you suppose that it was Mr. Henry Clayton's body?"

"It is generally supposed, sir."

"I asked what made *you* suppose so."

"I can hardly say—it came into my mind."

"You heard that a body had been found, and it came into your mind that it was Mr. Clayton's body?"

"Yes, sir."

"Why?"

"It was a very strange thing, his disappearing like that and never being heard of. It couldn't help but come into my mind."

"Who told you of it?"

"I heard two of the policemen talking."

"And you told your wife?"

"We both heard what they said."

March sat behind the table. Frank Abbott wrote. Miss Silver knitted placidly. Robbins, who had taken a chair with some reluctance, sat on the edge of it as stiffly as if he had a ramrod down his back. His linen house-coat made marked contrast with the dark pallor of his face and the strong black hair heavily streaked with grey. March thought, "An odd face. I wonder what's going on behind it." He said,

"Did you use these words to your wife—'It fare to serve him right'?"

"Why should I say that?"

"Your wife told Miss Elliot that you did."

"Mrs. Robbins was very much upset, sir. She'd known Mr. Henry from a boy. I don't know what she said to Miss Elliot, but she was in that state she might have said anything—right down hysterical."

March leaned forward.

"You haven't really answered my question, Robbins. Did you use those words—'It fare to serve him right'?"

"Not that I can remember, sir."

"Had you any reason, or did you think that you had any reason, to use such an expression with regard to Mr. Clayton?"

"Why should I, sir? I'd known him since he was a boy."

March leaned back, frowning a little.

"I'm sorry to touch on a painful subject, but I must ask you whether you considered Mr. Clayton was responsible for any trouble you had had in your family."

"I don't know what you mean, sir."

"I'm afraid I can't accept that. You did have trouble, didn't you, over your daughter? I am asking you if you thought that Mr. Clayton was responsible."

The man's face did not exactly change. It hardened. The deep lines were deeper.

"We never got to know who was responsible."

"Did you suspect Mr. Clayton?"

"We didn't know who to suspect."

"But it is true, is it not, that in January '41 you had news of your daughter being in London and went up to see her?"

"Who told you that, sir?"

"Mr. Roger Pilgrim informed Miss Silver."

Robbins turned towards the clicking neddles.

"Then I suppose he told you, miss, that my daughter was killed in an air raid."

Miss Silver coughed.

"He told me that you saw her in hospital before she died."

"It wasn't exactly a hospital—more like a First Aid station, miss."

"But you saw her there."

"Yes, miss."

March resumed.

"Did she tell you that Mr. Clayton was the father of her child?"

The dark face remained harsh and inexpressive. The eyes dwelt on a point a good deal lower than the eyes of the person to whom he spoke. He said, "She was dying when I got there. She didn't tell me anything."

Miss Silver coughed again.

"Major Pilgrim told me that she was able to speak to you."

Robbins turned that lowered gaze in her direction.

"No more than a few words, miss. She said 'I'm going'

and asked me to look after the child—not knowing it was dead.''

March said, "She didn't mention Henry Clayton's name?"

"No, sir. There wasn't time for anything like that."

"Do you mean that you would have expected her to mention Mr. Clayton's name if there had been time?"

"No, sir."

"There was no grudge against Mr. Clayton in your mind—no suspicion that he had treated your daughter badly?"

"No, sir."

"Then why did you use the words repeated by Mrs. Robbins—'It fare to serve him right'?"

"I have no recollection of saying any such thing. It's not an expression I should use, sir."

March said, "Very well. Now, will you take your mind back to the night of Mr. Clayton's disappearance. It was the twentieth of February, a month after your daughter's death and three days before the date set for his wedding. I have your original statement here—I should like to go through it with you. There are one or two points where I think you may be able to help us."

He took him through the telephone conversation of which he had overhead Henry Clayton's part and the subsequent short talk in the hall.

"Mr. Clayton went out just as he was, saying that he wouldn't be long, and not to wait up, as he would take the front door key and put up the chain when he came in?"

"That's right."

"Then you say that you went through to the kitchen to tell your wife that you would be late coming up. Why did you do that?"

"I was going to wait up for Mr. Henry."

"Why?"

"He was inclined to be heedless, sir. Mr. Pilgrim was very particular about the door. I told Mrs. Robbins I should wait up, and I come back to the hall."

"I see. Now how long do you suppose you were away from it?"

"Not very long, sir."

"Cast your mind back and go over just what you did and said. See if you can't get some idea of how long it would take."

"I went across the hall and down the passage to the kitchen. Mrs. Robbins was in the scullery. I went through to her. So far as I remember, I told her Miss Freyne and Mr. Henry had some sort of a quarrel on by what I'd just heard Mr. Henry say on the telephone, but he was all set to make it up. I said he'd gone round to see her, and she said it was pretty late. We talked about it a little, and then I come back to the hall."

"Do you think you were away five minutes?"

He thought for a moment.

"All of that, sir."

"Ten minutes?"

"It wouldn't be as much. Somewhere between the two is what I would say."

"And when you left the hall. . . . Wait a minute, what sort of lock have you got on that front door? Does it lock itself when it's shut?"

"Yes, sir."

"Then Mr. Clayton wouldn't have had to use the key to lock it when went out."

"Yes, sir, he would."

"How's that?"

"The old lock was still in use, sir. This one wasn't put on till afterwards."

March whistled.

"What was the key like?"

"A big old-fashioned key."

"Well, let's get back to you leaving the hall. Was the front door locked then?"

Robbins stared.

"Mr. Henry would lock it after him, I suppose."

"Was it still locked when you came back? Did you try it before you put up the chain?"

"Yes, it was locked."

"And from that time onwards the chain was up until— When did you open the door?"

"I couldn't open it, sir. I must have fallen asleep in my chair, because I heard twelve strike, and when I woke up it was striking six. The door was locked and the chain was up. I waited till eight o'clock, and then I informed Mr. Pilgrim. We couldn't open the door because the key was missing with Mr. Henry. We had to have the locksmith to it, and a new lock and key."

Miss Silver gave her slight cough.

"Did you try the door before you went to speak to your wife?"

"No, miss."

"Then how do you know that Mr. Clayton locked it afterwards?"

"That's what he took the key for."

"But you don't know that he used it—do you? You have just said that he was inclined to be heedless. His mind was full of going to see Miss Freyne, he might very well take the key and forget to lock the door—or consider that it was not necessary to lock it, since he did not intend to be very long. That is possible, is it not?"

For the first time Robbins shifted his position, sat a little farther back in his chair, and set a hand on either knee. His face showed nothing. The right hand moved on the stuff of his suit. Frank Abbott thought, "She thinks someone went after him and brought him back. If anyone did that, the door must have been open—Henry couldn't have locked it. That's the only time Henry could have got back into the house without being seen, that somewhere between five and ten minutes while Robbins was away—unless it's Robbins who called him back, Robbins who did him in. In which case he never left the hall at all—though why he should let Henry go out into the street and then call him back and knife him is just one of those things that don't make sense. He couldn't know that Lesley would be looking out of the window. I can't make head or tail of it. I wonder if Maudie can."

He heard Robbins say, "I don't know, miss," and he heard Miss Silver take him up.

"Robbins, no one would call you deaf, but I have noticed that your hearing is not at all acute. If Mr. Clayton had locked that door, you would not, I think, have heard the sound of the key turning?"

After a pause he said, "No."

"You are not accustomed to hearing that sound, so you would not miss it. In fact you would not have known—you did not know—that Mr. Clayton ever locked the door."

There was a longer pause. Then he said, "No," again.

The questions went on, but they brought out no fresh evidence. Just at the end Miss Silver asked one which seemed quite irrelevant. "You served in the last war, did you not? Were you in France, or did you go out to the East at all?"

He said in a surprised voice,

"I was a Territorial, miss. I got sent to India."

She inclined her head.

"I remember—Territorial regiments were sent out there. You were there for the duration, I suppose?"

"Yes, miss. Mr. Pilgrim kept my place open, and I come back to it."

As Robbins turned to leave the room, March called him back.

"Ever see this before?"

He was taking a key out of the piece of brown paper in which it had been wrapped. When it was free he laid it down on a sheet of paper—a handsome and distinctive piece of work, beautifully wrought with three lobes and a cockle shell in each.

Robbins stared at it gloomily and said, "Yes, sir."

"Old front-door key?"

"Yes." He paused, and added, "May I ask where it was found, sir?"

March looked at him very straight.

"Where do you think?"

"I suppose we could all make a guess, sir, but it isn't a matter for guessing."

"No—quite right, Robbins. It was found in Mr. Clayton's pocket."

The first Judy saw of Frank Abbott was when she met him in the upstair corridor. They stood and looked at each other for a moment before he said,

"March wants to interview Miss Janetta. I told him she'd want notice." There was a fleeting spark of amusement. "There was an old lady in Dickens who expired murmuring 'Rose-coloured curtains for the doctors,' wasn't there? Perhaps she was an ancestress."

"Miss Janetta isn't dying," said Judy demurely. Then all of a sudden she shuddered. "Don't talk about people dying—I just can't bear it."

"Well, she isn't going to. You've just said so."

He put an arm round her, took her along to the big empty state bedroom, and shut the door. When he had done that he put his other arm round her too and kissed her a good many times.

"Silly—aren't you?" he said in an odd unsteady voice.

"It's been horrid—"

"My child, I told you so, but you would come."

He kissed her again. This time she pushed him away.

"Frank—who did it? Do they know?"

"Not yet. Look here, Judy, I want you to clear out."

"I can't."

"Oh, yes, you can. You can come and do your work, but I won't have you here at night. I'll fix it up with Lesley Freyne—she'll take you in."

She said, "Penny is there. That's all that matters."

"Well, you matter to me. I'll fix it for you."

"No—I won't go. I'm next to Miss Silver, and I can lock my door. Besides, who's going to want to murder me?" Another of those shudders ran over her. "Don't look at me like that. I'm not going."

He said soberly, "I think you're being stupid. If Jerome gets one of his attacks, you have a bad night. I hear he had one a couple of nights ago."

"He didn't have one last night."

"Perhaps they gave him something to keep him quiet."

"So they did the other night, but he had one just the same."

He looked at her attentively.

"What was supposed to set him off?"

"Seeing Miss Freyne." Judy's voice was quite expressionless.

"He has one after seeing Lesley, but he doesn't have one after Roger falls out of the window, and he doesn't have one after they find Henry's body. Does that seem odd to you?"

"Very odd."

He kissed her again, lightly this time, and turned to the door.

"I mustn't dally. There are moments when being a policeman palls. Go in and ask Miss Janetta when she will be ready to see March. And it's no good her saying she isn't well or anything like that, because he means to see her, and Daly won't back her up."

He waited, and he had to wait some time, but in the end she came out to say that Miss Janetta would see Superintendent March in twenty minutes, and she hoped that he would make his visit as short as possible, as she was feeling terribly prostrated.

Frank Abbott got back to the study to find Lesley Freyne there. She gave him her hand and a friendly smile, and he thought, as he always thought, what a nice woman she was, and what a pity she hadn't married and had a pack of children of her own instead of having to make do with evacuees. Of course it was very nice for the evacuees.

He went to his place, took up his pad, and wrote down an interminable string of questions and answers. Sometimes he could have flinched for her, but she kept her quiet dignity and gave no sign, however near the quick the question must have cut. March was as considerate as he could be, but he had his duty to do, and to establish a motive for Henry Clayton's death was part of that duty.

"Miss Freyne, you will appreciate that I have to ask you questions which you may find it painful to answer. In the statements which were made at the time of Clayton's disappearance there were references to a disagreement which had taken place between you during the afternoon. Can you indicate the nature of that disagreement?"

"I am afraid not. It was a private matter."

"A good many private matters have to be disclosed in the

course of a murder case. When you made your original statement there was no reason to suppose that Clayton was dead. Now things are different. The body which was found in the cellars yesterday has been identified as that of Henry Clayton. His name is on a tab on the coat, and his signet ring has been identified by Jerome Pilgrim. There is no doubt at all that he was murdered. It seems likely that, for some reason, he returned to the house after having left it, and that he was stabbed in or near the lift going down to the cellars. The weapon was probably taken from one of the trophies in the dining-room and subsequently replaced. Examination has disclosed traces of blood close up to the hilt of one of the daggers. Scrapings from the floor of the lift show similar traces. In these circumstances, you must see that I have no choice but to press you. Anything that caused a disagreement between you and Clayton might throw some light on the motive for this crime.'

"I don't think it could possibly do that."

"You might not be the best judge. Will you not change your mind?"

She shook her head.

"It wouldn't be fair to do so. It might cause distress to an innocent person."

"You mean that your quarrel was about a woman?"

"It wasn't really a quarrel. It wouldn't help you to know about it. We took different points of view about something—that was all."

"Can you not particularize a little more than that? You need not mention names."

She seemed to be considering. After a while she said,

"Yes, I could do that. A case came up in conversation—I took one point of view, and Henry took another."

"What kind of case was it?"

"The case of the unmarried woman who has a child. I took the point of view that the child had claims upon both the parents which should override everything else."

"And Clayton?"

"He didn't agree. He said of course the man must pay, but

he didn't admit any responsibility beyond that. It is what a great many men would say. There wasn't any quarrel.''

March looked at her.

''Was the case you were discussing that of Mabel Robbins?''

She had a momentary colour in her face.

''No, of course not!''

''I don't know why you should say 'of course.' You must have known the girl.''

''Oh, yes, I knew her. She was very pretty and charming.''

''Then it would have been natural that you should have her case in mind—wouldn't it?''

''It was another case—a case in the papers.''

''It might have been another case, and yet you might have had Mabel Robbins in your mind. That would be natural, wouldn't it?''

''Mr. March, do you really expect me to be able to tell you just what was in my mind three years ago?''

''I think you would know whether you had thought about Mabel Robbins. Come, Miss Freyne—you were reluctant to speak of this disagreement because you didn't want to involve an innocent person. Will you assert that this person had no connection with the Robbins family?''

She said with composure,

''No. I had better tell you. I was thinking about Mrs. Robbins—I have always been so sorry for her. I didn't want to say anything to revive Mabel's story. Please don't misunderstand me. The case I discussed with Henry had nothing to do with the Robbinses, but I knew if I mentioned it that the Robbinses would be dragged in—as they have been now.''

He looked at her hard.

''Miss Freyne—did you know that Mabel Robbins was dead?''

''Yes—Mr. Pilgrim told me. He said the Robbinses did not want it spoken of. I never mentioned it.''

''But you knew. Did you know at the time of this disagreement?''

''No, I don't think I did. I think Mr. Pilgrim told me afterwards.''

''You're not sure?''

"Yes, I am sure that it was afterwards."

"Did you know who was the father of Mabel Robbins' child?"

"No."

"Did Mr. Pilgrim tell you anything about that?"

There was a long pause before she said,

"Yes."

"Did he tell you that he thought Clayton was the father?"

"He said he was afraid of it."

"Did he give you any reason for thinking so?"

She turned very pale indeed. She kept her voice steady, but it was very low.

"He said Robbins told him."

Chapter Eleven

When March knocked at Miss Janetta's door and went in he found Miss Lona Day in attendance. He was aware that the stage had been set and his part mapped out for him. He was undoubtedly the crude policeman blundering into a lady's sick-room. The curtains, half-drawn across the windows, were flowered in roses and forget-me-nots. Pink linen blinds half down converted the cold daylight into a rosy glow.

Just at first he couldn't see anything. Miss Day conducted him deviously amidst furniture until he reached the bed, where he was provided with a seat. After a minute or two his eyes cleared and he discerned Miss Janetta amidst pink bed-linen with an embroidered coverlet drawn up to her waist. She appeared to have sufficient strength to sit up. She wore a bed-jacket trimmed with a great many yards of lace, and not a hair of her elaborate curls was out of place. A boudoir cap composed of about two inches of lace, a rosebud and a bunch of forget-me-nots nestled coquettishly amongst them, and she wore several valuable rings. He reflected that she looked a good deal more like a Dresden shepherdess than a mourning invalid.

She was speaking to him out of the pink haze.

"You must forgive me if I have kept you waiting. It has been such a terrible shock. I am not as strong as my sister. You will not mind if my nurse stays in the room."

"I would rather see you alone, Miss Pilgrim."

She gave a fluttered sigh.

"Do you know—I don't really feel—I'm afraid I'll have to ask you to let her stay. Lona dear, my smelling-salts—"

Miss Day's eyes met his with sympathy. She said,

"I think you'd better let me stay."

He gave up. If he pressed her, she would probably swoon, and then it would all be to do again.

After producing a vinaigrette Miss Day had drifted tactfully over to the window. Miss Janetta addressed him.

"Just tell me what you want to know, and I will do my best. But I must save my strength—you will help me to do that?"

"I won't keep you longer than I can help. I wondered whether you could tell me what was the general feeling in the family with regard to the sale of the estate—when it was first suggested."

Miss Janetta forgot all about being prostrated. She said with surprising energy,

"It was my brother. I can't think how he came to think of such a thing. I never was so shocked in my life. And getting Roger to break the entail! I can't think what either of them were thinking about. We were all quite horrified."

"When you say *we*, to whom do you refer?"

The curls were lightly tossed.

"All of us—the whole family. Why, my sister would simply have broken her heart. She lives for the garden, and—of course you couldn't be expected to understand, but there have always been Pilgrims at Pilgrim's Rest."

He produced a sympathetic smile.

"Yes, it is very sad when these old places pass into other hands. But I gather Mr. Pilgrim intended to proceed with the sale."

Miss Janetta heaved a sigh. "He was very, very obstinate about it. He had a very obstinate character. If he hadn't died when he did, we should all have been turned out."

Miss Day had come back from the window. She said in a soothing voice,

"Are you sure you are not talking too much, dear?"

It didn't go down at all well. There was an acid edge on the voice that snubbed her.

"I think you had better go and see if Jerome wants anything. You can come back presently."

March felt a little sorry for Miss Day, but she was probably used to it. What a life!

She faded from the room, and he resumed.

"The sale fell through owing to your brother's death?"

She heaved another sign.

"Yes. It was quite providential. A terrible accident of course, but he was in failing health, and he has been spared all these terrible things—Roger, and poor Jack—and now Henry." A lace-edged handkerchief touched her eyes for a moment.

March would have bet his last sixpence that the gesture was purely ritual. He said,

"Yes." And then, "Roger was about to sell, wasn't he?"

A natural flush deepened the colour in her cheeks.

"And look what came of it!" she said.

"My dear Miss Pilgrim—"

The curls were tossed with vigour.

"I suppose you don't believe in things like that, but I do. My brother was going to sell, and he died. And Roger was going to sell, and he died. There's a verse about it. It's carved over the mantelpiece in the hall—

> 'If Pilgrim fare upon the Pilgrims' Way,
> And leave his Rest, he'll find nor rest nor stay.
> Stay Pilgrim in thy Rest, or thou shalt find
> Ill luck before, Death but one pace behind.' "

"Yes, I've seen it," said March drily. "Henry Clayton wasn't selling the estate though, was he? How do you account for him?"

The brightness went out of her eyes. They looked vague.

"My brother was trying to sell—it stirs up ill luck—you don't know where it will strike next. You mayn't believe in things like that, but I know they're true. If Jerome tries to sell, something will happen to him."

"I don't think it will," said March grimly.

"There must always be a Pilgrim at Pilgrim's Rest," said Miss Janetta.

He got nothing from her of any more value than that. She remembered the evening her nephew Henry disappeared. She had been very much fatigued by the large family party, and had gone to her room at half past nine. But not to sleep—oh, dear no! She was a perfect martyr to insomnia.

"Your windows look out to the street, Miss Pilgrim. Did you hear Clayton go out?"

It transpired that she had heard nothing.

"I feel the cold too much to have my windows open. Dr. Daly doesn't advise it."

March found it impossible to resist the belief that the insomnia existed only in her imagination. Anyone who was awake in this room would surely have heard that big front door fall to. He came downstairs a little later and went on with his interviews.

Miss Columba had taken her heavy heart to the garden. It was very heavy indeed. It was a relief to dibble in another row of peas under Pell's disapproving eye. He laid his peas in a trench and raked the earth over them. It aroused all his worst passions to see her using her middle finger as a dibber and making a separate hole for every pea. The fact that her rows usually did better than his was an old and gnawing grievance—one of the things which added bitterness to the tone in which he talked to William about "females." "Females wasn't never intended to garden—stands to reason they wasn't. 'Twas Adam was set to till the ground, not that flighty piece Eve. Childer and cooking—that's all that females are fit for. Getting in trousis and doing a man's job is clean flying in the face of Providence, and you can't get from it."

The dead weight which Miss Columba carried lifted percep-tibly as she put in her peas. In the house they were all sorry for her. All except Janetta, who never thought of anyone but herself. Even Robbins—no, she wasn't sure about Robbins. Dark—secret. Like a plant that has run to root. She remembered an apple-tree when she was a girl. Never bloomed or fruited, and her father had it taken up. Six foot of tap root. Dark—secret. Going down and down. They planted it again with a paving stone under it. It did all right after that.

Pell's voice came up out of the wordless grumbling which had accompanied his digging.

"That grand-daughter of mine's home."

Miss Columba poked a hole with her finger and dropped a pea into it. "Which one?"

"Maggie. Looks a show in her uniform. Against nature, I call it."

"Leave?"

Pell cleared his throat.

"Peck of rubbish! Calls herself a corporal—two stripes on her arm! Flying in the face of Providence, that's what I call it."

Miss Columba put in another pea.

"Maggie's a good girl."

"She was. No saying what she is now. Paints her mouth!"

"Girls do."

He gave a crowing laugh.

"Same as Jezebel! And what come of her—answer me that!"

Miss Columba made two more holes, dropped in two more peas, and said with finality,

"Maggie's a good girl."

It was all very soothing. Pell wasn't sorry for her. If the whole family was lying dead, he would be just as cross-grained and obstructive as he always was. It kept you in the world you were accustomed to, the world of normal disagreeable things—north east winds—May frosts—hail—drought—green fly—wireworm—Pell. Very steadying. Murder was not a normal thing. Something out of control. Something out of madness and nightmare. Wrenched loose. Threshing round. Killing. Don't think about it. Plant the peas. They'll put down roots and throw up shoots. Bloom. Fruit. Fade. Go back to manure the ground. Natural. Murder not natural. Don't think about it. Think about Pell. Think about Maggie.

She put in another pea, and said,

"I'd like to see Maggie. Tell her to come up and see me."

March got down to the net results of his interviews after lunch. Miss Silver in the convenient small chair which left her elbows free—arms can be very hampering when you are knitting—Frank Abbott posed negligently on the arm of one of the big leather-covered chairs and looking as if he had never done anything in his life except exist beautifully in a workless world, an appearance to which a pile of very neat typescripts at March's right hand gave the lie.

"Well, Abbott, I've been over all the notes you took, and I don't know what you think, but it looks like Robbins to me."

Frank nodded.

"We could do with some more evidence."

"Oh, yes. But I don't see where we're going to get it. However, I'd like to run through all the other possibilities. We may turn something up that way. Something may have struck you or Miss Silver."

She was finishing the right sleeve of Ethel Burkett's jumper. Her attention appeared to be wholly engaged by the ribbing at the wrist. March experienced a slight feeling of impatience. He was taking her into the fullest confidence, letting her in where he could without any complaint from her have left her out, and he thought a little response would not be out of place. There was no sign of it. She might have been in the next room. She might never have heard of Henry Clayton. She might have been in Timbuctoo. He didn't go quite as far as to wish her there, but he was well on the way to it. He picked up a sheet of foolscap covered with his own writing.

"I'll lead off with Robbins—just a close summary. I think there's no doubt he suspected Clayton of having seduced his daughter. She may have told him so before she died, or it may have been just suspicion. Miss Freyne's evidence is important on this point. She says Mr. Pilgrim told her that he was afraid Henry Clayton was responsible, and said that Robbins had told him so. Well, there's the motive. By all accounts he had been very hard hit, wouldn't have the girl's name mentioned, wouldn't have her and the child buried down here—Mrs. Robbins seems to have felt this very much—wouldn't even give out the fact that she was dead. All this is evidence that he was very deeply and to some extent abnormally affected. Then a month after the daughter's tragic death with her child in an air raid Henry Clayton comes down here to marry another woman. That strengthens the motive very considerably, I think. As to opportunity—well, Robbins had it if anyone did. His account of what happened after half past ten that night is corroborated at one point, and only one. Henry Clayton did leave the house. Miss Freyne saw him emerge into the street and come towards her. She says he was halfway between the door of the glazed passage and the gate to the stable yard when she turned away from the window. That distance is some ten to fifteen yards—I'd allow a margin because he was coming directly toward her and it was moonlight, both disturbing factors. In any case the distance was such that Robbins could either have called to him from the entrance to the glazed passage or run after him. Whichever it was, it is, I think, quite certain that Clayton returned to the house. What excuse Robbins used, we can't tell, but Clayton undoubtedly turned round and came back. Robbins may have had the dagger ready. He may have stabbed him at once, in the passage or in the hall, or he may have got him into the dining-room or into the passage where the lift is on some pretext or other. We'll never know about that unless he tells us. If he had it all planned, he would of course get him as far as he could. But there may not have been any premeditation—he may just have felt that he had got to have it out with him about his daughter. Clayton's going off like that to see Miss Freyne might have been the last straw. If Robbins suddenly taxed him with having ruined his daughter, that would have turned Clayton back all right. And he wouldn't want anyone listening in. There was the dining-room all handy, and on the opposite side of the house from Mr. Pilgrim's room and his aunts. And once they were in the dining-room all those daggers were very handy too. I think it happened that way.''

Frank ran a hand back over his immaculate hair.

"That's a point, about the position of the rooms, but it would apply to other people besides Robbins. I'm not disagreeing, you know. If the murder was premeditated, the dining-room would have been chosen anyhow, on account of having a door through into the stone passage just opposite that lift. If it wasn't premeditated, it was still the best room to have a quarrel in. You see, the room Judy Elliot is in overhead was empty. Henry was in the room Miss Silver has now. Then comes another empty room and Lona Day's. Jerome's room looks the other way, and isn't over the dining-room at all. Lona is the only one who could possibly have heard anything, and its unlikely she would, through these walls."

March nodded.

"Well, there we are. That's the case against Robbins as far as Henry Clayton goes. Passing to Mr. Pilgrim's death—I've see the groom William, and he says there was a thorn under the saddle, and it was a long black thorn from a tree hanging over the stable yard. But there's no real proof, and never will be, that the death was not accidental. If it wasn't, Robbins could have done it, just as anyone else in the house could have done it. Motive—Mr. Pilgrim was about to sell the house. If it was sold, the cellars would be cleared out and Clayton's body discovered. The person who killed him couldn't afford to let that happen."

Frank Abbott said, "Quite." Miss Silver did not lift her eyes from her knitting.

March frowned and went on.

"We come to Roger Pilgrim's death. If he was murdered, the same motive would apply. Without the discovery of Clayton's body, any coroner's jury would bring in a verdict of accident, with a feeling at the back of their minds that it was probably suicide, but kinder to the family not to say so."

Frank Abbott gave a short laugh.

"Who says we're not a sentimental nation?"

Miss Silver gave a slight reproving cough.

"Reluctance to inflict unnecessary pain can hardly be considered reprehensible."

March went on.

"The discovery of Clayton's body makes it a good deal more likely that Roger was murdered, because except for the death of Mr. Pilgrim, who really could not have had any motive for murdering his nephew, the household here was the same as at the time of Clayton's disappearance. And that means that there was probably someone amongst them who had already done one murder and had an extremely strong motive for covering it up by committing another. Now see how this applies to Roger's death. Miss Elliot saw Robbins go up the back stair at some time after six but before a quarter to seven. She thinks it was before half past six, but she isn't sure. She saw him go up, but she didn't see him come down. Robbins says it was only just after six, he wasn't in his room five minutes, and he came down by the stair in the other wing—which seems odd, because it's right out of his way on the other side of the house. He says Miss Freyne and Roger were together in the attic room when he came down. Miss Freyne says she left at six-fifteen. Well, there you are—he could very easily have waited to see her go, and then have gone in and pushed Roger out over that low sill. He had just seen him from his own room, right up there in the window. If he wanted to bump him off he couldn't have had a better opportunity. It all rather piles up against Robbins, you know. Take the fall of the ceiling. It would be the easiest thing in the world for him to pour water down on to it from the floor above—he and his wife had the whole place to themselves up there. And the business of the fire. It was he who took the tray of drinks along to the room which was burned out. Roger said the drink was doped. I gather that Jerome has sleeping tablets knocking about. It wouldn't be difficult for Robbins to get hold of one or two, and it would be the easiest thing in the world for him to come back, set light to the papers, and lock the door. That cross passage which runs in between the burned-out room and the lift is his own lawful direct way from the kitchen to the dining-room—he'd every right in the world to be going to and fro along it." He put down the paper he was holding and took up another.

Miss Silver had begun to cast off. Frank Abbott said, "Well, that's Robbins. What about the others?"

Chapter Twelve

March frowned.

"I don't know," he said. "The weak point is the initial motive. The only one who can be said to have had one besides Robbins is Miss Freyne."

Frank Abbott said,

"Oh, no—not in character at all."

"I agree. But we have to consider her. You see, I think it is quite clear that her disagreement with Clayton was a very serious one. I don't mean to say that she wasn't telling the truth about it—I think she was. But however much that disagreement began over an abstract case, I think it was quite impossible that those two people should have discussed it and disagreed over it without having Mabel Robbins in their minds, and this would mean that very passionate and bitter feelings might have been roused up. We don't of course know whether Miss Freyne already suspected Clayton of having been the girl's lover, but from her manner I thought so. It seemed to me that Mr. Pilgrim's subsequent disclosure had not really taken her by surprise."

Frank nodded.

"Henry was a bit of a lad all right—he'd be bound to be suspected. But you're wasting time over Lesley—she's one of the few people in the world who are constitutionally incapable of crime. But go on."

"Well, apart from that, she could have done it. But it would have had to be planned—perhaps on the spur of the moment after he telephoned. She looks out of the window, sees him coming, and goes to meet him. They go back into Pilgrim's Rest together. When they are in the dining-room she stabs him. She may have brought the knife with her, or she may have pulled one out of the trophy. It could have been done either way.''

Frank's eyes were at their iciest, his manner indifferent in the extreme. Miss Silver knew him well enough to be aware that he was angry. She drew her wool through the last loop and laid her hands down upon the completed jumper with a small satisfied smile.

Frank said casually,

''And when do you suggest that she locked the door? And how did she get out of the house when she had locked it? The key was in Henry's pocket. If Robbins didn't do the job himself, I take it we accept his statement that the door was locked and the chain up within ten minutes of Henry's leaving the house.''

March nodded.

''That's the weak point. Robbins would have had to let her out, or at any rate to lock up after her.'' He smiled. ''I am not seriously accusing Miss Freyne, you know——I agree with your estimate of her character. Well, now we come to the other people in the house. Miss Columba. The same general motive as the other relations, the same attachment to house and garden, but by all accounts a very particular attachment to her nephews. I really cannot see her murdering two of them. In the case of Henry Clayton, it is difficult to see any motive at all. This last consideration also applies to Miss Janetta. She is a vain and self-centered person without her sister's integrity of character. She has just described her brother's death to me as 'providential,' since it prevented him from alienating the property. But I really cannot see why she should have desired the death of Henry Clayton. I remember meeting him when I first came here, and I should say he was the type to be extremely popular with maiden aunts.''

Frank laughed.

''He was the blue-eyed boy all right! He'd a way with him, you know——stole horses where other people couldn't look over the hedge, and got away with it with a feather in his cap. But he did it once too often.''

March went back to his list.

''Jerome. Well, the only question here to my mind is

whether he is subject to fits of insanity. If he is, he could have done it all. I gather that his physical state hasn't changed very much. It would require a great deal of strength to stab a man with a sharp knife, to drag his body a short way, or to tip an unsuspecting person out of a window with a very low sill. No one who knew him would suspect him of doing any of these things if he was in his right senses. But the poor chap has had a bad head wound, and Daly tells me he gets what he calls nervous attacks. He says they are apt to come on at night after any exertion or excitement, that he hasn't ever seen him in one himself, so he has only the nurse's account to go by. On that, he says, there are no grounds for any suspicion of insanity. She says he has an aggravated form of nightmare, and wakes up very much distressed and dazed, but not at all violent.''

"That is so," said Miss Silver.

A little surprised at what was quite a dogmatic statement, he turned in her direction.

"I have both heard him and seen him in one of these attacks, Randall. The sounds are in the highest degree alarming. On the occasion on which I heard them they suggested a man violently attacked and violently resisting. There was also at least one scream. I say 'at least' because I am under the impression that it was a scream which had awakened me. My room, as you know, is not far from his. I understand now why the rest of the family sleep in the other wing."

Frank said, "Judy Elliot heard it too.'

"Yes, we both arrived in the corridor at the same time. Captain Pilgrim then appeared on the threshold of his room. His pyjama coat was torn open, he was clutching at the door posts, and he looked dazed and horrified. I reached him just as Miss Day came out of her room, which is opposite his. He was perfectly gentle, docile, and polite. When Miss Day told him that he had been dreaming again and had disturbed me, he was able to control himself sufficiently to say, 'So sorry.' ''

March nodded.

"Miss Day declares that these attacks never occur except in his sleep, and that he is never violent except in the first stage, when he thinks that someone is attacking him and hits out.

As soon as he is awake he is only dazed and distressed. The shouting and calling out is a constant feature. It therefore doesn't seem possible that he should have carried out a methodical murder like that of Henry Clayton, especially when you consider that it probably took place at quite an early hour when the rest of the household were either still awake or not yet fast asleep. Miss Day, for instance, says that she was reading in bed till past midnight, and that she heard nothing. I'll take her next. She came here at the beginning of December '43 to nurse Miss Janetta through an attack of influenza, and she stayed on to look after Jerome, who arrived from hospital on the twentieth. Henry Clayton came down for Christmas. She says she never met any of the family until she came here. Clayton was the merest acquaintance. She thought him very charming, but she naturally didn't see very much of him, as he only came down at week-ends and spent most of his time with Miss Freyne. On the night of his disappearance, she says, she left Jerome listening to the wireless at about a quarter past ten and went and had a bath. She was back in her room by eleven and read till nearly twelve. She didn't hear the front door shut, she didn't hear anything. There doesn't seem to be a shadow of a motive in Clayton's case, and if she didn't kill Clayton she didn't kill Roger. If Roger was murdered, it must have been to prevent the sale of the house and the discovery of the previous crime. In fact I don't feel able to believe in more than one murderer."

Frank Abbott said, "I agree."

March went on.

"I have left Mrs. Robbins to the last. You saw her and heard her statement. I don't think it's possible to suspect her. To my mind the thing that stuck out all through was her devotion to 'Mr. Henry.' Rather touching, I thought, poor woman. I think it is quite plain she more than suspected that it was Clayton who got her daughter into trouble. And look what she says."

He picked up another of the sheets which lay before him and read from it.

"Mrs. Robbins' statement—

" 'She never told me who it was—she never told me

nothing about it, just ran away and hid. But if it was Mr. Henry, I wouldn't blame her. He'd make any woman feel there wasn't anybody else. She done wrong, and she run away and hid. But Mr. Henry might have made any girl forget the way she'd been brought up.'

"And if you'll remember, that's where she burst out crying and it wasn't any use going on. For the rest, she said Robbins told her Mr. Henry had gone round to see Miss Lesley, and she went on up to bed and went to sleep and didn't wake up till the morning. She didn't hear anything, she didn't even know that Robbins hadn't come up. She'd had a lot to do all day, and she was dead tired and slept like a log."

He laid down the sheet in his hand and shuffled all the papers together. "Well, there we are. There's quite a case against Robbins, and none against anyone else."

Miss Silver was looking at the door. She got up now and went to it. It opened upon a passage which almost immediately turned into the back of the hall. She went to the corner and looked round. There was no one to be seen. Away to the left a stair ran up to the bedroom floor. Other doors opened upon the passage, other doors opened upon the hall. She went back to the study, to meet looks of surprise and a question from March.

"What is it?"

She went over to her chair and gathered up the finished jumper before she answered him.

"I thought the door moved," she said.

It was at this moment that it was borne in upon Frank Abbott that three was no longer company. All the time that they had been together in the study he had been aware of something in Miss Silver's attitude. He couldn't put a name to it, but she wasn't running true to form—he couldn't get any nearer to it than that. If she agreed with what March had been saying, why not chip in and say so with a bright quotation from the late Alfred, Lord Tennyson, or a home-made moral of her own? If she didn't agree, she had her own polite but quite pungent ways of saying so. Why, to quote out of her own book, should Maud be "faultily faultless, icily regular, splendidly null"?

And then all at once he got the idea. It was a case of "not before the child." She wouldn't disagree with Randall March or seem to criticize him in his own district in front of a junior officer from the Yard. Maudie had been very nicely brought up. She had spent a considerable portion of her adult life in bringing up the young in the way that they should go. She would rather die than display a lack of delicacy, especially if, as he suspected, she really had no solid grounds for either her delicacy or her disagreement. He thought perhaps it would be a good thing if the junior officer from the Yard were to make himself scarce. It occurred to him that he might achieve a word or two with Judy.

He said, "I'll be around if you give me a call," and melted from the scene.

Left alone, neither March nor Miss Silver spoke at once. He was putting his papers together, but presently he looked up from them to say,

"What is it?"

She had gone over to the fire and stood looking down into it, her knitting-bag slung over her left arm. At the sound of his voice she turned and said,

"Shall you be using this room any more, Randall? If you will, I had better make up the fire."

"No—yes—I don't know. You didn't answer my question. I said, 'What is it?'"

"And what did you mean by that?"

"As if you didn't know! You're holding something back, and I'd like to know what it is."

She stood where she was, looking at him with a grave and thoughtful expression.

"I am not happy about this case, Randall."

He met her look with a very direct one.

"Nor am I. But I wonder if we mean the same thing. I should be glad if you would let me have your point of view."

She said, "I do not think I have one. I will be quite frank with you now that we are alone. The death of Roger Pilgrim weighs upon me. He told the police that he believed his life to be in danger. He told me the same thing. He died. The police did not believe him—I did. I recommended a certain course of action which would, I think, have afforded him some protection. I refer to the sale of the property. I begged him to inform the household that he was not proceeding with it. Instead he made a very provocative declaration that the sale was going through.''

''Who was present?''

''Everyone—Miss Columba—Miss Janetta—myself—Judy Elliot—Miss Day—Captain Jerome Pilgrim—and Robbins. The scene took place at lunch.''

''Oh, there was a scene?''

''I think you might call it that. Miss Janetta flared up. If I remember rightly, she said that he couldn't do it, and that there had always been Pilgrims at Pilgrim's Rest. To which he replied with some heat that he was going to do it. I do not recollect whether he actually said, 'No matter what anyone says,' but undoubtedly that was the impression we all received. It was, I am afraid, a very unfortunate outbreak on his part.''

''Miss Freyne was not present?''

''No.''

''But Robbins was?''

''Yes.''

''How did he take it? Did you notice?''

''Yes—he appeared horrified. That would be natural, after thirty years' service.''

He made a non-committal sound that neither agreed nor disagreed. Then he said,

''Was the scene confined to Roger and Miss Janetta?''

''Yes. The others were, I think, shocked, but they made no protest.''

March said as if to himself,

''Miss Janetta—it's absurd—''

Miss Silver was silent for a time. She moved to put a piece of wood upon the fire. Then she turned back and said very seriously indeed,

''Will you do something for me?''

''If I can—''

''I would like you to have Miss Janetta's room searched.''

"Are you serious?"

"Quite, Randall."

He looked at her with astonishment and dismay.

"This is a red herring with a vengeance! What do you expect us to find?"

"Small pellets—perhaps in capsules—perhaps made up into pills—perhaps still in the rough, in which case they would, I think, have a greenish appearance."

A further access of surprise now ousted the dismay.

"My dear Miss Silver!"

She gave her slight cough.

"*Cannabis indica*, Randall."

He said in a stupefied tone,

"That's Indian hemp—hashish—what in the name of fortune?"

She coughed again.

"I may be wrong, but I do not wish you to accuse me of holding anything back. I have no evidence except that of my own impressions, and you will be quite justified in disregarding them."

He said, "This would be a lot easier if I knew what you were talking about."

"Jerome Pilgrim's attacks, Randall. I was told about them before I came down here. They were said to come on after any excitement or exertion. After I had witnessed one of these attacks Miss Day, who was very much upset, declared that it was Miss Freyne who had this exciting effect upon her patient. She said how awkward it was, and how difficult it made her position here, because the whole family was so fond of Miss Freyne. She appeared to be in genuine distress. If she was speaking the truth, her position was really a very difficult one. I made some discreet enquiries later on, and heard of three other instances where an attack had followed upon a visit from Miss Freyne."

March said bluntly, "Are you accusing Lesley Freyne of drugging Jerome?"

"Oh, no, I am not doing that—not at all. Too many hours elapse between the visit and the attack. It is not possible to relate them as you suggest."

"What makes you think he has been drugged? And why hashish?"

She answered the last part of the question.

"The painful and distressing dreams. *Cannabis indica* is, as you know, an illicit drug. It is not in the British Pharmacopoeia, but it is occasionally prescribed abroad. A friend of mine found it amongst the ingredients of a prescription given to her in India. The quantity was extremely small—quite microscopic in fact—but it produced the most terrible and distressing dreams. I have also heard of other similar cases. When I saw Captain Pilgrim at the door of his room I received a very strong impression that he had been drugged."

"Why should anyone want to drug him?"

"In order to separate him from Miss Freyne. That would be one reason. There might be another. The person who had killed Henry Clayton might find it very useful to provide a scapegoat. If a death from violence occurs, or has occurred, in a house which contains an invalid subject to acute nervous attacks, it is not too difficult to turn suspicion in his direction. As far back as three years ago neither of the two young girls employed here was willing to sleep in the house—Gloria Pell does not sleep in the house. And the reason given has been the alarming nature of Captain Pilgrim's attacks. Would not this be useful to a murderer, Randall?"

Looking at her doubtfully, he said,

"But—Miss Janetta—how in the world would she come by hashish?"

"That was naturally the first question I asked myself. If *cannabis indica* was being administered, who in the household could have been in possession of such a drug? There is no one who seems at all likely to be in touch with illicit drug distribution in this country. It has been for many years so strictly watched and so heavily punished that the risk, except to an addict who must have his drug at no matter what cost, is a very serious deterrent. There is no one in the house who can be suspected of being an addict. It then becomes a matter of past contacts which might have made a purchase possible somewhere abroad. Miss Day has been to India, Robbins spent nearly five years there during and immediately after the last war, and Miss Janetta wintered in Cairo in '38/'39. Any one of these three people could, I imagine, have obtained the drug. What the motive may at that time have been, I am not prepared to say, but in India or in Egypt *cannabis indica* would be procurable. I do not wish to go farther than that."

March said, "Miss Day—" in a meditative tone, and then, "In a matter of drugs one would naturally think first about the nurse. But what motive would she have for drugging her patient?"

Miss Silver coughed.

"There are several answers to that, Randall. She might wish to keep him—she might wish to keep a very comfortable situation. You will understand that I am not accusing Miss Day."

He drew his brows together in a frowning line.

"Are you trying to link up this suggestion that Jerome Pilgrim is being drugged with the deaths of Henry Clayton and Roger Pilgrim?"

She said very soberly,

"There is no evidence of a link, is there? There is, in fact, no evidence at all, only an unexplored possibility which I have asked you to explore. It may lead you into a blind alley—I am not prepared to say that it will not do so. But you will, I think, agree that when a serious crime has been committed anything abnormal should be investigated. It may not prove to have any connection with the crime, but that is no reason for neglecting it."

"No, of course not."

Miss Silver came up to the table and stood there, a small dowdy figure in olive-green cashmere. She said,

"If Captain Pilgrim were being drugged, it would be an abnormal happening, would it not? But the sudden cessation of the drugging would be abnormal too."

"What do you mean?"

"There has been no attack since the discovery of Henry Clayton's body."

"My dear Miss Silver, what does that amount to? We only found him yesterday?"

She coughed.

"I should have gone farther back. There has been no attack since Roger Pilgrim died." She set a hand on the table and leaned towards him. "Randall, there has been no attack since the police came into the house."

He smiled.

"No attack for two nights. Would that be so abnormal?"

It was the wrong answer. He was reminded of his school-room days. She said sharply,

"You are not giving your mind to it, Randall. It has been stressed that these attacks are the result of excitement or exertion. Consider the events of the last two days—the violent death of one person—the discovery of the murdered body of another—the necessity felt by Captain Pilgrim of assuming his place as head of the family. Could there be anything more conducive to an attack? Yet no attack has followed. Captain Pilgrim has exerted himself beyond what anyone would have considered prudent. He insisted on seeing Miss Freyne and breaking the news to her. The interview could hardly fail to be a most distressing one, yet there have been no ill effects. You will say that a nervous invalid may be roused and taken out of himself by a shock. That would be a possible explanation. But there is another explanation which is also possible. The presence of the police in the house, the careful scrutiny of everything and everyone, might quite reasonably alarm the person who had been using a drug and deter him or her from incurring any further risk."

March said,

"Him—or her?"

"That is what I said, Randall."

"Yes, but which?"

"That is not for me to say."

He said gravely,

"You've said a good deal. For instance, you offered an alternative reason for Jerome being drugged. You indicated that the attacks seemed to be connected with Miss Freyne. You suggested that someone wished it to be inferred that her visits had an upsetting effect. You said that someone might be trying to separate them. Have you any reason to suppose that there is anything between her and Jerome?"

"There is friendship and a deep affection—on his side, I think, a very deep affection."

"Do you mean that he is in love with her?"

"I cannot say. I have only seen them together on one occasion. He was like a different man."

"And who would wish to separate them? His aunts, his nurse? You know, if it was just that kind of jealousy, there might be no connection with the murder."

She inclined her head.

"Quite so."

"The aunts might be possessive—Miss Columba in particular is obviously devoted to him. The nurse might want to keep her job, or she might be fond of him herself—there might be no more in it than a jealous woman's trick. But why pick on Miss Janetta? She seems to me to have less motive than anyone else." He looked at her enquiringly.

She did not speak. When he became aware that he would get no answer he pushed back his chair.

"Well, I must be getting along. I'm to have the reports on the two post-mortems. And then—well, then, I think, I shall come back with a warrant and arrest Robbins. I'll leave Abbott and one of the men here—it had better be the sergeant. They can carry out your search. I suppose Miss Janetta can be induced to move into her sister's room whilst it is going on. I think it must be done as part of a general routine job—less upsetting all round—" He broke off and looked at her shrewdly. "All the same I would very much like to know why you have asked me to have just that room searched. Why not Jerome's room—the bathroom—and Miss Day's?"

Miss Silver coughed primly.

"Because I have already searched them myself."

Chapter Thirteen

Miss Silver came out of the study and went up to her room. The door to the back stair was open. She heard footsteps and voices, one of them Gloria's. She turned back to look and listen. There were two girls at the open bathroom door—Gloria pink-cheeked and chattering, and a sensible-looking young woman in khaki with a corporal's stripes on her sleeve.

Miss Silver drew their attention with a cough.

"Is that your sister, Gloria? I should like to meet her."

Maggie Pell was brought up and introduced.

"She's been seeing Miss Columba out in the garden and come in for a tidy-up. And Miss Collie says she's grown, and they don't starve her in the A.T.S. She says she looks ever so well. But Granpa, he don't half carry on about the uniform."

Maggie smiled, a nice slow smile. Her hair was much darker than Gloria's and very neat. She had blunt features and a thick white skin. Her brown eyes were kind.

"He's old," she said—"you can't expect him to change his ways."

Miss Silver looked at her, and took a decision.

"I wonder if you could spare me a few minutes," she said. "Is Gloria going out with you? Could you give me a quarter of an hour whilst she is putting on her things—if it will not make you miss your bus?"

Maggie shook her head.

"Oh, no, that's all right—there's no hurry. We're walking across the fields to see my aunt, Mrs. Collis, at Crow Farm."

She had a steady, quiet manner. Miss Silver approved. She took her into her room and shut the door.

"Sit down, Maggie. I expect you are wondering why I want to see you. You know, of course, what has been happening here."

Maggie said, "I'm sure it's dreadful! Mr. Henry and Mr. Roger both gone—I can't hardly believe it!"

"You were working here at the time that Mr. Clayton disappeared, were you not?"

"I wasn't sleeping in the house."

"No—I know that. It is all very shocking. And most necessary that it should be cleared up. Now I think you may be able to help us."

"I'm afraid I don't know anything about it."

Miss Silver gave a gentle cough.

"You cannot be sure about that. I want to ask you whether anyone sent a parcel to the cleaners just after Mr. Clayton was missing."

Maggie opened her mouth and shut it again. She brought her hands together in her lap and said,

"However did you know?"

"I thought something of the kind might have happened. Can you tell me who sent the parcel?"

"It was Miss Netta."

"Can you tell me what she sent?"

"Well, Miss Netta, she's very particular about her things—sends them away to be cleaned for next to nothing. There was a couple of dresses—one she had for afternoons, blue with a kind of mauve fleck in it, and one she'd been wearing of an evening, another kind of blue with some grey trimming."

"Were they badly stained?"

"No, they weren't. I packed them up, and there wasn't much wrong with them to my thinking. What was in a terrible mess was a warm purple dressing-gown she had that Miss Day had upset a jug of cocoa down. At least Miss Netta said it was Miss Day, but Miss Day was looking very old-fashioned about it, and I've got an idea it wasn't quite like Miss Netta said. She's like that, you know—if anything goes wrong, it's got to be someone else did it, not Miss Netta. So I've an idea that likely enough she tipped that cocoa over herself, especially as it went all over Miss Day too."

"Now when did this happen?"

Maggie Pell considered. She was a serious, simple-minded girl, and she was taking pains to be accurate.

"Well, it would be first thing in the morning, because that's when she has her cup of cocoa. Of course she has it at night too, the last thing. And Miss Day makes it for her on a spirit-lamp in the bathroom and takes it in—last thing at night and first thing in the morning. At least that's how it was in my time, and I don't expect it's been changed."

"So that the cocoa might have been spilled early in the morning or late the night before?" Miss Silver asked.

Maggie shook her head.

"I don't think so, because I remember Miss Netta said Miss Day made her have the dressing-gown round her for sitting up in bed because of its being such a cold morning. And so it was. I remember it was trying to snow when I came along and found them all in an upset over Mr. Henry."

"You are really sure about its being the morning?"

"Yes, I am now—because of what Miss Netta said about Miss Day making her have the dressing-gown round her. She was very put out about it—said it wouldn't have got stained only for Miss Day making her have it round her. I must say it was in a fair mess. You see, it wasn't just the cup of cocoa that went over her, it was the jug."

"Oh, there was a jug? Why was that?"

Maggie looked puzzled.

"Miss Day would be having a cup, I suppose. The jug broke all to bits. Miss Netta *was* put out! And she was putting it on Miss Day. But she said to me afterwards—that's Miss Day, not Miss Netta—she said, 'Well, you know, Maggie, she upset it herself, and my Chinese dressing-gown's ruined, for it ran all down the front.' "

"What was the dressing-gown like?"

Maggie's face lighted up.

"Oh, it was lovely—all birds and flowers and butterflies, worked on black satin. Done in China, she said. A lady she was with in India gave it to her."

"It sounds extremely handsome—too good in fact for everyday wear as a dressing-gown."

"Oh, but it wasn't—more like one of those house-coats really. She'd wear it for dinner in the evening when it was cold. Lovely and warm it was, with a beautiful silk lining."

"Then she did not usually wear it as a dressing-gown?"

"Oh, no, she didn't."

"Can you remember whether she was wearing it at dinner on the night Mr. Clayton disappeared?"

Maggie looked doubtful.

"I don't know—I don't think so. No, she wasn't. It was a green dress she had on—rather a bright green."

"Are you sure of that?"

"Yes, I am now."

Miss Silver looked at her. "Did Miss Day say anything to explain why she was wearing that handsome Chinese coat to take in Miss Janetta's early morning cocoa?"

Maggie stared.

"Oh, yes. It was because it was such a cold morning. It snowed as I came along. Lovely and warm that coat was, but it never looked the same after the cocoa."

"Did she send it to be cleaned?"

Another shake of the head.

"Oh, no, she didn't. I asked her what about putting it in the parcel, and she said no, she'd soaked it in water straight away and the worst of it was out, but the satin had rubbed and the colours run—in the embroidery, you know—and she was afraid it wouldn't ever look the same. And it didn't either—you could always see the marks. Cocoa's dreadful stuff to get out—kind of greasy, you know. I always thought it was a pity she put it in water, for Miss Netta's dressing-gown came back looking like new. But of course once you've started in to wash a thing, well, it doesn't give the cleaners a chance."

Miss Silver agreed. In a rather abstracted manner she enquired whether anyone else in the house had sent anything to be cleaned about that time—Mr. Jerome—Mr. Roger—Robbins or Mrs. Robbins—

Maggie had a quick "Oh, no" for that. She had done up the parcel herself, and no other parcel had gone. No clothes had been missing. As to the Robbinses, Mrs. Robbins didn't hold with cleaners—said they took the nature out of things. "If anything needed doing, she'd do it herself, or Mr. Robbins would. And what soap and water and benzine wouldn't take out, she'd say the cleaners wouldn't get out either. And I must say she was a very good hand at it.''

''Mrs. Robbins did a good bit of cleaning at home?''

Maggie Pell nodded emphatically.

''Oh, yes, she did—all her own things, and all Mr. Robbins'. She'd a sister a tailoress, and she learnt it off her. Mr. Robbins' suits, I'm sure they used to come up like new.''

It was now between three and a quarter past. After an interview with Jerome Pilgrim, March got into his car and went back to Ledlington, leaving Frank Abbott and the sergeant to conduct a search of the bedrooms.

Everything that happened during the afternoon was to be important—even the little things. When murder is abroad it is not easy to say which are the little things. A grain or two of dust, the smear of a damp finger, a speck of blood, a shred of torn paper—these weigh down the balance against a man's life. The murderer does not walk an easy path. He must keep the dust from his shoes, the stains of crime from his garments. He must not touch, he must not handle. But he must not only glove the bare skin lest it leave the mark of his guilty sweat—he must hood his thoughts and heed his tongue, he must mask his eyes from being the mirror of his mind, and walk the naked edge of danger easily. What to others are little things, sifted out afterwards by patient question and answer, are to him all the time an ever-present menace—the teeth of the trap which may at any moment spring to and catch him. He must watch everything and everyone. He must not appear to watch at all. With thought at its most abnormal, all that he looks, or says, or does must be so normal as to merge into an accustomed background and provide nothing that will catch even the most scrutinizing eye.

As Miss Silver stood at her open door to watch Maggie Pell cross to the back stair just over the way, Jerome Pilgrim came along the corridor. He looked pale and haggard, but she discerned a new air of resolution, as if the shocking events of the past few days had roused him—given him some needed impetus. He was wearing a coat and muffler, and informed her as he passed that he was going out into the garden. Miss

Silver commended this intention, observing that the air was quite springlike, but that it would be cold as soon as the sun went in.

He had a faint smile for that.

"Lona will be after me long before then. It if were not for my Aunt Janetta, she would be after me now."

Miss Silver hoped politely that Miss Janetta was not feeling worse. He replied that she was completely prostrated, and went on his way. It was Miss Silver's opinion that the more complete the prostration, the better for Captain Pilgrim. She considered him to be in some need of emancipation, and was pleased to observe that he was taking steps in that direction. She hoped that Miss Janetta would continue to absorb the greater part of Miss Day's attention.

As Jerome came through the hall he was aware of Robbins at the front door, his hand just rising to open the catch. At the tap of the stick Robbins turned, stepped back, and said in a voice that sounded aloof and cold,

"Is it by your orders, sir, that the police are about to search the house?"

Jerome said, "Certainly."

Robbins persisted.

"Have they your permission, sir?"

"Yes, they have." Then, as if he thought he had been too abrupt, he turned back to say, "The sooner they get down to it, the sooner they'll leave us alone. They asked my consent, but if it had been refused, they would have brought in a search-warrant."

"What do they expect to find, sir?"

Jerome said, "I don't know. I've said they had better begin at my room, and then I can get back there." He went on into the morning-room. "If there's someone at the door, hadn't you better see about it?"

From where he stood he could hear the catch click back. A cold air came in, and Lesley Freyne's voice, speaking to Robbins. He came back into the hall at his best pace and called to her,

"Come in, Les!"

She had a momentary impression of Robbins looking—

what was the word? It teased her because she couldn't get it. And then, when he had turned away and gone silently back across the hall and Jerome was taking her into the morning-room, it came to her. Remote—yes, that was it—as if he was a long way off and you couldn't reach him. It came and went again.

Jerome shut the door, dropped coat and muffler, and they went over to the fire and sat down on Miss Janetta's big couch. He said, "The police are searching the house. Aunt Collie's in the garden, and Aunt Netta's in her room. But you don't want them, do you? Will I do?"

She gave him her wide, warm smile and said,

"This is very comfortable, I think."

She was not prepared for his look.

"You are very comfortable, Les."

"Am I?" Her voice was rather sad.

"Yes. You are a halcyon creature—you have a circle of summer round you, very warm and comforting."

"St. Martin's summer, I'm afraid—"

"'Except St. Martin's summer, halcyon days'? But we're not quite into November yet, my dear. I shouldn't put us farther than July myself."

"I'm forty-three, Jerome."

"So am I, as near as makes no difference. It's a hoary age, but there is worse to come. You've no grey hairs, whilst I have thousands." His tone, half bantering, changed abruptly. "Les—don't let anyone keep you away from us."

"I won't if I can help it."

He said, "I don't know how it is—I feel as if I'd been in a dream. Now I've waked up. I want you to help me not to go back into the dream again. I think you can. When all this frightful business is over I want to get back to something like a normal life. Lona's been very good, but I think it's time she went. Aunt Netta doesn't need her, and nor do I. There is really no reason why I should be so much of an invalid. I'll get gradually back to doing things. There'll be a lot of business to see to—" He broke off. "Some day I'll write again. I feel as if I'd got a lot of ideas stored up, and they're beginning to knock on the door and want to get out."

"I'm so glad. I always thought—"

He said, "Do you think about me, Les?"

"Of course I do."

"How?"

"As my friend." Her voice went deep on the word.

He turned a little away from her.

"We were friends—great friends, I thought. And then Henry came, and he was something more than a friend."

She lifted her steady grey eyes to his averted face.

"He wasn't in love with me—never."

"Then why—"

She said,

"I'd like to tell you—it's all so long ago—I'd like to. You know what Henry was—he made you feel you were the only person in the world. I don't think he put it on—at least not much. Do you remember when we were children, if we wanted anything we used to put Henry up to ask for it. He only had to smile and everyone said yes. It didn't matter who it was—Mr. Pilgrim, the aunts, my father and mother, Mrs. Robbins—it was all the same, and it was very, very bad for him. I ought to have known better, but when he smiled at me, I said yes too."

"Did you care for him, Les?" The words were almost inaudible.

Her voice dropped too.

"Not with my heart. I was charmed and flattered, and—I was very, very lonely. The man I cared for didn't care for me, and—" the low voice shook—"I got tired of being unhappy and alone. I wanted a home of my own, and a life of my own, and children of my own. So when Henry smiled at me, I said yes. Only when it came to the point I couldn't do it, Jerome. Mabel Robbins stuck in my throat."

He looked round startled.

"Was it Henry?"

"Oh, yes. It came out when we were talking about a case in the papers. I don't mean that he told me—it just came to me. It sounds stupid, but all at once I could see that it wasn't just Mabel. It was something in Henry—he was like that, he had to have what he wanted, it didn't matter about anyone else. There would always be women like Mabel, and it wouldn't matter about any of them any more than it had mattered about her—any more than it would matter about me. The only person who ever had mattered, or ever would matter, was Henry. And I just felt I couldn't do it. I should have told him so that evening—only he didn't come—"

Jerome spoke without looking at her.

"You cared for someone?"

"Very much."

"Then why—my dear—why—"

"I've told you."

He half turned to look at her, half put out a hand, and drew it back. There was a pause before he said,

"Who was It?"

The colour rushed into Lesley's cheeks. She looked young and defenceless. She said, stumbling over the words,

"Have you—any right—to ask?"

He looked at her then, to see the Lesley of so many years ago—the colour, the wet dark lashes, might have been because he—and Henry—had pressed her unmercifully, teased her too hard. He—and Henry—there hadn't been anyone else. It was always he and Henry and Les. He said.

"That's for you to say." And then, "Les—I've always cared."

"You never told me—"

"You had too much money—and I'd too little." He gave a short, hard laugh. "A hundred a year, and my brains—which were going to make me a fortune! I was going to write a bestseller, or have a smashing success with a play and come back and shove it under your father's nose and say, 'What about it now, sir?' He warned me off, you know."

"He didn't!"

"Oh, yes, he did. 'Boy and girl nonsense, my dear fellow. She's going to be an heiress. You wouldn't like to have it said you were after her money—now would you?' And then a piece about liking me well enough but having other views for his daughter."

After twenty years his voice showed just how much his young man's pride had been pricked. The scene came up before Lesley as if she had been there—her father tactless and blundering, ambitious for her, without any real sense of what would bring her happiness; Jerome as proud as the devil, flinging off to make a fortune. Everything in her wept for twenty wasted years.

She said, "So that's why you stopped coming down then?"

"Yes. My smashing success didn't happen, but for a long time I kept thinking it might be round the next corner. I took care not to come down or see too much of you—I wasn't going to be told a second time that I was after your money. Then your father died—"

"Well?"

He lifted a hand and let it drop again upon his knee.

"That finished it. By that time I knew just about where I came in the writing line. Anyone who isn't a fool can measure himself if he will face up to it. I was a decent second-rater, and I wasn't going to be anything more. I could make five or six hundred a year, but I wouldn't ever be in a position to go to your father and tell him I wanted to marry you, and that being the case, I wasn't going to take advantage of the fact that he was dead and go to you. It sounds a bit highfalutin, but I suppose it was just my beastly pride. So I saw less of you than ever. I thought, 'What's the good of getting hurt?' You see, I never thought—I never thought I had a chance."

She said, "You let it go—"

"I suppose I did. And now—it's too late—"

"Is it—Jerome?"

"I'm all smashed up—"

The flush which had made her look like a girl again had and said,

"Do you still care for me? That's the only thing that matters—if you care."

He took the hands and held them in a grip that hurt.

"Les—"

It was half her name, and half a sob.

Chapter Fourteen

When Maggie Pell left Miss Silver she went part of the way down the back stair. At the turn she heard heavy feet coming up. She stepped back into the bathroom and saw Judy Elliot go by with a police sergeant and a tall fair young man in plain clothes. They went up, and into the corridor and along. The sound of their feet died away, a door opened and shut. Judy Elliot didn't come back.

Maggie waited a little. A wisp of hair had come loose. She took off her cap and made sure there were no more ends. If there was a thing she was faddy about, it was her hair. All very well for Gloria to go about with it flying every way, but it wasn't her style at all. Satin-smooth she liked it. The way some girls would go about in uniform with their hair all of a fuzz—well, she didn't think it ought to be allowed.

When she was quite satisfied she went on down the stair and made her way to the kitchen. Mrs. Robbins had been busy when she arrived, but she couldn't go away without seeing her. She might be in the kitchen, or in the housekeeper's room next door. She tried the kitchen first. It was empty, but the door to the scullery stood half open, and on the far side of it there were voices—Robbins' and Mrs. Robbins'. Well, Maggie would rather have found her alone, but you can't always pick and choose.

She was halfway across the kitchen, when she realized that the Robbinses were having words. Nothing so very out of the way about that when all was said and done. It was Maggie's opinion that Mrs. Robbins had done a bad day's work for herself when she married, and if a girl couldn't do better than that she'd best stay single. Give and take was one thing, but to have a man lay down the law to you till you couldn't call your soul your own was what there wasn't any need to put up with, not if you set a right value on yourself.

Robbins was undoubtedly laying down the law.

"Police in the house, and everyone knowing about it! And Mr. Jerome giving them leave to carry out a search! If Mr. Pilgrim was here he'd not have let them across the doorstep. They're in Mr. Jerome's room now for all I know. 'I've given them leave,' he says, 'and they can start on my room first.' And him the master of the house!"

Maggie Pell shared his horror. So that was what the police were doing upstairs. A good murder on the front page of your paper was all very well, but when it came down to searching people's bedrooms in a house like Pilgrim's Rest—well, it did bring it home to you and no mistake. She wondered if they'd search all the rooms, and if they did, whatever would Miss Netta say? She heard Mrs. Robbins give a sort of sniffling sob, and then Robbins again, very angry.

"What's the good of that? I tell you it's the end!"

"Don't speak like that!"

"I'll speak how I like, and you'll listen! And this is what I've got to say—you stop all this crying and whining about someone that's better dead!"

Her sharp cry stopped him there.

"Alfred!"

"Don't you Alfred me! He ruined your daughter, didn't he? And he's dead and damned, and nobody to thank for it but himself, and you go snivelling about 'poor Mr. Henry'!"

"Alfred—" It was just a frightened gasp.

Maggie was frightened too. She wished she was anywhere else. She wished she had never come, but she didn't seem able to go. She heard Mrs. Robbins break into bitter weeping. She heard the sound of a blow, and a wincing cry. She moved forward a step or two. She couldn't just stand there and hear a woman treated like that.

And then, short of the scullery door, Robbins' voice halted her. It wasn't loud any more, but it was all the worse for that. He said,

"Shut up! Do you hear—shut up! And you keep shut up—do you hear? I tell you the police think I did it, and the way you're going on is the way to make them think it. 'What's she carrying on like that for?' they'll say. 'What's anyone want to carry on like that for it they haven't got something on their mind? And what's she got on her mind?' they'll say. 'Why him'—that's what they'll say. 'And she knows who done it. And how would she know about it if it wasn't her husband? He done it'—that's what they're going to say. Do you want to put the rope round my neck? Because that's what you're doing. I tell you they think I did your damned Mr. Henry in. I heard them talking in the study, and that's what they think—they think it was me!''

Mrs. Robbins called out wildly.

"Was it?" she said—"*was it?*"

Maggie felt the trickle of sweat on her temples. She couldn't have taken another step forward to save her life. She heard Gloria's voice calling her in the passage.

"Mag—where are you? Maggie!"

She turned round and ran out of the kitchen.

Judy Elliot turned to the right at the head of the stairs and walked along the corridor a little ahead of Frank Abbott and the sergeant to the door of Jerome Pilgrim's room. She threw it open and stood back for them to go in. As they passed her, she took as much care to avoid looking at them as if they had been some plague come into the house. She stepped back lest they should brush against her.

It is not pleasant for a young man who is in love to be treated like this. Frank Abbott had a normally high opinion of himself. The girls whom from time to time he met, flirted and danced with, had done nothing to reduce it. Judy's attitude was galling in the extreme. What it amounted to was, "It's a low job searching people's rooms, and you're a low hound to do it."

As this idea forced an entrance, an icy anger cauterized his hurt. He walked past her not only as if she wasn't there, but as if she never had been there as far as he was concerned. Judy Elliott in fact just didn't exist. He had a job to do, and that was that.

Judy shut the door on them with laudable self-control. She could have banged it with the best heart in the world, but she remembered that she was a housemaid and restrained the impulse. She turned, to meet Lona Day coming out of her room across the passage.

"What's going on, Judy?" Lona's voice was distressed, her look anxious.

Judy's cheeks burned and her eyes were bright.

"They're searching the house."

"Oh—how unpleasant!"

"Horrid!"

"But why? What are they looking for? What do they think they're going to find?"

"I haven't the slightest idea."

A child of three could have seen that she had lost her temper and wasn't in any hurry to find it. Miss Day gazed at her soulfully and said,

"I suppose they know best. Where are they now?"

"In Captain Pilgrim's room."

"Oh dear—but he ought to be resting—"

Judy's shoulder twitched.

"He's downstairs. He told me to take them up."

Miss Day said, "Oh dear—" in a helpless sort of way, and then, "They won't disturb Miss Janetta?"

"She's to go into Miss Columba's room whilst they do hers."

Anger boiled up in Judy. Two men going through an old lady's things—sorting out her drawers! Revolting!

It took Judy a little time to get away. There were times when Lona was very much the nurse, practical, self-reliant and on the spot, and there were times when she wound herself about you and clung. Judy had no natural affection for clingers, but short of brutal rudeness they are very difficult to dislodge, and it wasn't really in her to be brutal.

Lona had got pretty far with explaining how sensitive she was to anything like crime or the police— this at any rate was how Judy put it afterwards—before she was sufficiently roused to say, "Well, you're not the only one. And we've both got jobs. You'd better go and break it to Miss Janetta that her room is going to be searched."

If she thought to provoke Miss Day she was disappointed. She got a heavy sigh and a look that asked for sympathy.

"Well, I don't know what she'll say. I wouldn't mind changing jobs with you, my dear."

Judy went down the back stair and fetched her cleaning things from the bathroom cupboard. The police having finished with Roger Pilgrim's room, she had swept it before lunch. She thought she might just as well work off some of her emotions on polishing the floor. It would take her away from the proximity of the search, since Roger's room was in the other wing, and the farther she could remove herself from Frank Abbott, the better she would be pleased. She got down on her hands and knees and began to rub with a will.

A little later than this Alfred Robbins left the kitchen with the intention of going upstairs to his room. He was pale with a sort of burned-in pallor, but his manner was composed. He had his foot on the bottom step, when he heard the garden door open at the end of a short passage running at right angles to the foot of the stairs. Miss Columba came in, walking as if she was carrying a weight which had grown too heavy. She sat down on the bench which ran a short way in from the door under a row of pegs and called to him, as he knew she would.

"You'll have to pull my boots off. I can't manage them."

From the moment he heard the door he had known how it would be. He had to put the best face on it and come back. But when he got there she wasn't in a hurry. She just went on sitting there, slumped down anyhow, with her shoulders in amongst the coats and mackintoshes hanging from the pegs above. He stood waiting, controlling the impatience that worked in him like yeast. Presently she said,

"Lord—I'm tired!" Then, after a pause, "There's a lot to be said for being a vegetable. Some people are. No more feelings than a cabbage. It's feelings that get you down. Better not have any."

Robbins stared at the ground. Everything in him said, *"That's right!"* His impatience boiled up. When he couldn't bear it any longer he went down on one knee and said,

"You ought to have those boots off."

But you couldn't hurry Miss Collie. He ought to have known that—she took her time. That was Miss Collie—it was her time, not yours, no matter what you felt like.

She sat there looking at him until he could have screamed. In her own time she said,

"You've been here—how long, Alfred?"

It wasn't often she called him that. He said,

"Thirty years."

"It's a long time."

After another pause she said,

"Pity we can't go back. But we can't." She thrust out a foot at him. "There—get these things off! They weigh a ton."

When she had put on the house-shoes which stood handy under the bench, he thought he was going to get away, but his luck was out. The catch of one of the windows in the morning-room was stiff—Judy Elliot hadn't been able to unlatch it. He'd better come along and do it now before it was forgotten.

He did his best to get clear.

"Mr. Jerome is in there with Miss Lesley."

"Well, he ought to be resting. I'll go and pack him off. You'd better come along and see to that catch."

It would never have occurred to Miss Columba that the two in the morning-room could have anything to say to one another that might not just as well be said when she was there. Lesley and Jerome had known each other for forty years, which is time enough to have said everything. She walked in bluntly, and might have had her mind changed if her tread had been lighter. As it was, even in house-shoes she was sufficiently audible to give Lesley time to withdraw a hand which was being kissed and get as far as the hearth, where she stood looking down into the fire and hoping that its glow would account for her burning cheeks. Such a flood of happiness had invaded her that she felt as if it must be shining through her for all to see. And she wasn't ready to share it yet. It was for her and Jerome, not for anyone else—not yet, not now, with all this dreadful business going on.

As Robbins went to the window, Miss Columba after giving her a brief friendly nod began telling Jerome that he ought to be up in his room resting.

Lesley had herself in hand.

"I must go back to the children. I only came in for a minute, and Jerome kept me."

She didn't look at him, but she heard him get to his feet.

"My room's full of policemen, Aunt Collie. I don't suppose I shall find it very restful."

"Policemen? In your room?"

"You gave them leave, didn't you? And so did I."

She stood there frowning, her corduroy slacks stained with earth, the great fisherman's jersey emphasizing her bulk. Lesley saw the square hands shake. But next moment they had gone for shelter to pockets which harboured a clasp knife, odd lengths of tarred twine, labels old and new. The hands had shaken, but the voice did not shake. She said gruffly.

"What do they want? What do they think they're going to find?"

"I don't know."

The catch of the window had jammed—Robbins couldn't move it. He heard Mr. Jerome go limping into the hall to let Miss Lesley out. Went right down the passage with her to the glass door on the street. If his mind hadn't been so much taken up he would have wondered about that, but all he wanted now was to get through with this fiddling job, to get away upstairs, to get Mr. Jerome alone if he could and have it out with him. He couldn't go on this way. If Miss Collie would go away, he could catch Mr. Jerome on his way back from the door. But Miss Collie didn't go. She stood there with the mud on her and her hands in her pockets and waited for him to finish with the catch. Murder in the house, and the Day of Judgment—the secrets of all hearts opened. And Miss Collie stood there and waited for him to finish with the catch of the window! He wrenched at it with desperate hands and it came over, and there was Miss Collie telling him to get a drop of oil and ease it.

As he passed through the hall, the big door stood wide. Mr. Jerome and Miss Lesley were in the glazed passage talking. If he made haste he might be able to catch Mr. Jerome before he went upstairs.

But when he came back with the oil the door was shut.

Only Miss Collie stood just where she was, with her hands in her pockets, frowning.

Even then she kept him. While he was about it he could oil the other catches and make sure of them. As it turned out, there was another as stiff as the first. He had to stand and loosen it with her eye on him. Queer sort of way she'd got of looking at you as if there wasn't anyone there. It didn't mean anything, it was just Miss Collie's way. But it put thoughts into your head. The secrets of all hearts—he'd never really liked to hear that read. A man's thoughts were his own if anything was. What he had in them was his own business. But Miss Collie didn't mean anything—it was just her way.

It was a quarter to four by the morning-room clock, all pink enamel and gilt amoretti, before he got away and went upstairs. By that time Frank Abbott and the police sergeant were on the top floor, engaged in searching his room. It is on record that he went to the door of Jerome Pilgrim's room but did not get speech of him. After which he went up into the attic from which Roger Pilgrim had fallen just under forty-eight hours before.

At between ten minutes and five minutes to four he fell from the same window, and to the same death.

Chapter Fifteen

Frank Abbott and the police sergeant from Ledlington heard a cry, and immediately on that the shock and sound of the fall. They had the drawers out of the chest in Robbins' room, and they had them stacked one over the other between them and the window. The sergeant barked his shin and brought the top drawer down. They had to shift them before they could get to the window, and then they had to get the two leaves of the casement open.

By the time they had done all this Judy Elliot was looking out of a window on the floor below, staring down at the body of Alfred Robbins, which lay on the flags where Roger

Pilgrim's body had lain. Pell was stooping over it and saying, "He's dead, certain sure."

Abbott called out, "Don't touch him—don't touch anything! We'll be down." And with that he drew back and made for the door.

But the door was locked. Frank stared at it, and the sergeant stared at him. There was no key on the inside.

The Ledlington sergeant stooped down and looked through the keyhole.

"It's there, on the other side. That's a queer start. It was this side all right when we came in—I'd swear to that."

Frank nodded.

"I thought so too, but I don't know about swearing. You didn't hear the door open, did you?"

The sergeant stood up.

"We shouldn't—not if it was when we were shifting those papers."

The contents of the bottom drawer lay out across the floor—piles of old papers, newspaper cuttings yellow with age—the *Pioneer,* the *Civil and Military*—Indian papers, dusty with thirty-year-old news of the last war—nothing later than 1918—the whole making an uneasy bed for the dead man's shirts. And, dropped down across them where it had fallen from Frank Abbott's hand, a brown leather wallet.

He turned for it as the sergeant stepped back for a kick at the door. The crack of the breaking lock came as he stooped to pick it up, taking it gingerly by the edges with the handkerchief he had let fall beside it. If it was what he thought it was, there wasn't any mystery about Alfred Robbins' death. Most men would prefer a drop from a window to a drop at the end of a rope.

He knotted the corners of the handkerchief and followed the sergeant down the crooked stair.

Pell had been perfectly right—Robbins was dead. But the death must be certified, reported, put on record. Police procedure must take its course. At the Pilgrim's Rest end of the telephone the police sergeant called up its ordered activities. His voice could be heard from the study by anyone standing in the passage or at the end of the hall—a good firm voice with a rasp in it, but matter-of-fact, as if what he had to report was mere routine.

"Superintendent there?... Yes, get him on the line... Smith speaking, sir. There's been another death.... Yes, the butler, Robbins—suicide.... Yes, the same window as Major Pilgrim. ... No, nothing's been touched. Sergeant Abbott and I were next door when it happened.... You'll be out? Very good, sir."

In this twentieth century, murder holds as exact a state as a medieval monarch. The exits and entrances are all laid down. Surgeon, photographer, fingerprint expert make their bow and play an appointed part.

Randall March played his. Once more he sat at the study table to hear statements and put questions. The two sergeants first with their report, Smith leading off.

"We'd finished in Captain Pilgrim's room. Nothing there. Then we went up to this attic bedroom, which is where we should have begun by rights, only Captain Pilgrim asked us to do his room first so that he could get back to it—and being an invalid, that seemed reasonable."

March said, "How long were you up there before the fall?"

The sergeant looked at Frank Abbott and said,

"Ten minutes?"

Frank nodded.

"About that."

Smith went on.

"We'd got the drawers out of the chest. Bottom drawer full of old newspapers and cuttings, which would account for us not hearing when he locked us in."

March exclaimed, "Locked you in!"

"That's right, sir. We're both quite sure the key was on the inside when we got there. He must have come along, opened the door without making any noise, seen what we were up to, and reached round the edge of the door for the key. Then he pulled it to, locked us in, went through to the next room and chucked himself out. He knew his number was up all right, but he'd a nerve opening the door and getting the key the way he did."

Frank Abbott said in his detached voice,

"It was what he saw when he opened the door, I imagine, which told him his number was up. I don't think his suicide was premeditated, or he wouldn't have come near us. He was scared stiff of course—too scared to keep away, so he came to see what was happening, and what he saw showed him the game was up. I don't think anyone would have planned to lock the door. It was done on the impulse, so as to give him time to take the drop his own way. After what he must have seen he'd know he was for it one way or the other."

"What did he see?" said March short and sharp.

Frank Abbott was unknotting the corners of a handkerchief. When he had them free he leaned over the table and laid the square of linen carefully on the blotting-pad. In the middle of it was a man's brown leather wallet with the initials H.C. stamped in gold. March repeated them aloud—"H.C." Frank said,

"Henry Clayton—the missing wallet."

"Was there a missing wallet?"

"Oh, yes. Roger told Miss Silver about it. Old Mr. Pilgrim gave Henry fifty pounds for a wedding present, spot cash over this table, and Henry took out his wallet and put it away—a brown leather wallet with his initials on it. Roger was in the room at the time, and so was Robbins."

"Where did you find it?"

Smith took up the tale.

"Back of the drawers in the chest. You know how it is, in a real good chest the drawer goes all the way to meet the frame, and this had been a good old chest in its time, but the back of the bottom drawer was broken away—worm in the wood. And this wallet had got down inside the frame, wedged between the bottom drawer and the back."

March looked down at it lying on the spread handkerchief.

He looked up suddenly, to catch a slightly quizzical expression in Frank Abbott's light blue eyes. Without quite knowing why, he experienced a sense of discomfort.

Smith had his answer ready.

"That's a criminal all over. Extraordinary, the things they'll keep. This Robbins now—how long is it since Mr. Clayton was murdered—three years, isn't it? And Robbins is in and out of a kitchen with a good roaring fire going for the whole of that time—all he's got to do is to push this wallet in the range any night after his wife's gone up. But he keeps it, the silly fool—sticks it in his drawer along with all those old papers. Likely enough he never looked at them, and never knew the wallet had gone missing. But when he saw it lying there right on top of what we'd turned out he'd know that the game was up. If there was anyone in the family that could swear to it—and probably all that's left of them could do that—well, it would hang him, wouldn't it?"

March said, "It's empty, I suppose?"

Frank Abbott answered.

"It feels empty. I thought they'd better go over it for fingerprints before we looked inside."

He got a brief nod of assent. March said sharply,

"What was it like behind the drawers? If there was worm, there'd be dust."

"You'd say so if you'd seen our hands!" said Smith. "Not just wood dust either—cobwebs and all sorts. Comes of being shorthanded in a big house like this. In the ordinary way all those drawers would come out at spring cleaning and the frame brushed down properly, but you could see these hadn't been done for years."

"Then why is the wallet so clean?"

"It mayn't have been there long—I shouldn't say it had. You see, there were these papers underneath, and his shirts on the top of them. He'd been opening and shutting the drawer every time he wanted one. The wallet would be shoved away at the back. Well, one day when his wife puts his laundry away the wallet gets pushed over the broken edge at the back of the drawer."

"Was there any dust on it?"

March looked at Frank Abbott and got a shake of the head.

"Clean as a whistle."

"Then it hadn't been there long."

"I should say not."

March knotted the corners of the handkerchief again.

"Well, that's as far as we can go until Redding has gone over it for prints. You'd better let him have it at once,

Smith. . . . Oh, just one thing before you go. How long between the cry and fall and your getting out of the room?"

"It's difficult to say exactly—two minutes—perhaps three. What do you say, Abbott?"

Frank nodded.

"We were on the far side of the room, backs to the door—window and door about equi-distant."

"But the wallet would be in sight of anyone opening the door?"

"Oh, yes. It's a sizable room for an attic, with quite an uninterrupted view. We were both down on our knees. I'd got the wallet laid out on a handkerchief and was just going to tie it up, and Smith was half inside the empty chest feeling in all the corners. We had to get up, and then the stacked drawers were in the way—Smith barked his shin on a corner and brought them down. We had to get to the window and open it. Judy Elliot was leaning out of the window below us, and Pell was bending over the body. We spoke to him, and it wasn't till after all that we found we were locked in. I picked up the wallet and knotted the handkerchief round it, and Smith kicked the lock out. I should say all of three minutes."

"Yes, it would be. And you've no idea when the door was locked?"

"None—except that the most likely time would be when we were shifting the papers."

"Yes. Well, that's that. Did you finish searching the room?"

"Yes, while we were waiting for you. Smith stayed with the body whilst I carried on upstairs. I thought Mrs. Robbins would be wanting to go up there. We'd left the floor ankle-deep."

"Find anything else?"

Frank held out a bulging envelope.

"This—at the back of the wash-stand drawer. Not the envelope—that's only cover."

Through the open flap a small cardboard box was visible—one of the sort which pull out like a match-box.

"Greenish pellets inside, like you said to look out for."

March said rather grimly,

"The whole bag of tricks! All right, Redding must go over

it. And the stuff must go to the analyst—but it looks as if Miss Silver had made a pretty good guess.''

Frank said, ''Do you think it's guessing? The Chief suspects her of—I don't like to say the black arts, because he really has an uncommon respect for her, but I rather think there've been times when he wouldn't have been surprised if she'd gone out of the window on a broomstick.''

March gave a half laugh.

''There've been times when I've felt like that myself! The fact is she comes to very close quarters with people—gets at them from the inside where we only get an outside view, and an artificial one at that, because by the time we come into it everyone concerned is hard at work covering up. We don't see people being natural—she does. By the way, where is she?''

Frank threw up a hand.

''With Mrs. Robbins. The detective sunk in the ministering angel! And she does it just as well. In fact 'age doesn't wither nor custom stale her infinite variety.' ''

March allowed himself a smile.

''And I wonder whether Cleopatra or Miss Silver would be the more disconcerted at the comparison. . . . All right, Smith, take the wallet and that envelope to Redding, and let me have them back when he's finished. I don't suppose there's anything left inside, but you never can tell. And just ask Miss Elliot to come here, will you. I'll see her next.''

Frank stood back against the mantelpiece. That he was expected to stay was obvious. He certainly had no intention of going. He was here on a job, and he meant to see it through. Briefly and bitterly he concluded that if Judy didn't like it she could lump it.

Randall March broke in upon this pleasant frame of mind.

''Why did Robbins leave that wallet where you were bound to find it? He must have known about the search. You were—how long in Jerome Pilgrim's room?''

''Certainly twenty minutes—probably more.''

''Then why wasn't Robbins up in his room getting rid of incriminating evidence?''

''Well, look here—he may have missed the wallet and

never thought of looking where we found it. He may have thought someone had taken it—his wife for choice. I hear she's been crying her eyes out over Henry Clayton. I think he'd suspect her before anyone. I think he'd suspect her, and hope she had destroyed it. And I think he'd let sleeping dogs lie. How's that?''

''I don't know—it might be—''

''As to his getting upstairs whilst we were in Jerome's room, he was trying to go up, but Miss Columba caught him and had him into the morning-room to do a job on the window-catches there. Jerome was in there with Lesley Freyne. I should think it was then between twenty and a quarter to four. Lesley went away, Jerome went up to his room where we had just finished, and Robbins did his job in the morning-room. He then went upstairs and knocked on Jerome's door. Lona Day opened it and asked him what he wanted. He said to speak to Mr. Jerome. She said he couldn't—he must wait—Jerome was resting. In fact, nurse in defence of patient, and the only-over-my-dead-body touch. I don't know what he wanted to say to Jerome, but it didn't get said. Robbins then went upstairs, locked us in, and chucked himself out of the window next door.''

March said, ''Pity Jerome didn't see him.''

''Yes. Soothing music was being diffused by the wireless, and she wanted him to rest. He heard the knock of course, but I don't think he took much notice of it. She went to the door, and then she went to her room. I gather she was backwards and forwards for a bit getting him his tea. She wanted him to have it at four, and then rest till supper-time.''

The door opened and Judy came in. She had taken off her overall and was wearing a dark blue skirt and jumper. Her hands were scrubbed and clean. There were dark smudges under her eyes. She avoided looking at Frank, but he looked at her with a long, cold stare. She may have felt it—it was that sort of look. She couldn't very well lose colour, because she had none. She kept her head up.

March was very nice to her. He made her sit down, and said,

"I'm afraid this is all very trying. I won't keep you long. I believe you heard Robbins scream and fall?"

Judy said, "Yes."

"Where were you, Miss Elliot?"

"In Major Pilgrim's room." She coloured a little. "The one he was using. The police told me I could clear up there, so I was getting it straight."

"Well, you heard the scream. Was it just a cry? No words?"

Judy said, "I don't know." She had turned very pale. "That sounds stupid, but—I really don't. It was a—a shock." She kept her eyes on his face as she spoke. "If you mean did I hear any words, I didn't."

He put her down as conscientious and intelligent.

"What did you do?"

"I ran to the window and opened it. I could see someone lying on the stones. I got a sort of giddy feeling. The next thing I knew I was half sitting, half kneeling on the floor by the window and Pell was running across the paved garden. And I called out to him, 'Who is it?' I don't know why I said that, for of course I knew because of the linen jacket. Pell said, 'It's Robbins!' And I asked if he was dead, and Pell said, 'As any door-nail.'"

"What did you do then?"

"Sergeant Abbott and Sergeant Smith called out of the upstairs window, and I ran down to the morning-room and told Miss Columba."

"Was she alone?"

"Yes."

"Where were the others?"

"Miss Janetta was in bed. As I got to the top of the stairs, Miss Day came out of Captain Jerome's room. I suppose I looked upset, for she came along the passage and asked me if anything was the matter. I told her what had happened, and she said she thought she had heard a cry, but the wireless was on and she couldn't be sure."

"Thank you, Miss Elliot."

He took Pell's statement next.

The old man stumped in, thick grey hair standing up in a

fuzz above the square weather-beaten face. The hair had been as red as Gloria's, and it was still as thick and curly. He had wiped his dirty hands on his corduroys. His small greenish-hazel eyes had an obstinate twinkle for authority. "Law-abiding I be, and no call to fear the law" would have just about hit off his mood. He planted himself squarely before the writing-table and kept that twinkling gaze upon the Superintendent's face. It did not change because March spoke him fair, any more than it would have changed under a browbeating. He was an honest man in his rights, and he knew what they were.

He was at the other side of the garden tidying it up. He heard both cry and fall. By the time he turned round, there was Robbins a-lying on the stones. He ran over to him—"And first Miss Elliot she pokes her head out of Mr. Roger's window and says, 'Is he dead?' and I says, 'As any door-nail.' And then the police puts their heads out of Robbins' room and hollers to me not to touch anything, which I hadn't, only to feel of him whether he was alive or dead."

"You didn't see anyone at any other window?"

"There wasn't no one to see, nor I wouldn't have seen 'em if there was. I was running, wasn't I, and looking at the dead corpse? You don't look at no windows with a corpse a-lying right in front of you on the stones."

There was no more to it than that.

March said, "I suppose you don't," and let him go.

He saw Lona Day after that, grave and concerned, but not so much concerned as to impair her complexion or its delicate make-up. Where Judy had been unbecomingly colourless, Miss Day was discreetly tinted. She did not overdo her lipstick, but the colour had been freshly applied. A plain dark dress with a severe white collar gave the effect of uniform and was surprisingly becoming. Her manner identified her sympathetically with the family, and made it plain that she shared the anxiety which pressed upon its members. March remembered that in his previous examination he had found her intelligent and exact.

"Where were you at the time of the fall, Miss Day?"

"Well, Superintendent, I don't know that I can say. You

see, Captain Pilgrim had the wireless on, and I was going backwards and forwards between my room and his room and the bathroom, and I didn't take any particular notice at the time. You know how it is, you don't when you're busy like that. But it must have been about a quarter to four when I came out of Captain Pilgrim's room and saw Robbins.''

"When you say you saw him, what exactly do you mean?''

The greenish eyes rested upon his face. He found himself thinking their colour unusual—and attractive. She said at once,

"He knocked at the door, and I opened it.''

"What did he say?''

"He said, 'I'd like to have a word with Mr. Jerome.' ''

"And what did you say?''

"I told him he must wait until Captain Pilgrim was rested. he had already done a good deal more than I thought wise, and I didn't mean him to see anyone else until he had had a good rest. As a matter of fact I was just hurrying to get his tea.''

"Do you usually do that?''

"No, he very often comes down, or if he has it upstairs, Miss Elliot or Robbins would take it up, or I might do so myself. There hasn't been any particular rule about it. But I often make an odd cup of tea—nurses get into the way of it, you know. I have a spirit lamp in the bathroom, and I always keep a supply of tea, and cocoa, and dried milk, and biscuits in the cupboard there. Miss Janetta likes a cup of cocoa the last thing at night and the first thing in the morning, and I make it for her.''

"Well, you were going to make tea for Captain Pilgrim. Did Robbins say anything more?''

"He said, 'I want to see him very particularly,' and I said, 'Well, you'll have to wait. No one's going to see him till he's had his rest.' He went off, and I heard him going up the stairs. I supposed he was going to his room.''

"Did you go back into Captain Pilgrim's room?''

"Just for a minute. I told him I was going to get him his tea. Then I went into the bathroom and put the kettle on.''

"And where were you at the time of the fall, Miss Day?''

"Well, I really don't know, because I didn't hear it."

"You didn't hear the cry, or the fall?"

"No, I didn't."

"How do you account for that?"

"The bathroom window looks to the side of the house, and the plumbing is old. I'd just been running water to fill the kettle, and the pipes make quite a noise. But of course I don't know that I was in the bathroom at the time. I was backwards and forwards to my own room, and the windows there look out to the front."

"But Captain Pilgrim's windows look on to the paved garden."

"Two of them do. It is a corner room, and there is another window to the side of the house."

"How do you account for Captain Pilgrim not hearing the cry?"

"He had the wireless on. But I think he did hear it, because when I went in to him—afterwards, you know—he said, 'What happened? Did someone call out?' So I thought it best to tell him what had happened."

"Who told you, Miss Day?"

"Judy Elliot. I saw her in the passage, and she looked so upset that I ran along and asked her if anything was wrong."

March turned to Frank Abbott.

"You were taking a shorthand note of what Miss Elliot said. Wasn't there something about Miss Day thinking she had heard a cry?"

"Yes, sir."

"Is that right, Miss Day?"

"Oh, yes, that's what I said to her. But, you know, I'm not sure about it—I couldn't swear to it or anything like that. And the more I thought about it, the more I felt, 'Well, perhaps it was just imagination,' because I honestly didn't think about it at all until Judy said there had been another accident." Her eyes dwelt upon March's face with an appealing expression.

He said, "I see." And then, abruptly, "Miss Day, have you ever suspected Robbins of taking drugs?"

She looked at him in a startled fashion. The word came

into his head and stayed there—she was startled, but she wasn't surprised. She said,

"Oh, dear!" And then, "Oh, I wouldn't like to say."

"I think you will have to. I am not asking you whether he did take drugs—or a drug. I am asking you whether it ever crossed your mind to suspect him of doing so."

She said with some appearance of relief,

"Well, then, it did."

"Did you suspect him of using any particular drug? And if you did, what made you suspect him?"

She looked distressed.

"He talked to me once about hashish. That's *cannabis indica,* you know, only he called it by the Indian name, *bhang.* He'd been in India."

"I think you have been there too, haven't you?"

"Yes—that is how he came to talk to me about it."

"What did he say?"

"He asked me if I had ever tried it. He said it gave you wonderful dreams. And of course I told him how dangerous it was, and warned him that it was illegal to use it in this country."

"And what did he say to that?"

Miss Day gave a slight shiver.

"He looked at me in rather a curious sort of way and said I wasn't to think he used it, only there were times you liked to feel you'd got something by you that would make you sleep. I felt sorry for him, because I knew that he and his wife were in trouble over their daughter, so I just warned him again as seriously as I could. I didn't repeat what he said to anyone."

"When did this conversation take place?"

"Oh, it was a long time ago—when I first came here, quite three years ago."

"Was it before or after Henry Clayton disappeared?"

She thought for a minute, and then said,

"I think it was after that—but not very long after."

"Miss Day, did you ever see Robbins under the influence of a drug like hashish?"

She took a minute over that. When she spoke, it was with

hesitation. "His manner was very strange sometimes. I couldn't say if it was due to a drug."

"What is the effect of hashish?"

The hesitation continued.

"It is—a narcotic—"

"But it induces dreams?"

"I believe it does."

"Does it sometimes have an exciting effect?"

"I have heard it does—I don't really know much about it."

"It might induce bad dreams as well as pleasant ones?"

"I suppose it might."

"Have you never heard of its having that effect?"

"Well—I have—"

"Miss Day, did it ever occur to you that Captain Pilgrim's nervous attacks might be caused by something like hashish?"

She cried out at that,

"Oh, don't! Oh, how dreadful!"

"Did it never occur to you? From what I have heard, the symptoms were all present—heavy sleep, from which he was aroused by distressing dreams to a dazed and abnormal state. That is so, is it not?"

"Yes, but—oh, how dreadful—how wicked!"

"Did that suspicion ever cross your mind?"

She was in considerable distress.

"Not—not until this last attack. I did think when I first came that perhaps the sedative he had been ordered for occasional use—I did wonder whether it was agreeing with him, and Dr. Daly changed it. He didn't have an attack for some time after that. But when he had this last one I did just think, just suspect—no, it wasn't as definite as that—I mean I couldn't really think it—there wasn't any motive—what motive could there be? Oh, I do hope it isn't true!"

"Would Robbins have had the opportunity of administering such a drug? You said just now that he sometimes took up Captain Pilgrim's tea. Did he take up his supper?"

"Oh, yes, always—unless he came down for it."

"It could, I suppose, be administered in anything that was highly seasoned?"

Lona's eyes were full of tears. She brought out a handkerchief and dabbed them.

"Oh, yes, I suppose so." She dabbed again. "I'm sorry, but it does seem so dreadfully wicked. I can't believe it!"

March said drily, "Well, it isn't a thing we can expect to prove. We shall see whether the attacks stop now."

She let a smile break through and said,

"That would be wonderful!"

March let her go.

Chapter Sixteen

As Lona Day went up the main staircase she met Miss Silver coming down, and stopped for a moment to enquire after Mrs. Robbins, and expressed pleasure at hearing that she was lying down and had fallen asleep.

"Judy is sitting with her."

Lona Day said, "That is very kind. But then Judy is kind—isn't she?"

She lingered for a moment as if she would have liked to go on talking, but receiving no encouragement from Miss Silver's silence, she put up a hand to her head and said,

"What a day! It feels like a year since this morning. I hope Miss Netta is having a little nap too—it will do her good. It is so sad that she and her sister are no help to one another. Well, I must go to my real charge, Captain Pilgrim. Those policemen will be coming up to see him any time now. He is being wonderful of course, but I can't help feeling anxious about him."

It was a pity that Frank Abbott could not have been there to hear his Miss Silver produce one of her moral maxims. She coughed slightly and remarked that anxiety produced an atmosphere sadly adverse to recovery. After which her beaded slippers took her firmly on her way.

Lona Day found her patient using the telephone extension in his room. She caught no words, but the tone of his voice was warm. As she came in, he said, "Yes—presently then. I'll ring up when they've gone." He hung up the receiver and turned, to meet an affectionate accusing gaze.

"You know you shouldn't—you really shouldn't."

"And why not? If you think it's restful to sit still and do nothing with this sort of thing going on in the house, well, I should say there was a hole in your training. You know, I am not really an invalid now."

He saw the tears come into her eyes.

"It's just that I'm—well, I expect it's silly of me, but you've come on so far—I don't want you to slip back. You mustn't run before you can walk, you know."

"I haven't run very far—have I?" He leaned forward and looked at her. "Don't think I'm ungrateful for all you've done for me, Lona, but I've got to walk. I don't say anything about running yet, but you never know."

The green eyes shining with tears met his.

"You mean that you don't want me any more?"

Jerome Pilgrim had been an invalid for three and a half years, but for nearly twenty years before that he had been a personable and attractive man. He could recognize an emotional danger signal. He said in a cool, friendly voice,

"My dear Lona, you are much too good a nurse to mean what that implies. You don't want me to remain an invalid in order to practise on me, do you? To lose a patient doesn't necessarily mean to lose a friend."

He heard her say under her breath, "They all say that." Then, more impulsively, "Oh, you know I didn't mean it that way! You couldn't really think so!"

He smiled. "I didn't think so."

"You mustn't ever. There isn't anyone in the world who wants you to get well as much as I do. You know, at first I didn't think you would. Only a nurse mustn't let herself feel like that, and when you began to get better I was so thankful. And then you didn't get on as fast as I hoped you would, but I kept on hoping."

Jerome had an uncomfortable feeling that the temperature of this interview was remaining obstinately high. He made another effort to bring it down.

"We all have a great deal to be thankful for. Do you know where the Superintendent is? I haven't seen him yet, and I should like to do so. I think when he arrived you told him I was resting." He smiled again. "That sort of thing isn't necessary, you know. I am quite ready to see him as soon as he finds it convenient."

For a moment he wondered whether she was going to flare up. She coloured, met his eyes with something of a blaze in hers, and then suddenly turned round and went out of the room, leaving him to reflect wryly that women were incalculable creatures. What a moment to choose for a scene! As if there was not enough without that! He supposed that all their nerves were strung up and ready to jangle at a touch. Only Lesley was herself—calm, strong, lovable, and loving. The thought of her was like fresh air to a prisoner, cool water to a thirsty man. The few words he had had with her on the telephone were a link with all that was wholesome, normal, hopeful. And presently she would come over, and they would have a quiet time together when all this police business had been got through.

He leaned back in his chair and gave himself up to thoughts of her and of their future.

Miss Silver entered the study with a slightly deprecating air. She found March looking over some papers, whilst Frank Abbott sat at the end of the table transcribing his shorthand notes. Both men looked up as she came in. Frank pushed back his chair.

"Pray do not let me disturb you." This was to both of them. Then, to March, "If you have a few minutes to spare—"

"Have you something to tell me?"

She sat down, folding her hands in her lap. The fact that she had not brought her knitting with her appeared to mark the occasion with solemnity.

"I have been with Mrs. Robbins, Randall."

"Had she anything to say?"

"A good deal, poor woman. I fear that her life has been a very unhappy one."

If March felt some impatience, he knew his Miss Silver too

well to make any attempt at hurrying her. She had her own ways of imparting what she had seen, and if among the gleanings there were opinions and deductions of her own, they were apt to disclose unexpected values. He therefore maintained a sympathetic silence, and was rewarded.

"She kept on saying that Robbins had been a hard husband to her. She blames him for their daughter's disappearance, and most particularly for hushing up her death. As she put it, 'It wasn't nothing to be ashamed of to be killed in an air raid, and he did ought to have brought her back here to be buried—her, and the poor little baby that I never so much as saw.' It appears that he did not tell her that he had news of the daughter, or that he was going to see her, but when he came back he told her that Mabel and the baby were dead. She said he was in one of his moods, and when he was like that you couldn't turn him any more than if he had had been made of iron. I took this opportunity of asking her whether she knew if he used any drug, and she said there was some stuff he brought from India—he'd take it once in a while, and it would make him queer for days. But she said he didn't use it much this last year or so. She thought the nurse frightened him about it. I asked if he had spoken to Miss Day about the drug, and she said yes, and she had frightened him. I asked her if she knew what it was called, and she said yes, it was an easy name to remember—'*bhang*.' And he had wanted her to try it when he first came back, but she never would."

March nodded.

"That corroborates what Miss Day says. She mentioned a conversation with him on the subject of hashish when she first came here, and said she warned him not to go on taking it. What I can't understand is why Robbins should have drugged Jerome Pilgrim—assuming that you're right, and that Jerome was drugged."

Miss Silver coughed.

"I feel quite sure that he was drugged, though I do not suppose that it will ever be possible to prove it."

March said, "Well, there's no need. I suppose that the case is closed. There will be a verdict of wilful murder against

Robbins in the case of Henry Clayton, and of suicide in his own case. Accidental death in the case of Roger Pilgrim—and no one will ever know just what happened, though I suppose we can all make a good enough guess. Personally, I don't believe Roger was murdered. He may have been, but that wouldn't be my guess. I think he was suffering from persecution mania and his nerve went. It doesn't matter now except to his relatives, and they can always salve their feeling with the theory that he turned giddy, which is the view I expect a jury to take. Robbins certainly murdered Henry Clayton and committed suicide when he knew that he was suspected and that the police had evidence to connect him with the crime. The wallet did the trick—there's no doubt about that. By the way, I've just got it back. Redding has been going over it for fingerprints. I don't suppose there'll be anything inside, but now that we can handle it, I'll have a look.''

The case was still in the handkerchief, but loosely wrapped. March laid it out flat upon the blotting-pad. There were two full-sized pockets and two small ones. The leather was good and fresh. The case had obviously been a new one—probably a wedding-present, three years ago. There was nothing in any of the four pockets, nor in the large outer one which ran the whole length of the wallet. March let it drop back upon the pad.

"There were no fingerprints," he said.

Miss Silver sat up a little straighter.

"But it was clean, Randall."

He was frowning a little

"I don't quite follow."

"It was found at the back of the chest. The back of the chest was dusty. The wallet was clean. How long do you suppose it would remain clean with dust all round it?"

"Not long. But it needn't have been there for long. The working theory is that it was somewhere at the back of the drawer, among the papers which filled the lower part of it, and that it got pushed over the broken-down edge when Mrs. Robbins was putting her husband's shirts away."

"You did not answer my question, Randall. I asked you

how long you thought it could have been there without gathering dust.''

Frank Abbott had stopped writing. He sat pen in hand, his eyes on Miss Silver's face.

March said, "I don't know."

"You are not, of course, in the habit of dusting your room. Any woman would tell you how quickly dust gathers upon any surface exposed to it. If the wallet had been in the place where it was found as much as an hour or two, it would, I think, have been dusty. If it had been there for twenty-four hours it would most certainly have been so. And it is five days since Mrs. Robbins last went to that drawer to put her husband's laundry away.''

There was a little pause before March said,

"That's not conclusive, you know. Robbins may have been to the drawer himself.''

"To take a shirt out. But that would not push the wallet over the broken edge at the back. That would only happen when shirts were being put into the drawer.''

"What are you implying?''

She looked at him very straight.

"I imply nothing, Randall. I state as a matter of certainty that Henry Clayton's wallet was deliberately placed where it was found—and that not more than a few hours ago.''

March's frown had deepened.

"You mean that Robbins hid it there?''

"No, I do not mean that. Why should he do so dangerous a thing? He could have burned it in the kitchen fire, cut it in small pieces and put it down a drain, to mention only two of the possibilities which would occur to a man of his intelligence.''

"You've got me out of my depth, I'm afraid. The case is a perfectly clear one. Robbins kept the wallet, heaven knows why, but if criminals never hoarded damaging evidence, a good many who are now in prison would be still at large. He kept it, and when he heard the house was going to be searched he hid it in what he thought was a perfectly safe place.''

Miss Silver coughed in a hortatory manner. He might have

just shown up a sum containing a particularly glaring mistake. The simile occurred to Frank Abbott, who waited enjoyably to hear the error pointed out.

"I think not, Randall. You forget that Robbins had been a house-servant for more than thirty years. As long as this house was properly staffed it would be part of his routine to supervise the regular cleaning of many rooms containing chests with drawers, such as the two writing-tables in the study, the bureau in the morning-room, the big sideboard in the dining-room. At any special time, as in spring-cleaning, all these drawers would be removed and the framework thoroughly cleaned out. No one who had seen this happen year after year would expect a police search to be less thorough. I am quite unable to believe that Robbins placed the wallet where it was found."

"Then who did?"

"Someone who meant it to be found there."

March sat back in his chair. "There's a perfectly clear case against Robbins, and you are trying to push it over."

"I am giving you my own conclusions from the facts. Perhaps I should not do so. But look at the facts and draw your own conclusions. It is known before half past three that the rooms are to be searched—"

March interrupted her,

"You say that it was known, but there's no proof that Robbins knew about the search as early as that. I saw Jerome Pilgrim, told him I wanted to have a search made, and got his permission. He asked to have his room done first, rang for Miss Elliot. I asked her to fetch Sergeant Abbott and Sergeant Smith, which she did. Do you know that she saw Robbins and told him there was to be a search?"

"No, it was Captain Pilgrim who told Robbins. They met in the hall when Miss Freyne arrived. Robbins came out to the kitchen and made an angry scene with his wife. She said he was dreadfully upset about the search and very angry with Captain Pilgrim for allowing it, because he said it was a disgrace to the house. She said he went on and on about it, and told her the police suspected him, and it was all her fault for taking on so much about Mr. Henry."

"But, my dear Miss Silver—"

"Wait a moment, Randall. Here you have his wife's evidence that Robbins did know about the search and was very much upset about it, and that he knew he was suspected by the police. If he had known that Henry Clayton's wallet was hidden in his chest of drawers, would he not have gone straight up to his room to remove it before the search could begin? Instead he goes out to the kitchen, where he stays for some time raging about the search and having words with his wife about her grief for Henry Clayton. Coming away from the kitchen, he meets Miss Columba, who takes him off to attend to the morning-room windows. Miss Freyne goes home, and Captain Pilgrim returns to his room. Robbins has allowed the search to go on for at least twenty minutes whilst he scolds his wife, and when he does go up it is not to his own room. Pray take particular note of this. He goes to Captain Pilgrim's door, knocks on it, and is very insistent that he must see Mr. Jerome. Miss Day sends him away, and it is not until then that he goes up to his own room. Do you really believe that any man would behave like this if he knew that evidence which would hang him was concealed where the searchers were bound to find it?"

Chapter Seventeen

Randall March took a glancing look at Frank Abbott, fixed his eyes upon Miss Silver's face, and dropped the last remnant of the official manner.

"Look here," he said—"what is all this? Have you, or have you not, got anything up your sleeve? In a word, what are you getting at?"

His gaze was met by one of reproach.

"Really, Randall!"

He gave a short grim laugh.

"What's the good of saying 'Really!'? I asked you a question, and I'm waiting in a perfectly respectful but determined spirit for the answer. I want to know whether you've got something up your sleeve, because if you have, I think you really must tell me what it is. On your own showing, this affair has cost four lives already. Whilst I am not entirely prepared to subscribe to that, you must admit that the business is far too serious—and dangerous—to play about with. If you know anything that I don't know, I must ask you to let me have it.''

She gave him her sudden and most charming smile. Frank Abbott had once remarked that it would melt an iceberg or pacify a hyena. She said,

''But of course—I would not dream of withholding information. I was about to tell you what I know, but I am afraid you may not think it of any great importance.''

''But you do?''

She allowed a considerable pause to elapse before she said, ''Important—unimportant? These are words, are they not? If you are piecing together a jig-saw puzzle, a small piece may be important, and a large one unimportant, to the design. It would all depend, would it not, upon the grouping of the other pieces?''

Frank thought, ''She's got something. I wonder what it is. It's something he isn't going to like—she's breaking it gently.''

March was smiling. ''I won't refuse the smallest contribution.''

She sat up straight, her hands still folded in her lap, her manner grave and intent—the teacher who addresses a problem which the class is going to find difficult.

''I have two small pieces of information and one exhibit. You may perhaps remember that Maggie Pell, who is Gloria's elder sister, was in service here at the time of Henry Clayton's disappearance—'' She paused, coughed, and repeated the words with a significant variation—''at the time of Henry Clayton's murder. She went into the A.T.S., and at the moment she is here on leave. She came up to see Miss Columba after lunch today, and I took the opportunity of having a talk with her.''

''And what did you talk about?''

''It occurred to me that the person who stabbed Henry

Clayton and afterwards concealed his body would scarcely have escaped without stains, perhaps very considerable stains, upon clothing which would have to be cleaned or destroyed. I thought that Maggie might remember the disappearance of a garment or garments, and that she would probably remember whether a parcel had been sent to the cleaners. I questioned her, and she had quite an interesting story to tell. That is to say, it interested me, and I think it ought to interest you. On the day following what we now know to have been the night of Henry Clayton's murder Miss Janetta Pilgrim was about to partake of her usual early morning cup of cocoa, when not only the cup but the whole contents of the jug were tipped over, with the result that the purple dressing-gown in which she was wrapped became very badly stained. The cocoa was, as usual, brought to her bedside by Miss Day, who is in the habit of making it in the bathroom, where she has a spirit-lamp. Miss Day was herself wearing a handsomely embroidered Chinese coat which she sometimes used as a dressing-gown. This also suffered from the deluge of cocoa. Miss Janetta was very much put out, and accused Miss Day of having tipped it over, but Miss Day told Maggie that Miss Janetta had done it herself. Later that day Miss Janetta told her to make up a parcel for the cleaners. There were a couple of dresses, not stained but in need of freshening, and there was the purple dressing-gown with the cocoa-stains upon it. Maggie asked Miss Day whether she wished to include her Chinese coat in the parcel, but she was told that it had been put to soak at once and the worst of the stains were out, though Miss Day was afraid that it would never look quite the same again.''

When she stopped speaking there was a silence before March said, ''And what do you make of that?''

Miss Silver's answer came quickly and firmly.

''That the garments of two people in the house were so deeply stained that one of them was sent to the cleaners and the other put to soak in water. That cocoa produces a stain which would more easily cover up and disguise a blood-stain than any thing else I can think of. That if there were blood-stains upon either of these garments, the tipping over of the cocoa provided a perfect excuse for sending one to be cleaned and soaking the other in water. That this adroit and ready use of a simple and domestic beverage argues no common degree of cleverness and resource. You were quite right, Randall, when you pointed to the danger of this affair."

March looked at her.

"You are accusing Miss Janetta of murdering her nephew? Or Miss Day? Because a jug of cocoa is tipped over and two dressing-gowns are stained? It is fantastic!"

She showed no offence.

"I have made no accusation. I am concerned with probabilities and facts. Do you, or do you not, consider it probable that the clothes of Henry Clayton's murderer would be stained with his blood? He is stabbed. His body must be dragged into the lift and dragged out of it again at the cellar level. It must be placed on the trolley, removed from it again, and packed into the trunk where it was found. The weapon must be handled, cleaned, and replaced. Do you think that all this could have been done without leaving stains upon the murderer's clothing?"

"Probably not."

She inclined her head.

"You were not bound to grant the probability, but you have granted it. You are bound to grant the fact that next day there are two stained garments in the house. It is true that an excellent excuse for the stains is forthcoming, but can you think of anything that would be easier to provide? Anyone can tip over a jug of cocoa. One of two women did."

His voice hardened.

"And how many times a day, on every day of the year, is something spilt and something stained?"

Miss Silver coughed.

"My dear Randall, you are supplying my reason for not being overanxious to produce this episode for your criticism. It does not suit the theories which you have formed, and it is very susceptible of being explained away. As I am anxious to be perfectly fair, I will inform you that if Robbins' coat or any other of his garments had been stained, there would have been no need to have recourse to a cleaner. It is a fallacy to imagine that blood-stains are very difficult to remove. If soaked in cold water before they are dry they come out easily enough, and a dark woollen material would show no after trace. Mrs. Robbins is reputed to be a skilful cleaner and presser. Robbins can hardly have been a manservant for thirty years without himself knowing something of these two useful arts.''

March smiled and said, ''Thank you!''

Frank Abbott was not writing now. He leaned back in his chair and enjoyed his Miss Silver—the perfect fairness of her mind, its just and equal balance, her avoidance of the easy score, the snatched advantage. He saw her return March's smile.

''Well, I have given you the first of my two small pieces of information. You do not think much of it. I will now pass to the second. You are probably aware that I am occupying the bedroom which used to be Henry Clayton's. No one had slept in it since he did. It struck me that owing to the shortness of staff the room, though tidy and clean, might never have been very thoroughly turned out. I made some discreet enquiries, and discovered that this was so. The chimney, for instance, had not been swept. In fact, the only bedroom chimneys attended to were those in Captain Pilgrim's and Miss Janetta's rooms, where fires were regularly lighted. In view of this I considered that it might be worth while to make a thorough search of the room.''

Frank said,

''We did go through all Clayton's things, you know.''

She gave her little cough.

''I supposed that you would have done so. But it was not then known that he was dead, and I thought it likely that any search would have been confined to going through his papers, most of which would be in London.''

He nodded.

''We didn't find anything here, or for that matter in town. The people where he lodged said he had been tearing up and getting rid of quite a lot of papers and letters just before he came down here. Spring-cleaning before getting married, I expect—goodbye to the bachelor life. Anyhow we didn't find anything. Did you?''

Miss Silver was not to be hurried. She turned to March.

"When you went back to Ledlington this afternoon I retired to my room, locked the door, and began my search. I had provided myself with a dustpan and brush so as not to leave any traces. Even when rooms are receiving the most thorough and competent attention a complete turn-out of shelves, drawers, bookshelves, and cupboards will produce a surprising amount of dust and debris. I went through everything, and I found nothing. There is a tall bookcase beside the fireplace. I took out every book and shook it face downwards with the pages spread. One or two small pieces of paper fell out into the hearth. As I did not wish to be seen emptying the dust which I had collected in my pan, I opened the window and tipped it out—an untidy practice which I do not defend, but which I considered in the special circumstances to be justified. I could not, of course, dispose of the small pieces of paper in this manner, so I had left them on the hearth, intending to gather them up. One of them was a good half sheet of notepaper doubled over. When I turned round from the window it had disappeared. Another small piece was actually in the air and on the point of vanishing up the chimney on the strong draught between it and the window. I closed the casement. One of the pieces then came down into the grate, but the doubled-over sheet did not. When I investigated I found it caught up on a brick ledge running round the chimney just out of sight. I used my brush to bring it down, and there came with it a letter, charred at the edges and down one side, but still quite legible."

Both men leaned forward. Frank said,

"A letter to Henry?"

"I believe so. I believe that he made an attempt to destroy it by laying it on the hearth and setting light to it. If the window was open at the time, the draught would have taken it up the chimney. Lodged against the damp brick—an unused chimney does become very damp—it did not continue to burn. The contents are quite legible."

March put out a hand.

"Where is it?"

"I will get it."

When she had left the room Frank Abbott gave March a quizzical look.

"She hadn't made up her mind about letting you have it or she'd have brought it with her, so it can't be plain evidence. There must be a snag somewhere, and I'm wondering what it is."

March looked past him.

"Well, we shall know in a minute."

It seemed longer than that before Miss Silver came back. She held edge upwards a piece of clean foolscap neatly folded in half. Laid out flat, it disclosed a sheet of writing-paper considerably discoloured by scorching. The top left-hand corner had been burned away. The paper had once been white. It was of a cheap quality and of the size which, doubled once, will fit the ordinary square envelope. So much could be seen at a glance. But as Frank came round to lean over March's shoulder, a second glance informed him that his suspicion was correct, and that there certainly was a snag. To start with, if there ever had been a date it was gone. It may have been up in the left-hand top corner, or it may not, but the left-hand top corner wasn't there. There was no heading. There was no form of address, and the writing, carried out in pencil, looked as if it had been done by a child of seven—the letters, the unformed capitals which such a child would make. Plain enough, but not easy to read because of the slight contrast between the pencil and the scorched page. By tilting the pad and getting it aslant to the overhead light March made the thing legible. It ran:

"I must see you again just this once more to say goodbye. You owe me that. As soon as it is safe. I shall be waiting. I must see you just once more. Burn this."

After a pause he said,

"Well, well, are you prepared to place any particular construction on this letter—I suppose we've got to call it a letter?"

Miss Silver took this temperately.

"I should prefer to hear your own construction."

With the remark that Henry was certainly a bit of a lad, Frank Abbott went back to his seat. March, conscious of anger and desirous of concealing it, looked hard at the paper and laid it down.

"It has neither address nor signature, the writing is disguised, and it bears no date. If Henry Clayton habitually occupied that room, there is some presumption that it had been sent to him, and that he tried to burn it—as requested. There is absolutely no evidence as to the writer, or to the time at which it was written. Clayton may have had the thing for years—months—weeks. He may have brought it down from London with him. He may have been clearing up here, as Abbott tells us he had already done in town. He was going to be married in three days' time, and he wouldn't want to have this sort of oddment lying about."

Miss Silver coughed.

"The letter says, 'Burn this,' and we find that an attempt had been made to burn it. This does not support the idea that it had been kept, and belonged to an earlier date."

March looked at Frank.

"You knew Clayton. How would he have been about a letter which a woman asked him to burn—punctilious, or careless?"

Frank's left eyebrow rose.

"That's a pretty difficult thing to answer. Strictly off the record and between ourselves, Henry was a careless chap—anyone who knew him would tell you that. And what strikes me is this, the woman who wrote that letter knew it, or why trouble to disguise her hand? It wasn't to deceive Henry. The only possible inference is that she knew he was careless and was afraid of his leaving her letter about. Printing is finger-breaking work—she didn't do it for fun. But—and this is a big but—if Henry got a letter like that three days before his wedding, I think he would have burned it—or tried to."

"We have no idea when he got it," said March wearily. "I'll get the handwriting experts on to it, but I don't suppose they can do anything with these printed capitals. As to fingerprints, after a scorching and three years of a damp chimney, it's no good expecting to find any."

Miss Silver had remained standing. She said,

"Will you show Miss Day this letter in my presence?"

"Miss Day?" His brows drew together.

"Miss Lona Day—who had to soak her Chinese coat in water on the morning after Henry Clayton was stabbed and his body concealed in the cellars. Miss Day who was in and out of Captain Pilgrim's room, and may very easily have been out of it at the moment when Roger Pilgrim fell from that attic window. A stair goes up to the attic floor between her room and mine. I advise you to see how long it would take an active person to run up to that attic and down again. Remember that Miss Freyne says she saw Lona Day at the end of the passage after leaving Roger Pilgrim, although Miss Day says she did not see Miss Freyne. But if she did see her, she would know that Roger was alone. She had only to run up those stairs and down again. The attic window was open, and the sill was low. Any excuse that would direct his attention to the garden would serve. It would require very little force to push him off his balance."

"My dear Miss Silver!"

She stood her ground.

"All this applies equally to the case of Robbins, with this significant addition—he came to the door of Captain Pilgrim's room, and there, but out of Captain Pilgrim's hearing, he spoke to Lona Day. We do not know what he said to her. She says he asked to see Captain Pilgrim, and that she told him he was resting. That is very likely. But, Randall, why did he want to see Captain Pilgrim? On the supposition that he was the murderer, I find it inexplicable. If he was guilty he should have had one object in view—to reach his room before the police began to search it."

"The police were already searching it."

"That is true. But he had wasted twenty minutes quarrelling with his wife. He knew that he was suspected by the police. If at this juncture he tried to reach Captain Pilgrim, I think it was because he knew something, and was no longer prepared to hold his tongue about it. Suppose for a moment that he knew something about Miss Day—something that connected her with the death of Henry Clayton. You have to remember that he was on duty in the hall that night, that he believed Henry Clayton to have seduced his daughter, and that now, a bare month after that daughter's tragic death, Henry Clayton was at Pilgrim's Rest to marry another woman. If he had seen or suspected something that night, do you not think it very possible that he would hold his tongue? But now it is too dangerous. He is aware that he is himself suspected by the police and he goes to his master to make a clean breast of what he knows. As I said before, we cannot tell what passed between him and Miss Day. He may have warned her that he could no longer hold his tongue. He must, I think, have said something which made her take a desperate risk to silence him."

Frank Abbott leaned forward.

"Are you suggesting that it was she who locked us in?"

She said soberly,

"I think so. I am unable to see why Robbins should have locked the door. Even if he had been seen, he had only to rush into the next room and fling himself from the window. But if it was he who looked in, he would know that you had not seen him. If it was his design to commit suicide, he had all the time he required. I do not believe that he had any such design. I think he went upstairs to go to his room. Hearing that the police were there, he turned in next door to wait till they had finished. And there he met the same fate as Roger Pilgrim."

March leaned back.

"Will you be offended if I congratulate you on your imagination? But you know, it won't do. It's an enthralling bit of fiction, but I'm a policeman and I've got to stick to facts. You haven't a leg to stand on—you really haven't. And what's more, you know you haven't. The only shred of fact in the whole of that very interesting piece of special pleading is that Robbins went to Jerome Pilgrim's door and asked to see him. You find this inexplicable, but speaking for myself, I do not expect to follow all the mental processes of a murderer who is about to commit suicide. He may have had some wild idea of confessing, of being helped to get away—I don't know, and to tell you the honest truth, I don't much care. He had a strong enough motive for taking Clayton's life, he had all the opportunity anyone could want, and the whole night in which to clear up after the crime. When you add to this that he was, at least occasionally, in the habit of taking hashish, a drug capable of producing mental derangement with in some cases homicidal tendencies, and, as a climax, that Clayton's wallet has been found hidden in his room, I think you would have to go very far to find a jury who would not convict him, or anyone who would feel a moment's uneasiness at their doing so.''

Miss Silver stood with her fingertips resting lightly on the edge of the table. She smiled benignly and said,

"Ah, yes—the wallet—I meant to tell you about that. It is extremely interesting.''

March restrained himself.

"What did you mean to tell me?''

"A very interesting *fact*, Randall.''

"Well?''

She gave her slight cough.

"In our previous discussion we were upon rather theoretical ground. As you produced the supposition that Robbins had concealed the wallet amongst his papers, I met theory with theory and held back my fact. To tell you the truth, I was doubtful of its reception and hoped to be able to reinforce it. Now that so much else has come out, I see no reason why I should not tell you what I know.''

"I am glad about that. What are you going to tell me?''

"That the wallet was certainly not in that chest of drawers this morning.''

Frank Abbott's faint sarcastic smile went out. March said, *"What!"*

"It was not there when I searched the room this morning.''

"You searched the room this morning?''

"Yes, Randall. I removed all the drawers from the chest, and I searched every drawer. The wallet was not then in any of them, nor was it lodged in the frame where Frank and Sergeant Smith found it this afternoon.''

March looked at her severely.

"You know, you really had no business—''

She gave him a disarming smile.

"I am aware of that, and prepared to hear you say so.''

Frank Abbott's hand went up to his mouth. He heard her say,

"That of course is why I preferred to hold my fact in reserve."

March was frowning.

"And now we've got it, what does it amount to? Evidence that Robbins concealed the wallet when he knew that the house was to be searched?"

Miss Silver shook her head.

"No, Randall—there was no opportunity after that. You spoke about the search to Captain Pilgrim and sent Judy Elliot for Frank and Sergeant Smith. Robbins was then downstairs. Mrs. Robbins tells me that he heard Judy give her message, and immediately after that the front-door bell rang and he went to answer it. As he crossed the hall he met Captain Pilgrim and asked him whether it was true that the house was to be searched. When he had let Miss Freyne in he came back to the kitchen, where he remained until Miss Columba took him to the morning-room. Before he had any opportunity of getting to his room Frank and Sergeant Smith were there."

She spoke in a pleasant, reasonable manner, but March's frown deepened.

"Then he put it there earlier—that's all. He would most likely be up in his room before lunch. The wallet could have been hidden in the back of the chest then—or after lunch. I can't pretend to give the exact moment, but there was plenty of time between your search and the official one."

She bowed her head as if admitting agreement.

"Plenty of time, as you say. And what motive? I cannot find one. Whereas Miss Day's motive would be very strong. Since it is certain that the wallet had been placed in the chest only a very short time before it was found there, you have, I think, to consider the motive very carefully. You have also to consider why so incriminating a piece of evidence was preserved. I believe that it was Miss Day who kept it, and that she did so with the intention of using it to divert suspicion from herself. If Robbins had been guilty he would have destroyed it long ago."

March waited until she had finished. Then he said with evident restraint,

"I am sorry, but I simply cannot agree. You have built up an ingenious theory without any evidence to support it. As you know, I have a great respect for your opinion, but you would not expect me to accept it against my own judgment. To my mind there could hardly be a clearer case."

Miss Silver shook her head slightly.

"Thank you for listening to me so patiently," she said. "I must not take up any more of your time."

She went to the door, smiled at Frank Abbott who stood there to open it for her, and was gone.

March went up to see Jerome Pilgrim, and went alone. Miss Silver had not convinced him, but she had disturbed his mind. The suggestion that after three, and possibly four, deaths the person responsible for them had remained unsuspected and was still at large was calculated to plant a thorn, and a very uncomfortable and irritating thorn at that. To vary the simile, he was in the position of a man who does not believe in ghosts, but does not rest easy in a haunted house.

He found himself sitting opposite Jerome and saying,

"I'm sorry to bother you."

"Not at all. I wanted to see you."

"I'm afraid this must have been a shock."

"To us all. It doesn't seem possible that it was Robbins, and yet I suppose—"

"I can't see that there's any doubt about it. But I'm anxious to know what you heard."

Jerome lifted a hand from the arm of his chair and let it fall again. "I can't be sure that I heard anything."

March looked over his shoulder.

"You've two windows looking out that way."

"Yes."

"You had the wireless on?"

"Miss Day had turned it on. I wasn't listening."

"What was on—music?"

"It was a band programme. I've looked it up since. I couldn't have told you if I hadn't."

"That argues an uncommon degree of abstraction doesn't it? Were you reading?"

"No. I was—thinking of other things." After a moment's hesitation he continued. "As a matter of fact Miss Freyne and I had just become engaged—my mind was entirely taken up with my great good fortune. I'm afraid I was for the time being completely oblivious to what was going on around me. As this is not exactly the moment to give out the engagement, I shall be glad if you will keep it to yourself."

March said sincerely, "I'm very glad. I can see no reason why it should be mentioned until you wish it."

"Well, that's the position—I don't know whether I heard anything or not. I have an impression that I did, but nothing to swear to."

"Will you tell me just what happened from the time Miss Freyne left?"

"Certainly. I came up here, found Abbott and Smith had finished and gone upstairs, and sat down where I am now. Miss Day came in in rather a fuss—an excellent nurse but rather inclined to pull on the leading-rein—"

March interrupted him.

"What do you mean by 'in rather a fuss'?"

Jerome laughed.

"She thought I'd been doing too much, scolded me about it, and ordered me to rest. She switched on the wireless and went off to get my tea."

"Did she come back again?"

"Yes. She was here when Robbins came to the door."

"Did you know it was Robbins?"

"Yes—I heard his voice."

"Did you hear what he said?"

"Only that he wanted to see me. I wish now—" He broke off, frowning. "He was upset about the search, you know. We met in the hall when he was going to let Miss Freyne in, and he asked me about it then. I thought he would just be wanting to harp on it, and I wasn't feeling like a wrangle, so I let Lona send him away."

"You didn't hear what she said to him?"

"No, just their voices. She went out of the room and shut the door."

"How long were they talking? Have you any idea?"

"I don't know that I have—I wasn't really attending. I do remember a vague impression that Robbins was making rather a song and dance about it."

"You thought it was Robbins who was doing the talking?"

"I had that impression. Look here, why not ask Miss Day about it? She'll know."

March nodded.

"Oh, yes. I just wanted your side of it. What happened next. Did Miss Day come back?"

"Almost at once."

"Did she stay?"

"No—just said Robbins wanted to see me and she'd told him he couldn't. Then she went off to get my tea."

"And how long was she away that time?"

Jerome smiled disarmingly.

"I'm afraid I have no idea. That was where I rather lost myself."

"When Miss Day did come back, did she seem just as usual?"

"No—she was upset and trying to hide it. I could see at once that something had happened. She brought in my tray and set it down, and I said, 'What's the matter?' She went over and turned off the wireless and said, 'It's no good— you'll have to know.' I said, 'What is it?' and she told me Robbins had committed suicide."

"She was upset?"

"Who wouldn't be? He'd just been speaking to her. I suppose it means he did Henry in, but I don't seem able to believe it."

March leaned forward.

"Look here, Pilgrim, will you give me a straight answer? Clayton was, I gather, a philanderer. Did you ever suspect that he took an interest in Miss Day?"

"I should have said he hardly knew her."

"That sort of thing isn't always a matter of time. The fact is, a letter has turned up—lodged in the chimney of the room

Clayton used to occupy—the one Miss Silver has now. An attempt had been made to burn it, but the draught had carried it up the chimney. Miss Silver suggests that it was written by Miss Day.''

"Surely the writing—"

"I'm afraid not. It's written in pencil with the sort of clumsy capitals of a child's copybook—no date, no address, no signature. It says, 'I must see you just once more to say goodbye. As soon as it is safe. I shall be waiting. I must see you just once more. Burn this.' "

Jerome's shoulder lifted.

"Well, you know, it might be from anyone."

"So I told her." March's tone was dry. "Imagination has its uses, but women have too much of it—they work it to death."

Jerome gave a short laugh.

"I wonder how many letters of this sort Henry had had in his time. I should say the only novel feature was the attempt to disguise the handwriting. Women are not generally so discreet, especially when they are working up for a final scene."

"You think it was that?"

"Looks like it."

There was a moment of silence. Then March said,

"Then you never saw any sign of mutual attraction between Clayton and Miss Day?"

"It never came into my head. Henry had that sort of manner with women—he looked at every girl he met as if he were head over ears in love with her. And of course they fell for it."

"Do you mean that he looked like that at Miss Day and she fell for it?"

"My dear March, he looked like that at my Aunt Columba—he looked like that at old Mrs. Pell, Pell's mother, when she wasn't far short of a hundred—he looked like that at Mrs. Robbins. And they all fell for it. I don't suppose Lona was any different from the rest, but as to anything serious—as you say, Miss Silver has too much imagination."

All the same, when March came out of Jerome's room and

saw Judy Elliot at the end of the passage he walked to meet her.

"Will you do something for me, Miss Elliot?"

"Of course."

"Could we go into your room for a minute?"

They went in. He left the door open, standing just inside where he could see the corridor and the door opening on the back stair.

"I just want to time something. I want to know just how long it would take anyone to run up those stairs, lock Mrs. Robbins' door, go into the next room as far as the window, and come back again. I want to time you whilst you do all that"

Judy looked doubtful.

"I think Mrs. Robbins is up there asleep."

"Well, try the locking business with one of the other doors. You had better go up first and prospect. I want you to know exactly what you are going to do, and to do it as quickly as you can. You don't need to go into the first room, only open the door just far enough to get the key, then put it in on the outer side and turn it in the lock. After that go into the attic from which Major Pilgrim and Robbins fell, walk across it to the window, stand there whilst you count ten, and then come down as fast as you can. I want you to start from just outside Captain Pilgrim's room and come back there. Abbott says you're to be trusted. I'm checking up on something, and I don't want it talked about."

Judy gave a little nod. "I won't talk."

"All right. Now go off and have a look at the course!"

When she came back he sent her to the end of the passage. "Turn when you get there, and I'll take the time from that."

A minute later she passed him running lightly, and was out of sight on the stairs. Standing there and listening, he could hear her. But if he hadn't been listeneing. . . . He wondered. And if she had taken off her shoes, there wouldn't have been anything to hear at all. The old builders built well and solidly. Not a stair had creaked, and the walls were thick.

He stood looking at his watch, and heard the light footsteps come again. She was back to where she had started in just two and a half minutes.

Chapter Eighteen

As Frank Abbott passed through the hall he was aware of Miss Silver at the morning-room door. She seemed to be emerging, but as soon as she saw him she stepped back. As she continued to hold the door open and looked at him with a smile, he rightly supposed that he was being invited to enter. When he had done so she closed the door and moved away from it.

"I am glad to have seen you. I was coming to ask Superintendent March whether a search of the other rooms was intended."

The formality amused him. *Superintendent March!* And she had been calling him Randall under all their noses for the last half hour! He wondered whether it was decorum or disapproval which dictated the change.

He said, "I don't think so," and saw her purse her lips. There was no doubt of the disapproval now.

"Frank, it is of the first necessity that Miss Janetta's room should be searched, and immediately. The Superintendent has seen Miss Day, has he not?"

"Yes, he's seen her."

"Will you tell me what passed—what he said to her, and she to him?"

"Well—I don't know—"

"Was the subject of hashish mentioned? Indeed you must tell me. It is of the first importance."

"Well—"

She interrupted.

"Was it mentioned?"

He smiled at her.

"You don't give me time—do you?"

She said very gravely,

"There may be no time at all. Was it mentioned?"

"Yes, it was."

"Pray tell me what was said."

"March asked her about Robbins—whether she knew that he had this drug, and whether she had ever seen him under its influence. Then he asked her whether she had ever suspected that Jerome was being doped."

"What was her answer?"

"She was much overcome. She exclaimed, 'How wicked!' " His voice was dry in the extreme.

Miss Silver said,

"That would be enough to put her on her guard. I am persuaded that she has a supply of the drug. She will now take the first opportunity of getting rid of it. It may already be too late, but Miss Janetta's room should be searched at once."

"Why Miss Janetta's room?"

Her look reproved him.

"My dear Frank, it is surely the obvious place. If you had an illicit drug to conceal, would you ask a better place than the room of a *malade imaginaire?* Miss Janetta enjoys her ill health and affords it a full complement of medicaments—the array of bottles in her room is quite staggering. How easy to hide the pin you wish to conceal in a box full of somebody else's pins! If I were in Miss Day's predicament I would certainly have placed my stock of *cannabis indica* in one of Miss Janetta's pill-boxes, and if I had not already removed and destroyed it I should at this moment be engaged in doing so."

He found the suggested picture an entrancing one. Maudie, the soul of rectitude, in possession of an illicit drug—Maudie suspected by the police and driven to the destruction of her secret store! The vision was delectable in the extreme. He gazed at her with admiration and said,

"You know, you're wasted on virtue. You'd have made the most marvellous criminal."

"My *dear* Frank!"

He made haste to placate her.

"Don't crush me—I'm a sensitive plant. I'm just having a

spasm of being glad you're not on the other side. Murder as
one of the fine arts wouldn't be in it.''

She shook her head at him. "There is no time to be lost.
Will you go to the Superintendent—''

"It wouldn't be any good. It would only put his back up.
He never did like the idea of searching that room. It's the sort
of thing that gets the police a bad name—invalid old lady
prostrated with grief howked out of bed and into hysterics.
Nobody but you would have screwed him up to it in the first
place. Mind you, to do him justice, I believe he'd face up to
any amount of adverse criticism if he thought it was called for
in the way of doing his job, but he's dead against stirring up a
lot of trouble for what he thinks is no reason at all. He gave in
to you and ordered the search because he respects your
judgment even when he doesn't agree with it. But all this was
before Robbins went out the window. As far as March is
concerned, that alters the whole case and puts a full stop to it.
If you ask him to have Miss Janetta's room searched now, he
will say no. He won't like saying no to you, and he won't like
being put in the position of having to say it. Speaking very
respectfully, I would suggest that it isn't good tactics to ask for
something that you know will be refused. You lose—prestige.
And prestige is always the ace in your hand when you are
playing this kind of game. No good throwing it away, you
know.''

She appeared to consider this gravely. Then she said,

"I did not contemplate making the request myself. I seem
to remember suggesting that you should do so.''

He broke into unabashed laughter.

"All right! He'll bite my head off, but I don't know that I
care. I must remember to tell the Chief when I get back. He
thinks I can do with quite a lot of taking down.''

Miss Silver regarded him indulgently, but ignored his last
remark. She observed brightly that there was no time like the
present, and that if a search was to be effective it must be
carried out without delay.

Frank turned to the door.

"All right, I'll ask him—play the idiot boy, I think, and

assume that the instructions stand. But there are no flies on March. I shan't get away with it, but no matter.''

As Frank had surmised, he did not get away with it. His very creditable assumption that the search of the house would now proceed, and that it would be as well to take Miss Janetta's room next and get it over, was quite firmly disposed of. March did not exactly say ''Nothing doing,'' but the effect was clearly conveyed. He then passed to his interview with Jerome Pilgrim, and stated that he had asked Miss Day to come down to the study as soon as she was disengaged.

''She's doing something for Miss Janetta at the moment, but she said she wouldn't be very long. When she comes down I shall show her the letter which was found in Clayton's room and ask her what about it. Miss Silver can be present. Do you know where she is?''

''Yes, I've just left her.''

March did not attempt to conceal a smile. ''So I imagined! What does she expect to find in Miss Janetta's room?''

Frank looked over his shoulder. They were in Roger Pilgrim's room, and he wasn't certain that the door had latched. When he had made sure, he said,

''Hashish—*bhang*—*cannabis indica*—placed there by Miss Day on the well-established principle of hiding a blade of grass in a hay-field. I'm told the place is a regular chemist's shop.''

''There is certainly a good deal of what Miss Silver might describe as medical paraphernalia.''

Frank cocked an eyebrow.

''If you want to quote Miss Silver, I can do it more directly than that. She says if she were Lona she'd be right on the spot at this moment getting rid of the stuff. And right on the spot is just where Lona is. What's the betting that Miss Netta's fire is at this moment burning with an exotic eastern flame? I don't know what hashish burns like, but I should expect it to be something in the green or violet line.''

March looked at him hard.

''You don't mean to say you believe this fantastic story!''

He got a shrug of the shoulder.

"Believe it, or don't believe it. There isn't any proof, and I don't see how there can be. And there is a most convincing scapegoat. Nobody is going to look past Robbins to find a highly chimerical murderer lurking in the background. But it's rather a staggering thought that perhaps, after all, there is someone there."

"It would be." March's tone was studiously quiet.

"Someone who bumped Henry off in a fit of temper, contrived old Pilgrim's death, pushed Roger out of the attic window, and then was all ready with her scapegoat. Talk about a ram in a thicket, Robbins fits the part to a hair—hashish in the wash-stand drawer, Henry's wallet in the chest, and a most convincing suicide to wind up with. Maudie says it happened like that. I don't say she's right, but I've got a very strong inhibition about saying she's wrong. And if she isn't wrong—" again that slight shrug of the shoulder—"if she isn't—well, we're letting something loose upon the world. That's one thing. And here's another—tigress having tasted blood and got away with it. Cheery prospect, isn't it? And not a thing that we can do about it so far as I can see, unless that letter knocks her off her balance and she gives herself away."

March said, "That wouldn't get us very far. She might have written that letter, or twenty others, and yet have no hand in Clayton's death." He changed his tone abruptly. "Let's stick to facts. There's a case against Robbins that would satisfy any jury in the world. There is no case at all against Lona Day."

Chapter Nineteen

Lona Day opened the study door and went in. She saw Superintendent March sitting at the writing-table with the overhead light shining down on his thick dark hair, and on the well-kept hand which was laying down a sheet of foolscap as she entered. On his right, at the short end of the table, was Sergeant Abbott, pencil poised and pad ready. He looked up at her, but he did not rise from his seat. It was a long, cold look. Away to the left, detached, remote, and prim, Miss Silver was completing the third row of a grey stocking destined for her niece Ethel's eldest boy. The blue jumper, finished off and nicely pressed, was now in a drawer which had once held Henry Clayton's shirts. Tomorrow, if all was well, it would be packed up and posted. In spite of current events the timing was excellent. If the post office did its part, Mrs. Burkett would receive her birthday present by the first post on the morning of that anniversary.

Miss Day cast a fleeting glance at the ball of grey wool in Miss Silver's lap. Then she came forward and took the chair she had occupied at a previous interview. As she did so, the telephone bell rang. March picked up the receiver. The ghostly rumble of a bass voice could be heard by the other three people in the room, but only he got more than that. He said, "What does she want?" and the rumble began again.

Presently he said, "Oh, well, I'll be here. What time did you say? . . . I see—then she won't be long. I'm not through yet anyhow."

He hung up and turned to Frank Abbott.

"Someone coming out here to see me. They don't know what she wants." Then, "Well, Miss Day, I have asked you to come down because I have something to show you. It has been suggested that you may be able to help us with an identification."

She looked faintly surprised.

"I? Well, of course if there's anything I can do—but—I really don't know—"

"Thank you."

He lifted the foolscap and disclosed, lying upon a second piece, the sheet of scorched notepaper. The clumsy pencilled characters caught the light. They were turned towards her so that if she would she might read them.

March said, "Can you help us at all with this, Miss Day? Have you ever seen it before?"

She had looked down at the paper. Now she looked up, the

grey-green eyes wide with what looked like surprise. Frank Abbott, on a hair-trigger of critical attention, could not suspect it of being anything else.

Miss Silver's needles clicked, but she was watching Lona Day. There was nothing to watch. If a shock was received, it had been absorbed. The hands lay quiet, the one against the dark of her dress, the other lightly on the table edge, no muscle tensed, no bone-white knuckles shown. The small nondescript eyes which saw everything continued to watch.

Lona said,

"Am I to read this? What does it mean?"

March answered her gravely.

"It is a letter. Do you know where it was found?"

"Oh, no. How could I?"

"I don't know. It was found lodged in the chimney of what used to be Henry Clayton's room. Some attempt had been made to burn it, but the draught must have taken it up the chimney. Will you please read the letter?"

She said at once, "Oh, I can read it—but what does it mean?"

"The writing is disguised. The writer appears to be suggesting an assignation for the purpose of saying goodbye. Since no place is mentioned, I think we may take it that this meeting was to be the last of a series."

She looked at him admiringly.

"How clever you are!"

Was there the faintest flavour of mockery behind the words? Frank was never sure.

What March thought he kept to himself. He disliked the whole business, and even as he proceeded with it he wondered why he had conceded so much to arguments which his reason derided. Not that he was beyond his duty if he confronted any or every person present in the house on the night of Henry Clayton's death with a letter which might be, however remotely, connected with it. But his mind informed him with unsparing clarity that all he now said and did was tinged with theories which he neither accepted nor shared. In other words, Miss Silver was using him, and he was allowing himself to be used. The position irked him beyond measure.

What he was doing was all right. The way in which he was doing it would have been all right if it had been his own way, but it wasn't. He could neither rid himself of his task nor accomplish it to his liking. All he could do was to pursue it with increasing reluctance. Behind everything else there was a compelling determination to have done with the matter once and for all, leaving no possible avenue through which any fresh pressure could be brought to bear.

With these things present in his mind he looked straight into Miss Day's attractive eyes and said,

"Did you write this letter?"

The eyes flashed, the hand on the table edge tightened, the voice rang clear with anger.

"Of course not!"

Well, no one could say that it hadn't been put to her, and no one could say that her reaction was anything but what was to be expected from an innocent woman. If there had been no flash and no anger, he might have begun to believe what he didn't believe. But if he had a right to suggest that she had been Henry Clayton's mistress, and perhaps his murderess too, then an innocent young woman had just as much right to be angry. He said,

"You know, I have to ask these questions. You were in the house when Clayton was murdered."

There was a bright patch of colour in either cheek. The eyes were bright too. Anger does not become everyone, but it became Miss Lona Day, who was certainly very angry. She said in a low, ringing voice,

"I was in the house with a man whose love affairs were notorious, and so—I had an affair with him! I was looking after two very sick people at the time, but that wouldn't be enough to keep me out of mischief! I was in the house at the time he was murdered, so I suppose I murdered him!"

Miss Silver looked quietly across her clicking needles and said,

"Yes."

Miss Day cried out sharply. She burst into hysterical sobbing.

"Oh! How dare you—how dare you?" She turned swimming eyes upon March. "Oh, she hasn't any right to say a thing like that!"

March was very much of that opinion himself. He found the situation awkward and unprecedented.

Miss Day continued to sob with a good deal of energy. Between the sobs she could be heard demanding what Miss Silver was doing there, and who she was anyhow—saying things like that about a nurse with her living to earn.

Frank Abbott noted sardonically that a good many layers of social veneer had come off with the tears. Or were there any tears? There was a handkerchief dabbed or pressed against the eyes, and the eyes were certainly very bright, but he felt some scepticism as to their being wet. At the moment they were fixed upon March as if he were her only hope on earth.

"Superintendent—I haven't got to listen to her, have I?"

He said in a grave, reluctant voice, "I think you had better hear what she has to say." He turned to Miss Silver. "I think you must explain or substantiate what you have just said."

Miss Silver had continued to knit. There were now several rows of dark grey stitches on her needles. She met his severe regard with a placid one, and replied, "It was an expression of my personal opinion. Miss Day made a statement in sarcasm. In sober earnest I agreed with her."

There was a short electric silence. Then Miss Silver added in the same equable tone of voice,

"Does Miss Day wish us to understand that she did not murder Mr. Clayton?"

Lona sprang to her feet. Her sobs had ceased. She looked only to March, spoke only to him.

"I have never been so insulted in my life! I came to this house more than three years ago to nurse a sick old woman and a badly wounded man. I have done the best for them that I could. I think I may say that I have earned the respect and affection of everyone in this house. I hardly knew Mr. Clayton. It is wicked to suggest that I had anything to do with his death. She has no right to accuse me and to leave it at that. I could bring an action against her for taking away my character. She ought to be made to prove what she says, and if she can't do it she ought to give me a written apology. My character is my living, and I have a right to protect it.''

March considered that the proceedings had now reached the border-line of nightmare. Miss Day was in her rights, and Miss Silver as badly in the wrong as if she had been tattling sixteen instead of sober sixty. That she could not substantiate her accusation he knew. That she should make an accusation which she could not substantiate staggered him.

Whilst Frank Abbott leaned back in his chair and put his money on Maudie, March said,

"Miss Silver—"

She gave her slight cough.

"Do I understand that Miss Day proposes to sue me for slander? It should prove a most interesting case."

March regarded her sternly, but she looked, not at him, but at Miss Lona Day, and just for a moment she saw what she was looking for—not anger, for that had been most patently displayed—not fear, for she had never expected fear—but something which it is difficult to put into words. Hate comes nearest—with the driving power of a formidable will behind it. It was like the momentary flash of steel from a velvet sheath, and it was instantly controlled.

Miss Silver continued to look, and saw now only what the other two could see, a pale insulted woman defending herself.

Lona Day stepped back from the table.

"If she has anything to say, why doesn't she say it? If she hasn't, I should like to go to my room. And I shall ask Captain Pilgrim if he wishes me to be insulted like this in his house."

March addressed Miss Silver.

"Have you anything to say?"

Over the clicking needles she gave him a faint, restrained smile. "No, thank you, Superintendent."

Lona Day walked to the door and made an exit which was not without dignity.

Miss Silver got to her feet with no haste. She appeared to be unaware of the disapproval which now filled the room like a fog. She met her former pupil's gloomy gaze with unruffled mien, and said cheerfully,

"Do you think she will bring an action, Randall? I do not. But it would be extremely interesting if she did."

Frank Abbott put up a hand to cover his mouth. He heard March say, "What on earth possessed you?" and Miss Silver answer, "A desire to experiment, my dear Randall."

"You can't bring charges of that sort without a shred of evidence!"

"She does not know whether I have any evidence or not. The more she thinks about it, the less secure she will feel. It takes a clear conscience to support an accusation of murder."

March said with real anger,

"You cannot accuse a woman of murder without one shred of evidence, and in the teeth of overwhelming evidence against another person! There is only one murderer in this case, and that is Alfred Robbins."

As he spoke, the door opened, disclosing Judy Elliot. She had a bright patch of colour on either cheek. Her voice hurried and shook. She said,

"Please, will you see Miss Mabel Robbins?"

There was one of those crowded silences. Four people's thoughts, shocked into immediate and vital activity, met and clashed there. Then Judy moved, and there came past her into the room a tall, dark girl in a fur coat with a small black hat tilted at a becoming angle. The coat was squirrel, the hat undeniably smart, and the girl would have been very pretty indeed if she had not been so dreadfully pale. She came straight up to Frank Abbott, put out both hands to him, and said,

"Oh, Mr. Frank—is it true about my father? They told me in Ledlington."

He took the hands, held them for a moment, and said,

"I'm afraid it is."

"He's dead?"

"Yes. We thought that you were too."

She drew her hands away.

"My father wanted it that way."

"He knew you were alive?"

She had very dark blue eyes. The long black lashes had

darkened them still more. They lifted now. She looked full at Frank and said,

"Oh, yes, he knew." Her voice was soft and pretty, with no trace of country accent. On those last words it was tinged with bitter feeling.

She turned to Randall March.

"I beg your pardon—I should have spoken to you. But I am sure you will understand. I have known Mr. Frank since I was a little girl, and I have just heard of my father's death—it was nice to see a friendly face. But of course I know you too—by sight. I used to work in Ledlington."

Her manner was perfectly simple and direct. In a situation beset with embarrassments she appeared to be unaware of them. When March asked her to sit down she did so. When he explained, Miss Silver's faint smile and the slight inclination of her head had a natural grace. When he enquired if she had something to say to him she lifted her eyes to his face and said,

"Yes, that is why I've come."

Away to her left Frank Abbott produced writing-pad and pencil. Above her knitting Miss Silver's eyes were bright and intent. March said,

"Well, Miss Robbins, what have you to say?"

Those very black lashes dropped. She said,

"A great deal. But it isn't very easy to begin. Perhaps I ought to tell you that I am not Miss Robbins. I am married, and—Superintendent March, will it be necessary to bring my married name into it?"

"I don't know. It depends on what you have to say."

She drew a long breath.

"It has nothing to do with my husband."

"Does he know you are here?"

She looked up again at that, quick and startled.

"Oh, yes—he knows everything. We talked it over. It was he who said that I must come, but it is I who don't want to bring his name in because it might hurt him in his profession. He is a doctor."

March said gravely,

"I can't make any promises—you must understand that.

Will you tell me what it is that you and your husband thought I ought to know? I suppose it concerns the death of Henry Clayton?''

The colour ran up into her face and died again. Just for a moment she had the beauty which takes you unawares. No one of the other three people in the room was insensible to it.

She said, ''Yes.'' And then, ''I was here that night.''

The few quietly spoken words produced almost as vivid a shock as her entrance had done. Frank stared. Miss Silver's needles halted for a moment. March said,

''You were here on the night that Henry Clayton was murdered?''

''Yes.''

''You really mean that?''

She smiled very faintly.

''Oh, yes, I really mean it.''

''Do you mean that you were present when he was— murdered?''

She caught her breath.

''Oh, no—not that!'' Another of those quick breaths, and then, ''Superintendent March, may I tell it to you from the beginning? You won't understand unless I do.''

''Yes, certainly—tell it in your own way.''

She had been leaning towards him over the table. Now she sat up straight, unfastening her coat and throwing it back. The dress beneath was of dark red wool, plain and good. She had taken off her gloves and put them down on the table. Her bare hands lay in her lap, the left hand uppermost. Over the platinum circle on the wedding-finger was a fine old-fashioned ruby and diamond ring. Mabel Robbins looked down at it and began to speak in a low, steady voice,

''I expect you know why my father wanted me to be dead. He was a very proud man, and he thought I had disgraced him. Henry Clayton made love to me, and I fell in love with him. I don't want to excuse myself, but I loved him very much, and I don't want to blame him, because he never pretended that he was going to marry me.'' She looked up with a startling effect of truthfulness. ''He isn't here to speak for himself, so I want it to be quite clear that he didn't deceive me. He never promised me anything. When I knew that I was going to have a child he provided for me and for the baby. I wrote to tell my mother that I was all right and well looked after, but she never got the letter. My father burnt it.''

Miss Silver said, "Dear me, what a very high-handed proceeding!''

"He was like that," Mabel said. Then she went on.

"I didn't know about the letter till afterwards. I only knew they didn't write. When my baby was a year old I wrote again and sent a snapshot of her. She is very sweet. I thought if they saw how sweet she was. . . . Well, my father came up he came to see me. It—it was quite dreadful. There was a very bad air raid. He wouldn't go to the shelter, or let us go. He sat there and told me what I was to do, and made me put my hand on the Bible and swear to it.'' She was looking at March now, her eyes big, and full on his face. "It doesn't seem reasonable now to think I promised what I did, but what with the noise of the guns, and the bombs coming down, and my father looking like the day of judgment, I did it. I was to be dead, and my baby too, so as not to disgrace him any more. I wasn't to write, or to come, or to do anything to show that I was alive. He said he would curse me if I did, and curse my baby. And he said it would be happier for my mother if she thought I was dead, because then she would stop worrying. So I promised, and he went back and told Mr. Roger, and Mr. Pilgrim, and my mother that my baby and I had been killed in the raid—he had seen us dead. Mr. Roger told Henry, and Henry came to see me and made a joke of it. We weren't living together any more, but he would come and see me once in a while. He had begun to take a good deal of notice of the baby. He used to say she was like his mother and she was going to be a beauty.''

She paused for a moment, as if it was hard to go on. Then she said,

"He stayed longer than usual, and we talked about a lot of things, but in the end he went away without saying what he had come to say. And when he had gone away he sat down and wrote it to me—I got the letter next day. He was going to marry Miss Lesley Freyne in a month's time, and he wasn't going to see us again."

There was a long pause. She looked down at her ring. The light on it brought up the brightness of the diamonds, the deep colour of the ruby—deep, steady, shining, like the lights of home. Presently she said in a low voice,

"I don't want anyone to blame him. He was getting married, and he didn't think it was right to go on seeing me. Only when it happened I didn't feel that I could bear it. At first I didn't do anything—I didn't feel as if I could. I lost a lot of time that way. Then I wrote and said I wanted to see him to say goodbye, and he wrote back and said much better not, it would only hurt us both, and he was going down to Pilgrim's Rest."

She put up her hand to her head for a moment and let it fall again—a pretty, well-cared-for hand with tinted nails.

"I think I was crazy, or I would never have done what I did. I couldn't sleep, and I couldn't get it off my mind that I must, must see him again." She turned from March to look, not at Frank Abbott whom she had known since she was a little girl, but at Miss Silver sitting there knitting in her low Victorian chair. "You know how it is when there's anything on your mind like that—you don't think about anything else—you can't—it just crowds everything out. I was working, you know. I used to leave my little Marion with my landlady. She was very good. Well, when I got away from the office that day—the day I made up my mind I couldn't bear it any longer, I'd got to see him—I just went to the station and took the first train to Ledlington. It seemed as if it was the only thing to do. I didn't plan it at all, I just went. Can you understand that?"

Miss Silver looked at her kindly and said, "Yes."

She turned back to March.

"There was an air raid, and the train was delayed. When I got to Ledlington the last bus had gone, so I walked. It was a good bit after ten before I got here. I heard the quarter strike on the church clock as I was coming into the village, and it wasn't until then that it came into my head to think what I was going to do next. You see, I had only been thinking about getting here and seeing Henry. I hadn't ever stopped to think how I was going to manage it.''

March said, "I see.'' And then, "What did you do?''

"I went and stood under the yew tree at Mrs. Simpsons' gate just across the road from here. It casts quite a deep shadow. It was bright moonlight, and I didn't want anyone to see me. I stood there for a long time, but I couldn't think of any way to get to Henry. I didn't dare go up to the house because of my father. I couldn't think of anything. I heard the half hour strike, and I just went on standing there. And then the door of the glass passage opened and Henry came out. I could see him quite plainly because of the moon. He hadn't any coat or scarf or hat on, and he was smiling to himself, and all at once I knew that he was going to her—to Miss Freyne. I had taken just one step to go to him, but I couldn't take another. It came to me then that it wasn't any use. I let him go. Then, all in a minute, someone came after him out through that glass door—''

"You saw someone come out of this house and follow Clayton? Was it your father?''

"No. But of course you would think that. My husband said you were bound to think it was my father. But it wasn't. It was a woman, in one of those Chinese coats. The moon was so bright that I could see the embroidery on it as she ran after Henry. She caught him up just by the gate into the stable yard and they stood talking for a moment. I couldn't hear what they said, but I could see his face when he turned round. He looked angry, but he went back with her. They went into the house.''

March leaned forward.

"Would you know the woman again? Did you see her face?''

"Oh, yes, I'd know her.'' Her voice was tired and a little contemptuous. "I knew her then. Henry talked about her quite a lot when she first came to Pilgrim's Rest to nurse Mr. Jerome. He said she was the most sympathetic woman he had ever met. He showed me a snapshot he had taken of her with his aunts. After that he stopped talking about her, and—I wondered.''

"You say you recognized her from the snapshot you had seen?"

"Yes. It was Miss Day—Miss Lona Day."

Frank Abbott took a fleeting glance at Miss Silver. He could discern no change in her expression. Little Roger's sock showed nearly an inch of grey ribbing. She drew on the ball of wool, the needles clicked.

March said, "Is that all, Miss Robbins?"

She looked up with an effect of being startled.

"Oh, no. Shall I—shall I go on?"

"If you please."

She kept her eyes on his face.

"I went after them into the house. You see, I knew that they hadn't locked the door, because from where I was I could see right into the passage and they didn't stop at all. They went right on into the house, and I went after them."

"What did you mean to do?"

She said as simply as a child,

"I didn't know—I didn't think at all—I just followed them. When I got into the hall the light was on. I looked to the left, and the dining-room door was still moving. I went up to it, and I could hear them talking. The door hadn't latched. I pushed it and went in." She stopped, leaned forward over the table, and said, "You've been in the dining-room—I don't suppose anything has been changed there. There's a big screen by the door—Miss Netta always said there was a draught from the hall. Well, I stood behind the screen and I looked round the end of it."

"Yes?"

"They were over by the big sideboard, Henry on the nearer side where the door goes through to the passage where the lift is. She was farther away on the other side. There was only the one light on, over the sideboard. I could see them, but they wouldn't see me as long as I was careful. I heard Henry say, 'My dear girl, what's the good? Better go off to bed.' And Miss Day said, 'Are you in such a hurry to go to her that you can't spare five minutes to say goodbye? That's all I want.'"

She looked at Miss Silver again. She was deadly pale.

"When she said that, it sounded like all the things I'd been saying in my own mind. I began to thank God I hadn't said them to Henry. He hadn't any reason, and he never would have any reason, to look at me the way he was looking at her. She cried out, and she whipped round and snatched one of the knives off the wall—you know there are a lot of them there, put together in a pattern—a trophy, I think they call it. She snatched the knife, and she called out, 'All right, I'll kill myself, if that's what you want!' And Henry stood there with his hands in his pockets and said, 'Don't be a damned fool, Lona!' ''

March said quickly, "You heard him use her name?"

"Yes."

"Are you prepared to swear to that? You will have to do so."

"I know."

"Go on, please.'

"Henry said, 'Put that knife back and come here! If you want to say goodbye according to all the forms, you shall, but it mustn't take more than ten minutes. Come along, my dear!' He held out his hand and he smiled at her with his eyes. She said, 'All right—that's all I want,' and she turned round and went up to the wall and put up her hand to the trophy as if she was putting the knife back. But she didn't put it back—she put it in the pocket of the Chinese coat.''

Miss Silver coughed.

"Those coats are not made with pockets, Miss Robbins."

She got a steady look.

"This one had a pocket—it will be quite easy for you to check up on that. She put the knife into it, but Henry couldn't see what she did because of all the heavy silver of the sideboard. He could only see that she reached up to the wall then stepped back again. But I saw her put the knife in her pocket.''

"You realize the gravity of what you are saying?"

She shuddered from head to foot and said, "Yes."

"Go on."

"She came to Henry and put her arms round his neck. I wanted to go away, but it didn't seem as if I could move. She said, 'You got my note. I was waiting for you. Why didn't you come to my room?' Henry said, 'Because it's all over, my dear.' Then he patted her shoulder and said, 'Come, Lona—be your age! We've eaten our cake—don't let's quarrel over the crumbs. We never gave each other any reason to suppose that we were very serious, did we? We'd both played the game before, and we both know when it's over.' She said, 'You're going to her—to Lesley Freyne.' Henry said, 'Naturally, I'm going to marry her. And, my dear, you'd better get this into your head and keep it there—I intend to make her as good a husband as I know how. She's the salt of the earth, and I'm not going to let her down if I can help it.' When he said that, I knew I'd got to get away. Everything she said and everything Henry said, brought it right home to me that I never ought to have come. I felt that if he saw me, I should die of shame.''

Her voice had fallen very low. It stopped. She looked down at her ring and drew two or three long breaths. Nobody spoke. After a little she went on.

''I stepped back towards the door. That was the last I saw of him, and that was the last thing I heard him say.''

She stopped again and put her hand up to her head—the same gesture which she had used before. It was borne in upon the two men that she was making a very great effort. Miss Silver had measured it from the beginning.

The effort carried Mabel Robbins into speech again. She said in her steady, low voice,

''As soon as I moved I began to feel faint. I had had very little to eat all day. I don't faint as a rule, but I was afraid I was going to then, and I thought I'd rather die. The door was ajar behind me. I got it open and I got into the hall, and there was my father coming through the baize door from the kitchen wing. He came up to me, and I don't know what he said, because the faintness was so bad I had to hold on to him. I remember he shook me and pushed me towards the front door, but when he saw how I was he let go and left me leaning against it. When he came back he had a glass with a pretty stiff dose of whisky in it. He made me drink it, and it brought me round. He took me out into the glass passage and said why had I come, did I want him to curse me for breaking my promise? And I said no. Then he asked if anyone had seen me, and I said no again. He said, 'You came to see Mr. Henry. Did you see him?' And I said, 'Yes, I saw him, but he didn't see me. Neither of them did. I stood there in the dining-room behind the screen, and I saw them, but they didn't see me. They're in there together—Henry and Miss Day. It's all quite over now—you needn't be afraid that I'll come back.' He said, 'You'd better not,' and then he put me out of the glass door into the street and stood there to watch me go. I don't know how I got back to Ledlington. The last train had gone. I must have just gone on walking along the London Road, because a motorist stopped there and picked me up. I don't remember anything about it, but he must have looked in my handbag and found my address, for he took me there. I can just remember my landlady coming out, and their helping me into the house, and his saying, 'I'm a doctor. You'd better get her to bed and I'll have a look at her.' That was how I met my husband.''

March looked at her hard.

''When you heard that Clayton had disappeared, did it not occur to you that you should communicate with the police? You've waited a long time to tell your story, Miss Robbins.''

It seemed as if she were feeling some relief. She was not quite so pale. She said, ''Yes. But, you see, I didn't know.''

''You didn't know that Clayton had disappeared?''

''No. I was very ill. It was two months before I could look at a paper, and there was no one to tell me about the Pilgrims any more. I was quite cut off from Holt St. Agnes. It was a year before I knew that Henry hadn't married Miss Freyne.''

''Who told you he hadn't?''

''A friend of his, a man I used to meet sometimes when I was with him. The way he put it, I never thought—'' She broke off. ''Indeed I didn't, Superintendent March. He said, 'So Henry couldn't stick it after all. Money isn't everything, is it? Do you ever hear from him now?' When I begged him to tell me what he meant he said, 'Oh, didn't you know? Poor old Henry, he jibbed at the last moment and went off into the blue. Nobody's heard from him since.' ''

''I see.''

"I thought that was all. It was the sort of thing Henry might do. I thought he had got too much tangled up with Miss Day, or perhaps Miss Freyne had found out. I never, never thought—I don't see how I could—it never came into my mind."

March said slowly and gravely,

"Just when did it come into your mind, Miss Robbins?" She moved to face him again.

"I've been married for about a year. I told my husband everything long before that. He has adopted my little girl. I could never tell you how good he has been. He has a brother who is a journalist—younger than John. He was in the army, but he was invalided out. His paper sent him down here when—when—" Her voice broke off.

March said, "When Clayton's body was discovered?"

"Yes."

"When did you hear of the discovery?"

Her colour had all gone again. Her voice had an odd note of surprise as she said,

"It only happened yesterday, didn't it? Jim—my brother-in-law—came in to see my husband this morning. He has a room quite near. He had been down here yesterday for his paper. He was on his way down again. I had gone to the office. Jim told my husband all about the case. The reason he came in was because he knew I came from that part of the world—he thought I might know some of the people." She caught her breath sharply. "He didn't know how well I knew them. He didn't know my story, or my real name. I had been calling myself Robertson before I married, and he thought I was a widow."

"The discovery of Clayton's body was in all the morning papers, Miss Robbins."

"I know. But I hadn't seen them—I never have time in the morning. I used to listen to the eight o'clock news whilst I was dressing Marion. Then I had breakfast to get. I never have time for the papers—it's always a rush to get off. I have a friend who looks after Marion with her own little girl, and I have to take her there on my way to the office. I usually only do a half day, but if they have a rush of work, I stay on. We are very busy just now, so I was going to stay.''

''Your husband saw the papers, I take it.''

''Yes—after I was gone. He didn't know what to do—he knew it would be a dreadful shock. Then Jim came in and told him all the things that weren't in the papers. He said of course there wasn't the slightest doubt that my father had killed Henry—though of course he didn't know he was my father. And he said all the newspaper men thought he had killed Roger Pilgrim too, to stop him selling the house, because if it was sold, the cellars would be turned out—'' She put up a hand and gripped the edge of the table. ''He said, 'Robbins will be arrested today there's no doubt about that.' ''

After a short pause she went on.

''My husband rang up the office and asked if I could come home—urgent private affairs. They said they couldn't possibly spare me then, but they would try to let me go by four o'clock. They didn't tell me he had rung up. When I went to fetch Marion my friend told me that John had asked whether she would keep her for the night. That was when I began to think something must have happened. I went home, and John wasn't there—he had had an urgent call. We have a daily woman—she gave me the message and said would I wait in for him, and he would be back as soon as he could. He didn't come until half past five. He told me about Henry, and what Jim said about my father being arrested. He said there was no question but that I must tell the police what I had seen and heard. He said I couldn't possibly stand out of it.''

''He was quite right.''

She said, ''Yes—I know that. I told him I would go down. He said he couldn't come with me, because of the case he had been called to—he would have to go back. But he said my brother-in-law would meet me. I don't know what he told him—enough to make him say he would keep in touch all day. He rang up again whilst we were talking, and John said I was coming down, and what train to meet. When I got to Ledlington he was there. He told me my father had committed suicide.''

Miss Silver coughed. Mabel Robbins turned to meet her eyes, very bright, very intelligent, very kind.

Miss Silver said,

"I am afraid I must give you another shock. Your father did not commit suicide. He was murdered."

If it was a shock, there was no visible effect, just another of those long sighing breaths, and then a low "I wondered about that—I couldn't see why he should kill himself."

She turned back to March.

"My mother—Superintendent March, I've told you everything I know—may I go to my mother now?"

Miss Silver said, "Someone must tell her first, I think. She believes that you are dead."

March said with authority,

"I am afraid that must wait. Miss Robbins, you are aware of the implications of this statement you have made. They are very grave."

She met his look with a perfectly steady one.

"Yes, I know that."

"In view of the fact that your father is dead and therefore in no danger of arrest—there is nothing you wish to modify?"

Her voice was tired and sad but as steady as her eyes.

"I've only told you the truth. I can't alter that."

He turned to Frank Abbott.

"Will you ask Miss Day to come down."

Chapter Twenty

Judy shut the study door and went back up the stairs. It seemed as if the day would never end, nor all the things that had to be done in it. That was what she had been feeling until the moment when she had gone to the front door and Mabel Robbins had stepped into the hall and given her name. And then everything else had been blown sky-high. It isn't every day that you open the door to someone who has been dead three years.

As she went upstairs she was still under the influence of that shock and she hadn't begun to think. Her mind was bubbling with unrelated ideas. How dreadful to come like that and find her father dead. How lovely for Mrs. Robbins to have her daughter back. And, "I wonder where she has been all this long time."

As she turned into the corridor and came to the door of her own room she met Lona Day in her outdoor things—fur coat, small dark hat, handbag swinging from her left wrist. She came up close and said,

"Who was that you let in just now? I heard the bell. Captain Pilgrim can't see anyone—not anyone at all. He's ill."

Judy said without any thought behind the words,

"It was Mabel Robbins. She isn't dead."

Lona took her by the arm and began to walk her back towards the stairs. As she did so she said in an indifferent voice,

"I knew that. Didn't you? Naturally she would come down, but I wasn't expecting her quite so soon. Hurry, Judy! Captain Pilgrim is very ill. I must fetch Dr. Daly to him. He's out at Miles' Farm, and they haven't a telephone. I must try and catch the taxi which brought that girl."

Judy hung back.

"You can't—it's gone."

She was hurried on again.

"I must get a lift in the police car then. It's a matter of life and death."

Past the foot of the stair, across the hall, out into the glass passage. As Lona opened the door to the street, Judy said,

"Aren't you going to stay with him?"

The door was open now, a biting cold air came in. The police car stood there at the left, black and empty. Lona said,

"No, no, no! I must get Dr. Daly! There's nothing to be done till he comes. You must drive—I'm not good enough in the dark. Get in—get in quick!"

She had the door of the car open now, and she had Judy by the arm.

"Get in—get in! Do you want him to die?"

With her foot on the step Judy turned.

"Miss Day, you can't take a police car like this! You must go back and ask."

It was Lona's left hand which was on her arm. The right came up now with something dark in it. They were just shadows, the hand and what it held—frightening shadows out of some horrid dream. They came up close. Something like a cold, deadly O was pressed against Judy's neck a little below her ear. Lona Day said,

"If you don't get in at once and start the car, I'll shoot. If you call out you'll be dead before anyone hears you. That's right! Now start the car!"

With all her heart Judy prayed that the switch-key would be gone, but she put up her hand to feel, and it was there.

The cold pressure was gone from her neck. Afterwards she called herself "Fool!" a dozen times, because just there she had her chance and missed it. But it all happened so quickly between one breath and the next. The door behind her opened and shut, and quick on that the pistol was pressing into her spine and Lona Day was saying, "Reach out and shut that front door! If you do anything more you'll be dead!"

Judy did it. What she ought to have done was to duck and slip out on the right the moment the pistol went. But she had missed her chance.

"Start the car!"

Judy said, "I can't do it."

The voice behind her took on a cutting edge.

"If you don't, I'll shoot you here and now. And then I'll get out and walk back to St. Agnes' Lodge and tell Miss Freyne you've sent me for Penny. She'll let her come all right—you know that. And what I do to her won't worry you, because you'll be dead."

Judy heard her own voice say slowly and stiffly,

"What good—would that—do you?"

The voice behind her in the dark laughed—once.

"Have you never heard of the pleasures of revenge, my dear? If you spoil my chance of getting away, I'll take Penny with me. I'll give you till I've counted five."

Judy put up her hand to the switch.

As the car slipped down the street and gathered way, Lona Day spoke again.

"I'm going to sit back now. That means you won't feel the pistol, but it will be there. I can see you quite well against the lights, and if you try anything on, I shan't miss—I'm quite a good shot. We'll turn off to the right in half a mile." After a moment she went on. "If you do just what you're told you won't come to any harm, and nor will Penny. I'm going to get away, and you are going to help me. Don't make the mistake of thinking you can play any game of your own and get away with it. The other people who thought they could do that are dead. If I have to shoot you, who will look after Penny?"

Judy heard the odd stiff voice which didn't sound like her own say, "Don't—talk—like—that."

Lona said, "I'm warning you. You couldn't get away with it—none of them did. Henry Clayton thought he could pick me up and drop me, like he did with the Robbins girl. I'll tell you about that, because it will show you that you can't play about with me. We're coming to that turning. It's a lane, and there's a narrow bridge a little farther on. You'll have to be careful."

Judy took the corner. The lane was arched by leafless trees rising from a dark hedgerow on either side. The sky was covered with cloud, but a diffused light came through from the hidden moon. The car was a Wolseley, and the lights the best that the black-out regulations allowed.

She was a good driver. Up to this moment everything she had done was automatic. Now she began to feel the car and her own command of it.

From behind her Lona Day went on talking.

"Now I shall tell you about Henry. He was going to marry Lesley Freyne because she had money. After me! She isn't the sort of woman anyone could be in love with—it was just the money. Henry and I had met in London when I was with my last case, so when I heard a nurse was wanted at Pilgrim's Rest I applied, and of course, with my testimonials, they snapped me up. And would you believe it, Henry was frightfully put out. But he got over that. His engagement was rather hanging fire about then, and as between me and Lesley

Freyne—well, I ask you! And then in February he had the nerve to tell me the wedding-day was fixed— Bear to the left here!"

The lane forked and twisted. Judy took the turn. Lona went on speaking.

"He came down for the wedding. I sent him a note to come to my room. But he didn't come, he went to her instead. I heard him tell Robbins and go out. Robbins went away. I ran after Henry and caught him up by the gate to the stable yard. He was angry, but he came back with me. We went into the dining-room. I pulled out one of the knives from the trophy by the sideboard and told him I would kill myself if he didn't say goodbye to me properly. He told me not to be a fool. I made him think I'd put the knife back, but I didn't, I put it in my pocket. I was wearing my Chinese coat. He always said it suited me. They don't have pockets as a rule, but I'd had one made. The knife went into it nicely. I wasn't sure up till then whether I'd kill Henry. I'd thought about it, but I hadn't made up my mind. If he'd been very sweet to me, I might have let him off, but he actually told me that Lesley Freyne was the salt of the earth, and that he was going to do his best to make her a good husband. That finished it. I got him to come into the passage behind the dining-room, and when we were there I said, 'What's that?' as if I had heard something. He turned round to look where I was pointing, and I took the knife out of my pocket and stabbed him in the back. It was quite easy. . . . There are cross roads coming now. Go right over and up the lane on the other side!"

Judy had a sick, impotent feeling. She could drive the car, and she could listen. There didn't seem to be anything else that she could do. Her mind was like a stopped clock—it was there, but it didn't work. It was just as if she had been switched over from the normal everyday world into a nightmare. She didn't know her way in it. There wasn't any law or any kindness, there wasn't any pity or humanity or feeling. A monstrous ego held the stage, strutting and posturing there.

They went over the cross roads and up a wooded hill to an open heath bare under the clouded sky. Lona Day went on talking. Her voice came and went in Judy's ears. Sometimes she heard the words as words, sometimes they just went to build up the picture which was slowly forming in her mind—the narrow passage behind the dining-room—the lift with its open door—Henry Clayton lying there, inert, heavy, dreadfully heavy—and Lona dragging him—

The voice behind her said,

"Nurses learn how to lift, or I couldn't have done it. And of course the trolley came in very handy."

The trolley was in the cellar. . . . Judy sickened, as if the cold of that underground place could reach her here. Thought glanced away at an angle. Cold. . . . She hadn't felt her body until now, but suddenly she became aware of it, rigid and chilled in an indoor dress, driving on for mile after mile through the February evening. She tried not to listen to Lona boasting of how she had hidden Henry Clayton's body in the tin trunk and piled up the furniture in front of it—"And I locked the front door and put the key back in his pocket, so of course nobody dreamed he had come back into the house." But whether the words got through or not, the dreadful picture went on forming in her mind.

". . . and no one suspected anything. At least it turns out now that Robbins did, though he was asleep when I locked the door, because that daughter of his, the one he gave out was dead, was there—running after Henry, the impudent creature! And it seems she saw us in the dining-room, but I didn't know that until this afternoon. Whatever Robbins may have thought, or whatever he may have guessed, he hated Henry and he held his tongue. So everything was quite all right till Mr. Pilgrim took it into his head to sell the house—and of course I couldn't have that. I managed very cleverly about him. Even if they had found the thorn under his saddle they couldn't have traced it to me. And I was lucky too, because the fall proved fatal. And then Roger came home and began the whole stupid business over again. Really, men have no sense. Of course he had to go, but I wasn't so lucky as I had been about Mr. Pilgrim. He really seemed to have a charmed life. I failed twice, but I brought it off the third time. It was quite easy. I just waited for Miss Freyne to come down from the attic, and up I ran. He was looking out of the window. He never even turned round. He thought Miss Freyne had come back. He said 'What is it, Lesley?' in an absent sort of way, and he never knew who pushed him. Of course when they found Henry's body something had to be done about it. Robbins was the natural person to suspect, so I worked on that. I had kept Henry's wallet because I had always felt it would be useful if things turned out awkwardly. As soon as I heard the house was going to be searched I ran up and put it in behind the bottom drawer of the chest in the Robbinses' room. And then something happened which might very easily have knocked me off my balance. Only it didn't. I must say I feel pleased about that. Anyone can plan a thing if they have plenty of time, but it's how you act in an emergency that shows what you are. When Robbins came to the door and said he wanted to see Captain Pilgrim I knew at once that something had gone wrong. I came out of the room and shut the door behind me. He said, 'Look here, I'm not going to hold my tongue any longer. You were in the dining-room with Mr. Henry that night—my daughter Mabel saw you.' I said quite simply, 'Your daughter Mabel is dead'—just like that. And he said, 'Oh, no she isn't. That's what I gave out to stop the talk. She's alive, and if I say the word, she'll come forward and say what she saw and heard. I'd no cause to love Mr. Henry and I've held my tongue, but I'm not going to swing for him, and that's flat. You can have from now till supper-time to get away if it's any use to you, but that's as far as I'll go, and farther than I've any right to.' And he turned round and went away upstairs. I gave him a couple of minutes, and then I slipped off my shoes and went after him. I could hear the police in his room. I opened the door a chink and looked in. They had everything out of the chest of drawers, and Henry's wallet was lying there on the top of a lot of old papers. They had their backs to me, so I thought it would be a good plan to lock them in. The key was on the inside, but I got it—it didn't take a moment. Then I went in next door, and there was Robbins over by the window, leaning out. Of course I could see what it was—he was trying to hear what the police were saying there in his room.''

From behind her Judy heard a low rippling laugh—quite a pretty laugh.

"Well, he never knew who pushed him either. Let me see—we're coming to the end of this common, and I must watch the road and not talk so much. There's rather a steep lane down, and then the road forks and you go to the right. Pretty, wooded country, but the primroses will hardly be out yet, I should think. After that—let me see—"

Judy heard the rustle of paper behind her. A map was being unfolded and hung over the back of her seat. A flash reflected from the windscreen disclosed the presence of a torch. A little flicker of hope sprang up. If Lona Day had to manage a map and a torch, would she be able to keep the pistol aimed?... The hope flickered out. She felt the pistol again, pressing steadily against her spine. The map hung over the back of the seat, and that left a hand for the torch.

They came off the heath down a short, steep lane that ran between hedges. Judy found herself wondering whether there was a ditch under the hedge. If there was—suppose she ditched the car.... The answer to that one was easy, Lona would shoot her out of hand. She simply couldn't afford to let her go—not after all the things she had said. But suppose she could back into a ditch—there might be a chance that way. If she could do it quickly enough—if she could make an excuse for reversing and do it then, Lona might be knocked off her balance and there would be just a chance of getting away. It was the only chance she could think of.

There was a click behind her and the torch went out. Lona said in a satisfied voice,

"Yes—that will be all right. I hope you see how stupid it would be to try any tricks with me—you simply wouldn't have a chance. I have everything planned. I've known for three years that I might have to get away in a hurry, though I didn't expect to be quite so rushed as this. I didn't think that Mabel Robbins would have been in such a hurry to give her evidence. After all, she doesn't come out of it particularly well. I meant to get away later on tonight, but as you see, I can meet an emergency, and now it is going to be quite all right. The police will never find me, because I shall just become someone else. I have my ration-book and my identity-card—and I am sure you would like to know how I got them, but I shan't tell you. Well, perhaps it doesn't matter if I just give you a hint, because you'll never be able to tell anyone will you? You see, Lona Day isn't my real name, and there was nothing to prevent my getting my ration-book and identity-card in my own name, was there? And I banked Henry's fifty pounds in that name too, so you see I thought of everything. . . . Now this is where the road forks."

Judy found herself slowing down a little, her eyes following the line where the ditch would be—if there was a ditch—she couldn't be sure. And then all at once a rabbit came scuttering out of the shadows and across the front of the car. The fork of the road was just ahead. She thought the rabbit came out of a ditch on the right. She slowed down a little more and took the left-hand fork. At once the voice behind her said,

"Stop—stop—that's wrong! I told you to keep to the right."

The pistol pressed so close that it hurt.

Judy stopped dead. In spite of the cold a wave of heat went over her and her hands were sticky with sweat, because she hadn't been sure whether Lona would shoot her when she took the wrong turn. She had to chance it, but she hadn't been sure. She thought it would all depend upon where they were and how much farther the car was meant to go. She said,

"I'm sorry. I'll back to the fork—it won't take a moment."

The last words seemed to ring a warning bell. There was only a moment now—perhaps only a moment to live. The thought was in her mind as she put the car into reverse and pushed her foot down on the accelerator. She couldn't feel the pistol. Lona must have moved it.

The car ran back evenly, and then she jammed her foot right down. There was just time to feel a sudden exhilaration as they shot back, before the hind wheels bumped and came down hard in the ditch.

Something smashed at the impact with the bank—a bumper, glass, perhaps both, she didn't know. High above everything

Lona's scream—a sound of rage, not fear. In the instant before the crash Judy's hand had gone out to the catch of the door. The next thing she knew, she was slipping down over the running-board on to the road with a deafening noise in her ears and the glass of the windscreen broken. She thought there were two shots, and one of them very near. The car was all slumped and tilted up.

She ran for the ditch—any wild thing making for shelter. It must have been deeper than she thought, and there was a bank beyond it. She scrambled down one side and up the other, and heard another shot go off behind her. She didn't know where it went but the next might find her.

There was a hedge on the top of the bank. If she had been less desperate she wouldn't have got through—thorn, and holly, and something that smelled rank as she bruised it. Her dress tore, and caught, but she got clear as another shot came past her. It was so close that she felt it go by her left cheek, and with it there came the most horrible sound she had ever heard from a human being, the sound of a snarling fury which wasn't human at all. If it had words, no sense of them reached her. And all at once she felt that it didn't matter about being shot, but if this ravening creature were to touch her something would happen—she wouldn't be Judy any more. She put out her hands to shield her face and ran into the wood.

There were no big trees, just light growth of hazel or alder, with a tangle of ivy under foot, and here and there a black mass which was holly. She stubbed her foot in its thin houseshoe and came down, her hands flung out—catching at last year's leaves, wet moss, a fallen branch. She held on to this as she got up. It was short and heavy.

It wouldn't be any use at all against a pistol, but there is an old, old instinct to have something in your hand when you turn to face an enemy.

She had to stand for a moment to take her breath, to check the panic which would have sent her running wild—perhaps to fall again and be taken—helpless—

Something was coming through the hedge. The knowledge came to her through her ears and spread tingling over her whole body, every sound sharpened, every panting breath almost as close as her own. The horror came down on her again. If the hands which were forcing a way through the hedge were to touch her . . .

She was gripping the stick she had picked up. She flung it now as hard as she could to the left of where Lona was coming through the hedge. She could see her just clear of it, a shadow to be distinguished from the other shadows only because it moved. Quick on the sound of the thrown stick striking some bush or tree came the crack of another shot. That made five. Judy didn't know how many more there would be.

The shadow began to move in the direction from which the noise of the falling stick had come. As it moved, Judy moved too—towards the hole in the hedge. If she could get back on to the road whilst Lona thought she was still in the wood, she would really have a chance. You can't move amongst undergrowth without being heard. She set down each foot as if she were treading on egg-shells. A snapped twig would give her away—

Lona was calling to her now. The snarling animal sound had gone out of her voice.

"Don't be such a fool, Judy! You might have killed us both. But perhaps it was an accident. If it was, we won't say any more about it. Come along back and see if you can get the car out of the ditch. You're so clever with cars—I've never had enough practice. You needn't be afraid of the pistol—I've fired my last shot. You're not hurt, are you? It would be rather funny if you were dead. It would be a marvellous shot if I had really hit you in the dark. I'm afraid I lost my temper, and that's a thing I very seldom do. It doesn't pay, you know—one must always keep control. But I'd been flung against the back window, and if the glass had broken, I might have been most seriously hurt. Now, Judy, don't be stupid! Where are you?"

Judy had reached the hedge. She began to crawl backwards through the hole she had made. As she did so she was wondering what Lona had done with the torch, because she had had a torch in the car. She must have dropped it, lost it—something, or the beam would be stabbing to and fro in the wood looking for Judy Elliot.

She was through the hedge now. She slipped on the bank and came down into slime just covered with water—not enough of it to make a splash, but enough to mire her to the ankles. She stumbled up on to the road. No good to go back by the way they had come. No help in all those miles of heath and country lane. No use to take the way which Lona had meant to take, because it was a lonely road that she would choose.

She skirted the car. The torch was still in her mind, but she didn't dare to stop and look for it. And then her foot touched it, there in the dark on the road. She felt it roll, and knew what it was before she bent to pick it up. Odd that it should give her the first real feeling of hope. She didn't know how it was going to help her, but something deep inside her said. "It's all right now." On muddy, halting feet she began to run along the left-hand fork.

Frank Abbott went out of the room and shut the door. There was no sound after that. Miss Silver had laid her knitting on her knee. Mabel Robbins, who was Mabel Macdonald, leaned back against the hard wood of her chair. But she didn't feel that it was hard, she didn't feel anything. Her mind was empty and released. The years had given up their burden. She had done what John wanted her to do and she was free of it.

March had leaned back too. His right hand reached the table and stayed there, clenched into a fist. When he became aware of this tension he made a deliberate effort and relaxed. He looked across the papers which lay in front of him to the clear, colourless face of the woman who had just told this amazing story. It would knock the bottom out of his case against Alfred Robbins. As a theory it was practicable to suppose that she might be putting it forward to shield her father's name. But in practice you could pick a dozen juries a dozen times over, and every man jack of them would believe her. She was a witness who compelled belief. With his case toppled in ruins, he believed her himself.

His thoughts swung to Miss Maud Silver who had done the trick again. "She knows people. She starts where we leave off. Sees something—discerns some motive, some mainspring, and then starts looking for the evidence. I suppose that's the way it works, but I don't know. She had nothing to go on here that I can see, and yet it all fits in. Well, I suppose we must be thankful this girl turned up before the inquest. We'd have made a holy show if she'd come along afterwards!"

He turned to look at Miss Silver, and met her warm and friendly smile. They sat on in silence, each with his own thoughts, until the door opened a little more quickly than it had closed. Frank Abbott, extraordinarily pale, halted upon the threshold and said in a hard, controlled voice,

"She isn't in the house. Judy's gone too. And the car—they've taken your car."

March pushed back his chair and got up.

"Did anyone see them go?"

Frank shook his head.

"It must have been just after Mabel came. I heard a car go down the road. Jerome doesn't know anything—hasn't seen Lona since we had her down. We put the wind up her and she's bolted. But Judy—how did she get Judy to go?"

Miss Silver said, "Judy may have gone to see Penny."

Frank turned stony eyes on her.

"She hasn't. Lesley Freyne is here with Jerome—I waited whilst she rang up her house. Penny is asleep. Judy hasn't been over." He turned to March. "Look here, we'll have to take Daly's car—it's the nearest. Will you ring him up? God knows what's happening—and how she got Judy to go. Jerome says she's no hand with a car. That's why she's taken Judy."

Judy had stopped running. She didn't know where she was, or where she was going. The sweat of terror had dried on her and left her chilled beyond belief. When she stood still and listened she might have been the only living person in the world. Of all the sounds which man makes not one reached her—no faintest droning of a distant plane, no noise of wheels on road or rail, no sound of human foot, no sound of human speech. Into this vacuum there crowded all the sound which man banishes with his loud dominance—the light air moving in the leafless trees, the stir of a waking bird, the cry of the owl, and all the small shadowy noises of all the creatures that are abroad in the dark with their living to get.

She went on walking, and wondered where she was, and whether there was any end to this long, empty lane. It wasn't dark any longer. The clouds had rifted and the moon shone bright and cold. The over-arching trees were left behind. There was only an endless low hedge on either side, broken here and there by some sentinel holly. Shock, fatigue, and the moonlight made the whole scene unreal. The moon plays tricks with us, touching the commonest scene with enchantment—or horror—according to what has tinged our thoughts. It played now upon Judy's senses and caught them away into a haunted world full of shadows of evil. The most dreadful part of it was that she was alone there. There were no people, no shelter.

When she heard the car behind her it seemed like something which breaks violently in upon a dream. She was shocked awake, and uncertain what to do. If it was Lona— how could it be Lona? The car was ditched and she could never have got it out. The word "alone" slipped into her mind—Lona could never have got it out alone. Supposing someone had come by and helped her—

She suddenly saw twin lights come sliding down the lane.

Her mind was violently wrenched. She had the torch, and she could signal to the car. If she signalled, and it was Lona—if she didn't signal, and let help go by. . . . In a moment it would be too late. She must make up her mind— now—

But it was made up for her. Afterwards she didn't know whether she had tried to move her hand—to find the switch of the torch. She only knew that she had no power to do so. She felt the cold metal against her palm, but her fingers had no power to move. She stood frozen in the shadow of the hedge and saw the car go by.

It was the car she had driven and left in the ditch. Lona

was driving it at a low, careful pace. She went by. The glow of the lights held Judy's horrified gaze. The red tail-light was gone. She watched the glow until it was out of sight. Then she turned back along the way by which she had come.

Frank Abbott, driving Dr. Daly's car, had turned off the Ledlington road where Judy had turned.

"She won't dare risk the villages. This goes up to St. Agnes' Heath. If I were in her shoes I'd take it, get within walking distance of Coulton or Ledstowe, and shed the car. She's had forty minutes' start, and I shouldn't think she would reckon on getting more than that."

It was up on the heath that they saw the lights of a car coming towards them and stopped it. It contained two friendly Americans who were quite willing to admit that they had helped a lady out of a ditch a couple of miles back.

"She was sure glad to see us. Might have been there all night. It's a lonely bit of country. . . . Oh, sure, she was alone. . . ."

They were rather bewildered by the speed at which they were passed and left behind. March said, "Do you know the place—the fork they mentioned?"

"Yes. I should have thought she'd bear right, but they said she took the left-hand fork?" He broke off suddenly. "What's that?"

It was Judy, standing out in the middle of the lane and flashing the torch. Dr. Daly would have been horrified at the suddenness with which the brakes came on.

Lona Day drove on until she came to what she was looking for, the right-hand turn which would take her back to the Coulton road. She had to get back to it because she was going to Coulton, but she had not felt able to risk taking the right-hand fork under the eyes of the helpful young men who had got the car out of the ditch for her.

She was quite sure now that Judy had ditched it on purpose. Every time she thought of it she felt a burning surprise and anger. That the girl should have dared, and having dared, that she should have brought it off! She ought to have known that she hadn't a chance. She ought at this moment to be dead with a bullet in her brain.

She wasn't dead. She was alive, with a tattling tale to tell. Never mind, Lona would get away in spite of her. She hadn't killed four men, to be beaten by a tattling girl. She had made her plans. Her new name, her new place in the world, were waiting for her. Once she had slipped into them, the police might whistle but they wouldn't find her. In a way it was gratifying that they should know how clever she had been, and how she had diddled everyone for three years.

She went on slowly and carefully past the turning until she came to the narrow lane on the left which ran across the fields to Ledham. If she left the car just beyond it, the police would think she had gone that way. She drew up by the side of the road and walked quickly back to the right-hand turn. A mile to the Coulton road, and three miles on—farther than she cared to walk, but not too far for safety. When she was in sight of the Coulton road she would make her adjustments. A pity about her fur coat, but it would be the first thing in the description they were sure to circulate.

Twenty minutes later she was stripping it off and pushing it well down inside a hollow tree. Her hat followed it. Just a bit of luck that the moon had come out, for it wouldn't have been at all easy to find the tree in the dark. Seven—no eight months since they had picnicked here and pushed the sandwich papers down out of sight. She felt cold without her coat, though the coat and skirt she was wearing made a thick suit. Thick and new—no one at Pilgrim's Rest had ever seen it. The moonlight robbed it of its colour, but in the day it was a good shade of sapphire which took the green out of her eyes and made them look blue.

She found a comb in her bag and proceeded to deal with her hair, taking it up straight, away from face and neck and ears, before slipping on the dark wig which changed her quite beyond belief. Demure, smooth waves coming down to a roll at the back. Not nearly so ornamental as the chestnut curls, but oh, so respectable.

The woman who came out of the wood on to the Coulton

road was no longer Lona Day. A short three miles lay between her and safety.

Frank Abbott was taking tea with Miss Silver. There was a cosy fire. A comfortable twilight veiled the *Soul's Awakening* and the *Monarch of the Glen*. The rows of silver photograph frames which enshrined past clients and their babies caught a reflected glow from the firelight.

Miss Silver, neat and smiling, dispensed tea from a small Victorian teapot with a strawberry on the lid. Her tea-set, of the same date, displayed a pattern of moss roses. Since Emma never broke anything, it remained as she had inherited it from her great aunt, Louisa Bushell, that formidable pioneer of women's rights in an age which saw no reason why they should have any, since a gentleman could always be relied on to give a lady his seat. The tea-set lacked one cup of its original twelve, this having been broken by Miss Bushell's vicar, who set it down on its saucer with a slam at the climax of his argument that the original misdemeanour of Eve entailed continuous subjection upon her daughters. There were, however, a few occasions when Miss Silver entertained so large a party as to be reminded of this painful incident.

Frank now looked gloomily at her across the cups and said, "She's done the Macbeth act—made herself air."

Miss Silver coughed.

"Not quite an accurate statement, I think. She has merely become someone else. You will remember I said all along that there was a very clever, unscrupulous mind at work. I feel convinced from what Miss Day said to Judy that she had very carefully prepared a line of retreat."

Frank continued to look gloomy.

"Well, we can't pick up any trace of her in Coulton, Ledstow, or Ledham. No one answering to her description boarded a train at any of these places, and unless she got a lift in a car she couldn't have got any farther afield. It was too late for her to catch a bus."

"I do not imagine that the description which has been circulated will correspond with her present appearance. Our sex has an advantage over yours when it comes to a change of identity. Different colouring, another way of doing the hair, will completely alter a woman's appearance. At Pilgrim's Rest Miss Day wore green or black, both of which emphasized the red in her hair and the greenish tint of her eyes. You should look for someone with brown or dark hair, and I should conjecture that she would be wearing blue. The hair might of course be grey, but I fancy she has rather too much vanity for that.''

"I wonder who she'll murder next," said Frank Abbott.

Miss Silver lifted the lid of the teapot and added a little more hot water to the brew before she answered.

"She will be very careful for a time at any rate." After which she enquired brightly, "And how is Judy? I hope she is now none the worse for her very alarming experience.''

Frank leaned forward and set down his cup upon the tray. Perhaps he was afraid of emulating the vicar.

"She's staying on at Pilgrim's Rest," he said in rather a jerky voice. "You wouldn't think she'd want to, but she does.''

"She gave her evidence remarkably well at the inquest. And so did that poor girl Mabel—Mrs. Macdonald. I was much relieved that it was not considered necessary to publish her married name. Whilst one cannot approve of her conduct with Henry Clayton, one must remember that she was a young girl, and he by all accounts a particularly fascinating man. Inexperienced young women are sadly liable to be carried away by specious arguments on the subject of free union and companionate marriage. They fail to realize until too late that though civilized marriage laws may sometimes prove irksome, they nevertheless exist for the protection of woman and the family.''

Frank's gloom relaxed a little. Maudie discoursing upon the Moral Law enthralled him. He accepted another cup of tea and returned to Judy.

"Lesley and Jerome are getting married in about a month. Judy is going to stay on with them. There's been a frightful pow-wow about where they were to live and what was to happen to the house. I don't think Lesley was a bit keen on Pilgrim's Rest and I don't blame her, but Jerome dug his toes in. So they're going to have six assorted ophans in the attics with Lesley's matron to look after them. That ought to lay the ghosts. The aunts are going to stay put. Lesley and Jerome will have the other wing where his room is now. Mcals together, but separate sitting-rooms. Judy will have Penny and stay on. Ditto Gloria. Mrs. Robbins, who has taken a new lease on life, says she'll stay and cook. She doesn't hold with going to live with a married daughter, sensible woman. A let-off for Macdonald, who nobly offered to have her. So that places everyone. Happy ending." His voice was at its most cynical. He stared into the fire.

Miss Silver said gently,

"You would not have made one another happy, Frank."

"Probably not. At the moment the possibilities seem all the other way."

"You are not really suited."

He gave a short hard laugh. "What you mean is that I don't really suit! I'm a policeman, you see—a sordid profession."

"My dear Frank!"

He nodded. "That's what she thinks, you know—and I'm not so very sure I don't agree."

Miss Silver said, "Fiddlesticks!"

Frank laughed again, more naturally this time.

"I never heard you say that before."

"I never heard you talk so much nonsense."

This time he returned her smile.

"I'm sore, you know. But I'll get over it. You're quite right—we don't suit. We both thought we were going to, but we don't really, so it's better as it is. In fact,

> 'He who loves and rides away
> Will live to love another day.' "

Miss Silver beamed.

"I hope so," she said.